the heebie-jeebie girl

the heebie-jeebie girl

by susan petrone

THE
ST■RY
PLANT

The Story Plant
Studio Digital CT, LLC
P.O. Box 4331
Stamford, CT 06907

Story Plant hardcover ISBN-13: 978-1-61188-285-8

Visit our website at www.TheStoryPlant.com

First Story Plant Printing: April 2020

Printed in the United States of America

0 9 8 7 6 5 4 3 2 1

To Youngstown and those who love her.

Youngstown

I can hear you, you know. I can hear the rumble of cars and trucks, the jumble of notes from your radios and record players and instruments, the constant hum of you walking and talking and yelling and crying. I feel you too, your voices and all the things you've made, the clang and bang and burn of the mills and the trains that feed them. You are in me. I can feel your vibrations — don't think that I don't. I feel your parades and festivals and your fires too. Some cities sing, some play, some are filled with constant motion and tourists and people and fancy food. Me, I'm filled with fire, soot, and melting iron ore.

Sometimes I listen to you and your conversations, your arguments, your long, rambling talks about life and philosophy over a few beers, your quiet talks with your kids right before they fall asleep. Hell, I've probably heard you making love with your sweetie. Think about that next time you hop in the sack.

Some of your conversations are more interesting than others. Some of *you* are more interesting than others. I'm not God or your mother; I'm allowed to play favorites. I watch you the way you watch television.

I'm not old, not like some cities. I'm no Rome or London, and they'd be the first ones to say so. I'm not saying they're snobs, but they like to pretend that they're a little better than the rest of us. They act like they're only filled with the best and the brightest, like their streets are whitewashed, like they've never had streams of piss and blood and vomit in their gutters.

I know better.

We all have our secrets and our slums. I may not be ancient, but one hundred seventy-five years is nothing to sneeze at. I'm not some Johnny-come-lately new suburb out in the boondocks or one of those crazy planned retirement communities down in Florida. And I'm not a ghost town. There's real history in me, things worth noticing, worth knowing. Writers and musicians and movie producers and real estate tycoons have called me home. You know the Warner brothers? The ones who started a movie studio and named it after themselves? They were my boys. So was Harry Burt. You say you don't know who Harry Burt was? Have you ever eaten an ice cream bar on a stick from the Good Humor man? Of course you have, and you can thank Harry Burt for that. And for all you young punks, I have two words: Stiv Bators. Also one of mine.

You might say plenty of cities can lay claim to famous sons and daughters. You might say that I'm dirty and worn out and unloved. Maybe. But does your city have magic? Not pretend, not some cheap sleight-of-hand, pay-no-attention-to-the-man-behind-the-curtain crap, but genuine can't-be-explained-by-logic-or-reason magic?

I thought not.

Joe
August 1977

Hope gave the first lottery number to me.

We were out in the garage one Saturday while I worked on Ralph Krasniak's '72 Charger, which he needed to get to work on Monday. I had to get it done in one day because my sister, Dolores, is big on keeping holy the Lord's Day and all that. Technically the house belongs to her, and I live there under her good graces, so it's usually her way or the highway.

Those Chargers are so finicky that they can't run right unless it's seventy degrees, dry, and sunny. It had been a humid summer that looked to be a wet fall. Ralph was stalling out left and right, and I was tired of having him stop by every other day asking me to tinker with the choke setting or the float level. I kept doing it for free because he drives three other guys to work. The way things have been going down at the Sheet & Tube, they'll all lose their jobs if the car doesn't run. You never want to see a man lose his job, so I finally decided to rebuild the whole darn carburetor.

Hope is smart as a whip and could name half the parts by the end of the afternoon. At one point, she was holding the hi-lo screws, one in each hand, and moving them up and down like they were soldiers in a parade. Hope had been making little marching noises while she did this, but then she suddenly stopped. I glanced over at her, and she looked like she was thinking hard about something. We looked at each other for a second, as though we were both trying to figure out what the other one was thinking. Then she asked, "Want to hear a secret, Uncle Joe?"

"Sure," I said, keeping one eye on her and one eye on the bowl in my hand.

"The daily number is going to be two-two-zero." Hope has wispy blond hair that's always hanging in front of her eyes, but as she said this, she tucked her hair behind her ears so she could look at me a little better. "You should go to McGuffey's and play it. It's going to win."

"Since when does a little girl know about playing the lottery?"

"Grandma plays it sometimes."

"My sister wastes her money. She'd be better off putting it in the bank instead of hiding what little she has in a cigar box."

"Why does she hide her money in a cigar box?"

"Because she doesn't trust the bank."

"Why not?"

"Because fifty years ago all the rich guys running the country overspent and the stock market crashed, then everybody pulled all their money out of the banks, so the banks crashed and people lost lots of money."

"That was the Depression, right?"

"Right."

"Grandma talks about it all the time. She said everybody was poor then."

"They were," I replied as I grabbed the venturi.

"Were you poor?"

"Uh-huh."

"Well, if you play two-two-zero, you'll win and then you'll have some money," she said, and she sounded so confident and grown up that I almost believed her.

Hope is kind of an unusual kid. Her mother, Ruth, is my niece, and she tells me stories about how Hope says she once saw the Virgin Mary standing in her room. Ruthie and Dolores say it's true. Ruthie's husband Phil doesn't say anything. I say it's just Hope being a little girl with a big imagination. Kids like to make things up; it's what they do.

I saw it too. It looked just like the statue of Mary they have over at Saint Columba's. Honestly, I don't know who else it could have been.

Hope watched me work a little longer, then she got bored and went inside to bother my sister for a cookie. About ten minutes later, I saw them walking down the street in the direction of McGuffey's.

When I went in for dinner that evening, after Ruthie had picked up Hope, I told Dolores about Hope picking number two-two-zero. Dolores was hunched over the stove, spooning haluski onto my plate. Just as I suspected, she said that Hope had given her the same number. "We went down to McGuffey's to play it," she added. "Just to make Hope happy. And I needed a few things anyway."

Although I don't like to see anyone waste a dollar, it's Dolores's Social Security check, not mine. I didn't say anything else. Later that evening though, I couldn't help but wander into the living room after the six o'clock news. They have a little two-minute program where they pick the daily number, and wouldn't you know it? Two-two-zero came up. "Well I'll be dipped," I said. "Hope got lucky."

"Dipped nothing," Dolores said. "Hope is beloved by God."

Hope was at the house again the next Saturday. She spent some time with me while I repaired the steps to the back porch. The basement has a walkout to the backyard — a couple of four-foot Bilco doors on an angle that lead to the root cellar. It's right next to the porch stairs, and every child that's ever lived in or visited this house wants to walk up and down those doors like they're climbing some great

13

big mountain. You would have thought Hope was climbing Mount Everest. Then she asked if she could help me hammer, so I started a few old nails into a piece of scrap wood, got a small hammer, and let her have at it.

For a few minutes, Hope was silent. I glanced over at her, and she was holding the hammer in both hands and tap-tap-tapping at the nails. Then she looked up at me and said, "I start school this week. Second grade."

"I think I knew that," I said, not looking up from my work. "Everybody starts school around Labor Day."

"Labor means work, right?" she asked. I nodded. "So why is everybody *off* from work on Labor Day? Why doesn't everybody *go* to work on Labor Day?"

"Because it's a celebration of the people who work. The workers. You can thank the unions for that. People work hard, and for a long time the people who owned the factories took advantage of them until people got organized and demanded better treatment. That's why we have a forty-hour workweek and a minimum wage and why a child your age isn't allowed to work."

In another life, Joe Steiner probably would have ended up as one of the leaders of the American Communist Party, but the world has a habit of beating notions about equality and fairness out of young men. He started out at the Sheet & Tube, working alongside his best friend, Louis Nagy, who married Dolores back in '28. They both got fired and blackballed for union organizing in '30. Joe went off and became a mechanic, and Louis hopped on a freight train and didn't come back for eight months.

"Oh," she replied, and went back hammering the scrap wood. Hope is a smart kid, but she's still just a youngster. It's not as though we were going to have an in-depth conversation about the history of the American labor movement.

"Did you play two-two-zero last week, Uncle Joe?" she asked as she took a good whack on the scrap wood.

"No, I didn't get a chance," I said.

"It came up," she said. "Grandma won."

"So I hear. That was a lucky guess."

She stopped her hammering. "No, it wasn't." I looked up at her sitting on the wrap-around front porch that I should have gotten around to painting this year. She stared right back at me. "It wasn't a *guess*."

"Did you know that two-two-zero was going to come up?" I half-expected her to tell me the Virgin Mary showed up in her room again and told her the daily number.

"Not exactly ... " she said. I waited as she looked off in the distance for a second like she was trying to make up her mind whether or not to tell me a secret, but she just said, "All the numbers I gave Mommy and Grandma this week have come up."

I've spent enough time around kids to know that you can't argue with them and you can't reason with them. Children are going to believe what they're going to believe. We all learn soon enough that we don't have magic or superpowers or whatnot, so why go around disappointing them when they're only seven? I said that was a mighty impressive trick and left it at that. Hope went back to pounding on the piece of scrap wood while I pulled the measuring tape out one more time before I started cutting. "Forty-two ... " I muttered.

"What's forty-two?" Hope asked.

"Forty-two inches. That's the width of the step."

"Know what seven-five-five is?"

"Nope."

"The number for today. It's going to come up."

"Is that a fact?"

"Uh-huh," she said, and started banging on the piece of scrap wood again. We were happy enough out there until Ruth and Dolores came out on the porch.

"Hope!" Ruthie screamed. You would have thought I'd let the child get run over by a truck. "Put down that hammer this instant."

"But Uncle Joe said I could use it."

Ruth scurried over to the corner of the porch where Hope was squatting in front of the scrap wood and took the hammer away from her. "You could hurt yourself."

"Joseph," my sister said. "Why are you letting a little girl use a big hammer like that?"

"I'm letting her have fun."

"What if she hit her finger?"

"Then she'll learn not to hit it the next time."

"I like hammering, Mommy," Hope said.

"You've done enough hammering," Ruthie said and took her by the hand. "Besides, you and Grandma and I have some errands to run."

"Oh, all right..." Hope said, and she sounded just like her mother when she was a teenager. What goes around comes around, especially for parents.

The three of them bustled off together in Ruthie's car. My sister has never learned to drive, but two of her kids still live in Youngstown, so Ruthie or Eddie comes and takes her shopping if I don't have time to do it. They went off to Sparkle to get groceries and I don't know what else. Nobody mentioned the number, but later that evening, I heard the sound of the television and the daily number drawing. I wandered into the living room just in time to see my sister shoving a few lottery tickets back into the pocket of her blue flowered housecoat. The television screen showed the daily number as seven-five-five.

"Did you win?" I asked casually.

"Never you mind," my sister replied.

It seemed like a pretty big coincidence that Hope would pick the winning numbers for over a week. I wasn't sure what to make of it. I've never been much for gambling, but every gambler hits a lucky streak once in a while, Joe DiMaggio hits in fifty-six consecutive games, the Miami Dolphins go undefeated for an entire season, and a little girl picks the daily number a few times in a row. Sometimes things like that happen.

I didn't think about the lottery again until Dolores and I went over to Ruthie and Phil's house for a Labor Day picnic. My nephew Eddie and his three kids were there too. Eddie is the youngest of my sister's four kids. The other two live up in Cleveland.

For years, everybody called Eddie "Baby Eddie," until he got married, fathered a few kids, and had his wife leave them all high and dry. Then we realized he wasn't a baby anymore. Eddie and his kids lived with us for a few years, until the youngest started school and Eddie had saved the down payment for a new house. That's why I moved out to the garage in the first place, to make room for Eddie and the kids, but now the garage feels like home.

Cleveland never lets me forget all the people it's taken from me. I got something to tell Cleveland: bigger ain't always better. At least Mayor Hunter's hair never caught fire. At least the Mahoning River never caught fire, not like in *some* cities I know.

Hope ran around with her big cousins while the adults relaxed on the patio. At one point she ran over to the table in between Dolores and Ruthie and took a big gulp of pink lemonade from her cup.

"Hope, sweetie," Ruthie whispered to her. "Do you have a number for Grandma?"

Hope took another slurp of lemonade, said "six-nine-five," and went back to playing freeze tag with the other kids.

"Sorry, Mom," Ruthie said.

Dolores gave a little *c'est la vie* shrug and said, "Ask her again tomorrow."

"What's the matter?" Eddie said. "She gave you a number."

"Hope's numbers only come out when they have two of the same digits, like two-two-zero or five-five-two. And you have to play it the same day Hope gives it to you," Ruth answered.

"You've got it down to a science," I said.

"She's given us numbers that don't come out too." She looked a little defensive, like having Hope give her numbers was some kind of child abuse.

"How many times have you hit the daily now, Mom?" Eddie asked.

Dolores shrugged it off. "Just a few. Hope just likes giving the numbers. It's fun for her."

"She's sure good at it," Eddie said.

"Kind of gives you heebie-jeebies, doesn't it?" I said. There was dead silence, then Eddie sort of snorted back half a laugh.

"A little," he said. "No offense, sis," he added quickly.

Phil and Ruth looked at each other. Sometimes you can tell a lot about a relationship by how a husband and wife communicate without words. Phil has a wry sense of humor. Ruth takes after my sister and takes everything too seriously.

"We've talked about it at length," Phil said finally. "I do find it a little... unusual. But Hope's adding to her college fund, so I can handle unusual." Phil heads up the circulation department for *The Vindicator*. He's a sensible person, and since there's kind of a dearth of those in our family, he was a welcome addition to the clan.

"Good planning," Eddie said. "Make sure you call me the next time Hope gives you a number. At the rate I'm saving, I might be able to afford to send my three to Youngstown State for about an hour each."

Even Ruthie and Dolores had a good chuckle about that. From the other end of the yard, we heard a low "Wooooww ... " from the kiddie contingent. I glanced over and saw Eddie's three kids gathered around Hope, who was squatting on the ground. I couldn't see what they were looking at.

"What's going on over there?" Eddie asked.

"Do it again!" Lou said loud enough for half the block to hear. Whatever it was that Hope had done, she clearly didn't want to do it again because she jumped up, tapped Lou on the arm yelling "Tag! You're it!" and ran away. Edie and Nico scattered in opposite directions. Lou looked startled and then started chasing his sisters and cousin.

Sometimes it's nice to just watch kids playing. It reminds you of what it's like not to have a care in the world. All of us adults fell into a contented silence, just listening to the sounds of birds singing and kids playing. I couldn't imagine anything nicer.

"Hey, I heard the O'Keenes moved," Eddie said. "Is that true?" I can't either. You got no idea how hard it is to get you people to shut your traps and listen.

I nodded. "The university made offers on all the houses on that block. They're expanding."

"The university is already big enough," Dolores muttered. I agree.

"Do you know where they moved to?" Ruthie asked. She used to pal around with the youngest O'Keene girl.

I looked over at Dolores. "Somewhere in Columbus. Helen gave me their new address," she replied. "I'll give it to you next time I see you."

"Please do. I haven't talked to Betsy O'Keene in ages." Knowing Ruthie, she'd actually write a card to her old friend. Me? I'd think about it and never do it. Enough people have come in and out of my life that I know I don't have time to go writing letters to all of them.

Ruthie excused herself to go inside and get dessert ready. And then Phil asked if Eddie had heard any news regarding the Sheet & Tube. "I've heard some rumors about lay-offs, but nothing confirmed," Phil said. "I was just wondering if you had heard anything from any reliable sources."

Eddie's a news producer down at WFMJ, so he generally knows what's going on in the city. "The reliable sources are all back in the old neighborhood," Eddie said, and they both looked over at Dolores and me

"I don't like to think about it," Dolores said and went in to help Ruthie with dessert, leaving the three of us men to sort out all of Youngstown's problems.

"I was working on Ralph Krasniak's car a couple weeks ago," I said. "He's still over at the Campbell Works. He said everybody there is pretty nervous."

"Wow, Ralph Krasniak," Eddie said. "I remember him, He played for Chaney when I was at Ursuline. Hard hitter. I hated playing against him, but he always seemed nice off the field. I didn't know he was still at the Sheet & Tube."

"For the time being," I said. "He said there's a lot of talk about lay-offs."

"That's what they're saying down at the paper," Phil said.

"Here's to all the guys down at the Sheet & Tube," Eddie said, and we raised three bottles of Iron City beer in their honor. Then the three of us were quiet again until the ladies brought out the dessert.

There wasn't a Daily Number drawing that day, and the number the next day wasn't six-nine-five. But on Wednesday, Dolores got a quick phone call from Ruthie and then she hurried down to McGuffey's. That night, when they drew the number, my sister yelled "Holy Jupiter!" She usually only yells that when someone takes her picture and the flash blinds her.

The number was three-three-zero. I figured she must have bought a bunch of tickets for her to yell "Holy Jupiter." A few days a week, there'd be a late morning phone call, a quick trip to McGuffey's, and a "Holy Jupiter!" that evening when they drew the number. Dolores hit the number enough times that I could almost believe Hope really *did* make the number come up. Hope is a sweet girl, but she's a little different, what with the lottery numbers and how grown-up she seems sometimes and the whole thing about seeing the Blessed Mother in her bedroom.

I couldn't figure out how she was coming up with these numbers. None of us could. There was no logical explanation. Hope was picking two or three numbers a week right out of thin air. Either she had a direct line to the lottery commission or she was the luckiest kid I've ever met. I tried talking to Dolores about it one night over supper. I just asked casually "How do you think Hope picks all those numbers?"

Dolores' eyes slanted just a hair. "What do you mean?"

"I mean, how does she do it? You've got to admit, she's picked more winning numbers in the past month than most people pick in a lifetime. It defies the laws of probability." I may only have a tenth-grade education, but I know enough about mathematics to know that the odds of any three-digit number coming up straight are a thousand to one. And Hope was beating those odds on a regular basis.

"She doesn't always win," Dolores said, as though I was the village idiot. "Sometimes she gives Ruthie and me a number that doesn't come out."

"Those are the ones without the double digit. Every time she gives you a number with a double digit, it comes out."

"Well obviously the odds are better when one of the numbers repeats."

I about threw up my hands at that comment. "Look, dear sister, there are ten balls in each hopper numbered zero through nine. The chance of any one of those balls coming up is the same — one in ten for each digit. Multiply ten by ten by ten, it equals one thousand. It doesn't matter if the three-digit number is five-five-five or one-two-three or zero-zero-zero. The odds are still one in a thousand that the person buying the lottery ticket will pick the winning number — those three digits in that particular order."

"You're forgetting that Hope is a very special girl," Dolores said as though that were the end of the conversation.

Sometimes I almost feel bad for Dolores Steiner Nagy. There's a small hump on her back that she always said was an injury from bumping around in a roller coaster when she was younger. Something about her spine getting twisted. It's probably that scoliosis. The hump's gotten bigger as she's gotten older. During the Depression, she was on her own with her kids and her parents while her husband rode the rails like so many other unemployed, lost men did. He came home every couple of years and got her pregnant then went back out on the road. He didn't find a steady job or stay home for more than four months at a time until '38. As for the roller coaster injury, the bumping around might have injured her spine, but it couldn't shake the baby out of her. She ended up having to marry Louis Nagy anyway.

"All of your grandchildren are special. You've got a couple of musical prodigies, two mechanical geniuses, I don't know how many artistic prodigies..."

"You know what I mean."

"No, I don't. Hope is a fine child, but you have thirteen other grandchildren who are just as good." I didn't mean to get annoyed, but Dolores tends to play favorites among her grandkids. When Eddie and his kids lived with us, Dolores used to get mad at the oldest, Edie, because she looks just like Eddie's ex-wife. That isn't the child's fault. I don't like seeing people play favorites, especially not with family.

Dolores primly wiped her mouth with her napkin and put it back in her lap. "Hope is especially beloved by God."

"Because she said she saw the Blessed Mother in her bedroom and she picks the Daily Number?"

"Yes. You just keep reading all your science books and studying engines. You won't find an explanation for this. There are some things in this world that you just have to take on faith."

Sometimes I wish I shared my sister's faith in God. Life would be a lot simpler if I did. I don't mean to say that Dolores is simple minded. She isn't. But the Catholic Church got its hooks into her good and early, and she's content there. Myself, I have my doubts. Way back in the dark ages, I was an altar boy at St. Cyril and Methodius. Back then, just about everything in our life revolved around the church — school, sports, social life, everything. I spent most of my waking hours there. I remember more than once seeing a couple of the priests drinking up a storm on a Friday afternoon, smoking cigars and cussing when they thought no one could hear them, even though drinking and smoking and cursing were things they kept telling us kids not to do. I don't fault them for it, but it made me realize that priests are just people like the rest of us. They're no closer to God than I am.

Putting too much faith in anything will get you into trouble. I've seen banks fail, lived through two World Wars and a couple other wars to boot, watched one president and some other good men get shot and another president resign in disgrace. And the day after that conversation with Dolores, I saw a company kill an entire city in one fell swoop. One Monday in mid-September, the first shift showed up for work at the Sheet & Tube Campbell Works and found padlocks on the gates. The Campbell Works was only a few miles down Wilson Avenue from us — half the neighborhood worked there.

We were one of the few families in Smoky Hollow who didn't have someone working at one of the mills. My sister's late husband, Louis, and I both worked at Republic Steel for a short time back when we were arrogant young men. Louis got blackballed for union organizing. I didn't like the heat and the noise, so I quit when he left. I guess it was somewhere between solidarity and getting out while the getting was good. At any rate, that was the family's last excursion into the world of steel mills. Dolores made sure all four of her kids got an education and steered them away from any sort of factory work.

Even if you didn't work in one of the mills, you couldn't escape them. Youngstown is full of steel mills, and the Sheet & Tube was the granddaddy of them all. The blast furnaces and railroad tracks were part of the landscape — you saw the steel and smelled it every day. If you were close enough, you heard it. If you were in there, you felt it. And everybody breathed it. When the wind was right, we'd have to sweep super-fine black steel dust off the front porch. The mill was everything. And then the owners just closed up shop, leaving five thousand workers and their families out in the cold.

You're probably expecting me to say something now, aren't you? Next time someone rips your heart out and tramples in it the dirt, I'll be sure to ask you how you feel.

The Sheet & Tube still had the Brier Hill Works, but it was smaller and way up on the North Side. A handful of guys managed to get transferred over there, even though a fool could see the Brier Hill Works wasn't going to be around much longer. A few transferred to mills in other states, and the whole city protested the closing, but everybody knew the Sheet & Tube wouldn't reopen.

Dolores and I were both on Social Security, and the house was paid for years ago. Plus I still made a little money under the table as a mechanic. We could get by the same as we always had. But half of our neighbors went on unemployment overnight, and everybody started wondering if it was time to take the university up on the offer to buy their house because nobody else was going to.

A few weeks after they closed the Campbell Works, I spent an afternoon fixing the timing belt and doing a quick tune-up on Joey Vincenza's Dodge and then walked down to McGuffey's to get a bottle of beer.

When John McGuffey rang it up for me, he shook his head. "Gee, Joe, with all the money your sister's won lately, you think she'd at least give you the money for a six-pack."

Dolores' money is Dolores' money. I leave it alone, so when I asked, "Do you know how much she's won?" I honestly wasn't sure.

"I don't know. A lot. She cashes in a bunch of tickets every Saturday. What's her system?" He lowered his voice. "Does she have a line on the Super Lotto? You know, the million-dollar jackpot?"

"Not that I know of. I think this is all just a run of good luck," I said.

"Well, tell her to bring you along instead of Hope next time she cashes in. She shouldn't be carrying around all that dough on her own with just a little kid with her. Not these days."

Granted, it doesn't take a lot of money to impress a cheapskate like John McGuffey, but Dolores had to be winning more than I suspected for him to say something like that. When I asked her if she wanted me to go with her the next time she cashed in her tickets, she shrugged me off.

"I know everybody for eight blocks," she said. "Nobody is going to mug me when I'm walking home from McGuffey's."

She was right. Nobody mugged her. Instead they came to the house.

II

I still spent a couple days a week working over at Bob Javorsik's garage. He didn't have enough work for a full-time guy, and at my age I just want to get out of the house once in a while, so the arrangement suited both of us fine. One morning about a week before Thanksgiving, I spent a few hours trying to keep Vito and Millie DiNardo's '71 Chevy Vega from falling apart. It's nothing but a bucket of rust on four wheels and the valve stem seals keep cracking and leaking oil, but it's the only car they have and they can't afford another. Javorsik doesn't pay me much, but then he doesn't have to charge the DiNardos much either.

Once I got the rust bucket off the lift, it was only about one-thirty, but I told Javorsik I was done for the day. Most people wouldn't be so cavalier with their boss, but I'm twenty years older than Bob, and I work cheap. I can do whatever I want.

I hadn't had lunch yet, and on the drive home all I could think about was making myself a giant Dagwood sandwich. We had some leftover roast beef that was calling my name all the way down Wick Avenue.

The first thing I noticed when I pulled in was that the back door, the one facing the garage, was open. We're a corner house — the front door faces Audubon but the drive is on Adams. Dolores would leave the back door open in the warmer weather, but my sister is one of those women who is always cold. And she isn't one to waste money by heat-ing the entire neighborhood. We hadn't had much snow yet, but it was cold enough that even a fool would keep the door closed, yet there it was, wide open.

You know that little feeling in your gut like something's wrong somewhere? That was the feeling rattling around inside me as I walked across the yard and up the new steps to the back porch. The house is divided by the staircase that's almost directly across from the back door. The kitchen is to the right, and to the left is the dining room and beyond that the living room. The old wood screen door squeaked a little when I opened it, but other than that, everything was silent. I stood for a moment and waited, trying to see if I could hear anything or anyone. My sister is one of those people who's always busy. She cleans even when the house doesn't need it just so she has something to do. And with Thanksgiving coming up next week, she actually had some baking to do. But there was nothing. I couldn't smell anything either. Nothing baking, no lemony-fresh Pine Sol or whatever it is she uses to clean the floor. No gas — the oven wasn't even on. But I did hear water running in the bathroom upstairs.

For some reason, I went up the stairs quietly, slowly. There was no logical reason to be wary. Dolores was obviously in the bathroom and couldn't hear me. At the top of the staircase, I glanced in the open bathroom door. The bathroom was empty, but the faucet in the tub was running. I went in and turned it off. Our house isn't big — three rooms down, three rooms up. You can stand in the bathroom door and look right across the hall into Dolores' bedroom. She has a beautiful set of mahogany bedroom furniture that came from our parents — a bed, a dresser, and a wardrobe. The wardrobe door was open. On the floor in front of it was a wooden cigar box, the one where Dolores hides all her money. It was lying on the faded red and brown carpet that she's had in there since the Truman Administration. I walked in and picked up the cigar box. It was empty.

"Dolores?" I called once, then again, a little louder the second time. From way down in the basement, I heard someone call my name, very faintly, like she was down in a deep hole. I may not move as fast as I used to but let me tell you, I was down the stairs, across the kitchen, and down to the basement in record time. I went so fast I almost tripped over my sister, who was lying at the bottom of the basement stairs.

"Jesus, Dolores!" As soon as I said it, I knew she must have been in terrible pain because she didn't even scold me for taking the Lord's name in vain, she just said, "Joe, help me."

I tried to lift her up to help her up the stairs, but she screamed in pain the moment I moved her. Hearing that made me feel my insides were getting ripped right out of me. "I'm sorry, I'm so sorry that hurt," I said, trying to help her lie comfortably on the old linoleum floor. Her rose-and-white house coat had slipped up above her knees. I pulled it down for her. "Dolores, I'm going to run upstairs and call an ambulance, then I'm going to come right back here and wait with you, okay?" I said.

Dolores closed her eyes and nodded. My sister has seen a lot of hard times in her life. When we buried our parents, she was the one who stood up in the church as straight as she could and didn't shed a tear, at least none I ever saw. When Louis died, her kids were grown but they still went all to pieces. It was Dolores who held them together. This was the first time I had ever seen her look hurt or vulnerable since we were kids. I ran upstairs, called the ambulance, then went back downstairs and sat on the floor with her until we heard the sirens coming.

When we got to the hospital, they took Dolores into an exam room while I started making phone calls. When I was done, they already had Dolores set up in a hospital room. A nurse who said her name was Michelle was getting her ready for surgery. Michelle didn't look old enough to legally buy alcohol, but what do I know?

28

"I broke my hip," Dolores said. It sounded like they'd already given her some happy drugs, because she sounded tired and a little loopy.

When we were waiting for the ambulance, I had asked her what happened, but she was in too much pain to answer. Now I asked her again. This time, she wanted to talk.

I'll admit to being a bit of an ambulance chaser. A girl can only pay attention to so much — it might as well be something interesting. Joe followed the ambulance to St. Elizabeth's and then had the job of calling Dolores's kids. I'm not sentimental, but I can never hear someone on the telephone say, "There's been an accident," without feeling a little trembling deep in the furrows of my being. How can you not? These are my people. Bombay and New York and Beijing might have bodies to spare. I don't. I don't want to lose any of you.

"The fellas from the water department ... " I could hardly understand her.

"The water department?"

"They came to give me my money back," she mumbled.

"What?"

Dolores sighed. "My refund. I paid too much so they came to give me a refund but they didn't have any change. I made change."

It was all starting to make sense — the water running in the tub, the empty cigar box. She'd been scammed and robbed. My stomach did a turn or two like I was on one of those whirligig rides at Idora Park.

If Dolores said anything else, I couldn't hear her. The nurse started saying something about the aide coming in to take Dolores to surgery at the same time that Eddie showed up and started asking questions. Then Ruthie showed up with Hope in tow. I knew Hope was only there because Ruthie probably couldn't find a babysitter on short notice, but I was glad she'd brought her along to the hospital. Youngsters ought to see the good along with the bad.

Ruthie and Eddie were peppering the nurse with questions and asking to talk to the doctor, even though everybody knows that nurses are always the ones who know what's going on. Hope took my hand and asked if she could talk to her grandma. "You can try," I said, "but I think she just fell asleep. They gave her something for the pain and some medicine to make her sleepy before her surgery."

We went and stood over by Dolores's hospital bed and it was our own little circle of quiet while everybody else was chattering away.

"Is she going to be okay?" Hope asked.

"Oh sure. She broke her hip, but they're going to do surgery in a little bit to fix it."

"Your hip bone is right here, right?" Hope asked, putting one hand on her side.

"A little lower." I moved her hand down to her hip. "Your grandma fell down the basement steps. The first thing I'm going to do when I get home is check those steps to make sure it doesn't happen again."

Hope didn't say anything else, just stared at Dolores really hard. I thought I heard her whisper something to her grandmother. It was a sweet little moment, and then they came and wheeled Dolores away to the operating room.

When we were alone in the room, I switched on the television to keep Hope occupied and told the adults what Dolores had said and about the empty cigar box and that it looked like their mother had been tricked and robbed.

"Those bastards ... " Eddie grumbled.

Ruthie made a sort of groaning sound. "Oh Lord! She kept all her money in that stupid box." She didn't say it like an accusation, just as a matter of fact.

Eddie and I looked at each other. Hope had been picking the daily for Ruthie and Dolores for nearly three months, but I'd never asked either of them what Eddie asked, "How much money have you two won on the Daily Number?"

Ruthie bit her lips until they almost disappeared. "Almost ten thousand dollars each," she said quietly.

"Uncle Joe, you need to call the police," Eddie said as

I didn't tell Dolores to keep her money in the house. I didn't tell her not to trust the bank. The banks are part of me like any other building, but they aren't me. It's not my fault some people never trusted anything but what they could see and touch.

though I wasn't already picking up the phone to do just that. I could hear Hope asking her uncle what a bastard was as I told the whole story to the police. There wasn't much to go on, but they said they'd send someone to the hospital in the morning to talk to Dolores and that they'd meet me at the house the next day to look for evidence. The surgery lasted a couple of hours, and afterwards, Dolores was in no condition to talk. The doctor said it'd be best to just let her rest, so I spent the night in the easy chair in her hospital room.

Ruthie and Eddie got there bright and early the next morning after their kids went to school — I guess he ditched work for the day. There's devotion for you. Poor Dolores was all trussed up with an IV in one hand and some tubes in her nose to help her breathe. My kid sister looked beat.

She ate some of the scrambled eggs and applesauce they gave her for breakfast and perked up a little. After the orderly took the tray away, the four of us sat there staring at each other. "I don't like this place," Dolores said.

"Of course not, Mom," Eddie said. "Nobody likes the hospital."

"I do," I said. "Free food, all those cute nurses fluffing up your pillows." Ruthie rolled her eyes like I was some naughty child. No one in my family ever likes my jokes except the kids.

"I don't like this place," Dolores said again. "It's dirty." She sounded different, almost angry. I figured it was just the pain medication talking.

"Mom?" Ruthie asked. "How did you fall? Did you slip?"

Dolores was gazing out the window, looking at the parking lot of St. Elizabeth Hospital. "No, they pushed me. One of them pushed me."

"Mom, those guys weren't from the Water Department ... " Eddie started to say.

Ruthie shushed him. "She knows."

Dolores' gaze came back into the room, and it was like her brain took its time following her eyes. "Oliver Hardy pushed me."

"What are you talking about?" Eddie asked.

"Oliver Hardy pushed me."

I had a hunch of what she was talking about because Dolores and Louis used to love going to the motion pictures together when they were courting, and she always liked Laurel and Hardy. It didn't make any sense but I asked her if she meant he was fat.

Dolores nodded. "Oliver Hardy pushed me. Stan Laurel went upstairs to check the water."

"Was one of the guys skinny and one fat?"

She nodded again.

Ruthie and Eddie looked at each other and then at me. "What else do you remember about them?" Eddie asked.

"Oliver Hardy had a caterpillar on his cheek," Dolores said. "And he pushed me."

When I was a kid, I didn't think anything of teasing my younger sister. If she cried, so what? When you're young and careless, those things don't matter. You skin your knee or someone doesn't pick you for their team? You cry for a minute and then you move on. But when Dolores repeated "he pushed me," a tear dripped down my sister's cheek and sent me over the edge. I promised myself right then that if I ever found the guys who did this, I'd cause them as much pain as they were causing my sister.

When the kids and I talked to Dolores' doctor a little while later, we asked him why she was speaking in riddles when she'd been fine before the hip surgery. He was a young guy with a big moustache that he probably thought made him look distinguished. I thought it made him look like an idiot. "A lot of patients have what we call postoperative delirium after hip surgery," he said. "About ten percent of patients have longer-term cognitive or neurological alterations. It's exacerbated when you have an elderly patient."

"My sister is only sixty-eight years old." She's two years younger than I am. If Dolores is elderly, what does that make me?

"She's over sixty-five," the doctor said, like that was an explanation for everything.

"What does this really mean?" Ruthie asked. "Is this temporary? Will she be okay?"

The doctor put one hand to his chin and gave his huge moustache a thoughtful little stroke. "It's too early to tell."

I didn't want to say "thanks for nothing," but I sure thought it.

I was scheduled to meet the police back at the house so they could search for evidence. When I walked in the back door, it felt like I was walking into somebody else's house. The officer on the phone had said it was a crime scene and not to touch anything the thieves might have touched. A crime scene is something you see on a television show. It isn't supposed to be your home.

I figured the fellow who pushed Dolores might have left fingerprints on the water meter. I steered clear of the basement and went upstairs, making sure not to touch the bannister in case there were fingerprints on it. The wood is worn shiny smooth from three generations of Steiners going up and down, but it's as solid as the Rock of Gibraltar. I've made sure of that. Just because something is old doesn't mean it has to be weak.

I had touched the faucet in the bathtub the day before but nothing else. And nobody had been back to the house since we went to the hospital. The empty cigar box was still on the bed in Dolores' room where I put it the day before. I wondered if the police would need to take my fingerprints too. I didn't want to be in the house, so I sat on the porch in the cold for two hours until the police arrived. The sight of a squad car in the drive made me feel like some of the hillbilly trash who started moving into the neighborhood a few years ago. They always seem to have shouting matches in the middle of the street and garbage in the front yard. I say if a man can mind his own business, take care of his friends, and hold his liquor, he never needs to talk to a police officer.

Seems like Joe conveniently forgot that wasn't the first police car to ever grace their driveway. Louis moved back to his family permanently after Eddie was born. After that, the house at 602 Audubon would regularly have squad cars pull up and deposit a drunken Louis Nagy in his front yard. Young Eddie was with him on occasion because he was too young to drive his father home from the horse track or wherever he'd taken the boy. Nothing more than a slap on the wrist ever came of it. Louis was saved by being a charming drunk. And it didn't hurt that he had been friends with the deputy sheriff since they were kids.

One of the police officers took a statement from me while the other poked around the house a bit and dusted things for fingerprints. That was it. It wasn't like on *Columbo* or any of the other detective shows. Apparently when the police came to talk to Dolores at the hospital, she told them Stan Laurel sounded like Rudolph Valentino. Now I know for a fact that Valentino never said a word onscreen. I tried to explain to the police about how Dolores had been speaking in riddles since she came out of surgery and that she probably meant the skinny guy had an accent. The police said they'd put out the description — two guys, one medium height, heavy-set Caucasian with a birthmark on his cheek and one tall and skinny with some kind of accent — but you could tell they were just going through the motions to make some hunched-over old lady with a broken hip feel better. With all the real crime and arson and everything else going on in the city, a scam robbery wasn't going to be a priority. They said we were lucky it wasn't worse.

Dolores was supposed to stay in the hospital for about a week to make sure she was healing properly, then they were going to send her to a rehabilitation center. She still sounded kind of loopy even a couple days after the surgery, but Dr. Distinguished Moustache thought everything would work itself out and said she'd be home in a month or two. I kept hoping him and his moustache were right.

Ruthie and Eddie both asked if I wanted to come stay with one of them for a little while, but I knew Peggy would be coming down from Cleveland to stay with her sister and be with her mother. My oldest nephew, Louis, was going to come in from New Jersey. He'd probably stay with Eddie, who had enough going on with his kids. I made a joke about living the bachelor life for a while. Usually I move back into the house when the weather gets cold, and the *Farmers' Almanac* was forecasting this winter to be a doozy, but the house didn't feel the same anymore. I stayed in the garage. I didn't tell anyone about the robbery, but everybody in Smoky Hollow knew just the same. People find things out.

Dolores typically does the shopping because she always worries I'll spend all our money on beer or whiskey or cheese twists or something frivolous. We couldn't have survived all these years with a solid roof over our heads and three squares a day if I were that careless, but Dolores likes to have something to complain about. Three days after the robbery, I found myself at home with some time on my hands and no beer in the house, so I took a walk over to McGuffey's. The garage has a hot plate and a refrigerator. I can live out there pretty comfortably, but I can't make dinner out of nothing.

The first thing John McGuffey said when I walked in the door of the store was "Hey, I hear you got robbed." He didn't even say "Hello."

"Yeah, we did," I replied and went about my business. McGuffey's isn't all that big — it's not a full grocery. You have to drive a few miles over to Sparkle for that. And I'll be dipped if John McGuffey didn't follow me around the store's five tiny aisles, up and down, asking a new question in every aisle: Did the cops catch the guys who did it? What happened? What did they take? Did they break in? How's Dolores?

I stopped walking and looked at him. "Do you realize I've been in here ten minutes and you've asked half a dozen questions and just now got around to asking about Dolores? For crying out loud, she broke her hip. A decent man would have asked about my sister first."

McGuffey mumbled an apology and rang up my groceries. Next to the register, he had a display of candy and gum and on top of it a little chalkboard where he wrote the winning lottery numbers for the past two weeks. The big lotto jackpot was over a million dollars, but for that one, you had to pick six numbers between one and forty. I don't think Hope ever gave Dolores any numbers for that. I didn't like the idea of making money off a child, but ho-ho-ho, the cars I could buy with a million dollars would keep me happily occupied for the rest of my natural days.

One of the daily numbers from the previous week was ooo. McGuffey caught me looking at the chalkboard. "Ain't that something?" he said feebly, as though we had been having a pleasant conversation the whole time. "Zero-zero-zero. What are the odds?"

"About the same as any three numbers coming up," I replied.

McGuffey finished putting my groceries into bags and handed them over without looking at me. "Guess you're right," he said quietly.

"Damn straight I'm right. You're a businessman. I would think you'd know basic math." I didn't say anything else to him. Just took my groceries and walked home.

Dolores was scheduled to move from the hospital to the rehab center on a Saturday. Ruthie insisted on being there for the move. Phil had to work during the week, so he could really only visit on the weekend. Plus Peggy was in town from Cleveland to help. Hope would just get in the way, so I told her to bring the kid over to the house for a few hours while they did the whole move. My time is my own — I could go to evening visiting hours later in the day.

Even though I wasn't spending much time in the house, it seemed like a good idea to keep it clean. If the house was dirty when she came home, Dolores would have a conniption fit. Especially because she wouldn't be able to clean for a good six to eight weeks.

Hope helped me run a mop on the floor in the kitchen, then she got bored cleaning, so we played Go Fish in the living room. I let her deal, and we played for a few minutes. Then Hope lowered the cards from her face and kind of gazed off into space for a moment. I could almost hear the gears turning in her little head as she absent-mindedly scratched her chin with the cards. "Daddy said that somebody stole Grandma's money."

"That's true," I replied.

"Why do people steal?"

Sister Felicitas, nee Gertrude Farmer, taught religion and theology at Ursuline for forty-six years. She entered the convent at age fourteen because her mother decided that God deserved at least one of her four daughters. If Mrs. Farmer had had more than one son, God probably would have gotten a priest out of the deal too. After four-and-a-half decades of trying to get bored teenagers to think about the persistent questions of life, Sister Felicitas realized she wasn't any closer to real answers than her students. The Mother Superior said Sister Felicitas died suddenly in her sleep. I know better.

When kids ask big questions like this, I always opt for what Sister Felicitas back at Ursuline High School called the Socratic method. It's the only way to avoid embarrassing yourself by admitting you have no idea. "Why do *you* think people steal?"

"Because ... the other person has something they want?"

"Probably."

"Stealing is a sin. We learned that in school. We're learning all about sin and stuff this year."

"Do you have any twos?" I asked. She didn't. As I pulled a card from the mixed-up pile in between us, I asked "As I recall, you just made your First Confession, didn't you?"

"Yep. A couple weeks ago. That's why they taught us about sin. Do you have any queens?" I did, and handed her the Queen of Hearts, which had been sitting in my hand from the get-go. "I knew you had a queen. I remember that was the very first thing you asked for," she said.

"Good memory. Do you have any fives?"

"Thank you. And no. Go Fish."

We played for a few minutes and then Hope asked if the police had found the men who robbed Grandma. "No, they haven't," I replied.

"But they're looking for those guys, right?"

"Maybe. There are a lot worse things happening in the city right now. I'm sure the police have bigger fish to fry."

"What does that mean?"

I sometimes forget that even a smart kid like Hope is still figuring out the English language. "It means that when you have a lot of things to do, you have to prioritize, or figure out which thing is the most important and do that first."

"Does that mean the cops don't think finding the guys who robbed Grandma is important?"

"They think it's important. But maybe not as important as finding, say, somebody really dangerous."

"I guess so. But I still want them to find those guys."

"So do I."

Hope's eyes grew big and excited looking and I swear I saw a little lightbulb go on over her head. She dropped her cards on the floor and sat up tall. "Why don't we look for them? Why don't *we* find them?"

"You and me?" Somehow the idea of playing detective with a second grader seemed like an exercise in futility.

"We could go to Grandma's room and look for clues. Or could we go to Mr. McGuffey's and *question* him," Hope said. "Like the Bobbsey Twins or Sherlock Holmes."

"We aren't detectives."

"Oh fine," she sighed.

It occurred to me that Hope had gone to McGuffey's with Dolores practically every week. If someone had noticed Dolores consistently cashing in winning tickets, maybe Hope had noticed him. "Hope, I need to ask you something very important. When you and Grandma go to McGuffey's to play the number, who do you see?"

"We haven't done that for a while," she said dreamily as she picked her cards back up. "Do you have any tens?"

"Go fish," I said.

Hope screwed her face up like she was thinking hard, and I thought she whispered something to herself as she held her hand over the pile of mixed-up cards on the coffee table. I was looking at her face, but a little bit of movement on the table caught my eye, as though she was digging around for a card at the bottom of the pile. Except her hand didn't move. Obviously, it must have moved because she was suddenly holding a single card and cards don't just hop into little girls' hands of their own accord.

"How'd you do that trick?" I asked

"What trick?"

"It looked like you moved a card without touching it, like it came to you instead of the other way around."

She turned the card in her hand so it faced me. It was a ten. "Look, I got my wish!"

"Lucky girl."

"It isn't luck." She paused for a second in that way some kids have when they're about to tell you a big secret. Then she kind of sighed and said, "Yeah, it was. Still my turn. Do you have any aces?"

"Nope, go fish."

She drew another card, but I noticed she didn't whisper to herself before she drew. "Did you get an ace?" I asked.

"No."

We played the game for a minute, but I was still curious. "I know you and Grandma don't go to McGuffey's to play the lottery anymore, but when you did, who did you see?"

"Mr. McGuffey," she replied.

"Besides Mr. McGuffey. Did you ever see some people there more than once?"

She thought for a minute, holding her cards up and covering her eyes with them, her face scrunched up. "Well, there's Mrs. Antonelli. She always asks me how school is going and if I've made my First Communion yet. And there are some big boys who ride their bikes everywhere and smell all sweaty, but they always hold the door open for Grandma so I guess they're okay, and there's the chubby man who said Grandma ought to buy me candy because she just won the lottery. He said it twice."

"Twice in one day?"

"No. I saw him two different times and he said the exact same thing both times. I don't think he's very smart. It's your turn, Uncle Joe."

"Oh, um ... do you have any kings?"

"Nope! Go fish!"

I pulled an eight out of the pile and thought for a moment. How much could it hurt to find out a few more details? "A chubby guy, huh? Did Grandma know this chubby guy?"

"She didn't see him. We were over by the candy and stuff, and Grandma was at the register because she likes to talk to Mr. McGuffey about how much things cost. Do you have any eights?" she asked.

"Aw shucks, I just drew that! Here you go ... " I said, handing her the card.

"Thank you," Hope replied politely, as though she knew I had drawn an eight on my last turn. "I go again. Do you have any twos?"

"I do," I replied and handed it over. "Say, did this fellow have light skin or dark skin?"

"Light." Hope was concentrating intently on the cards in her hand and didn't look up.

What else did he look like?"

"He had brown hair and a birthmark, right *here*," she said, pointing to her left cheek, just on top of her cheek-bone. "I think it had a *hair* growing out of it. It looked like a little caterpillar on his face," she added. She said this last thing kind of quietly like, she was talking to herself, but boy oh boy did I hear it.

"Wait, what did you say?"

"It looked like he had a caterpillar on his face."

Hope hadn't been in the room with us when Dolores was talking about Laurel and Hardy, but I had to check.

"That's a crazy description. Where did you hear somebody say that?" I figured she'd say that her mother had repeated what Dolores said, but instead Hope looked at me with that look young children sometimes get when they realize grown-ups might not be as smart as they thought.

"Nowhere. I made it up because that's what it looked like," Hope replied.

That was enough for me. "Would you recognize him if you saw him again?"

"Sure. Do you know him, Uncle Joe?"

"No, but your Grandma said the exact same thing about one of the fellows who robbed her."

Hope threw all of her cards into the air. "Maybe it's the same guy!" she screamed. "Let's go find him."

"How?"

"Let's ask Mr. McGuffey."

"Hold your horses. Plenty of people have birthmarks. It's not much to go on."

"But it's *something*! Come on. Please can we go to McGuffey's? *Please*?"

If there's one thing I can't stand, it's when a kid starts to whine. In this case, I didn't mind giving in. I was more than ready to stop playing Go Fish anyway.

It took all Hope's self-control to put the cards away, put on her coat and boots, and walk to McGuffey's instead of running like a wild banshee. I told her that when we got to McGuffey's, she should talk to Mr. McGuffey like she always does and not mention anything about being detectives or looking for clues. "While we're there, do you want to buy a lottery ticket for your Grandma?" I asked. "Just for fun? We can bring it to her later."

"I don't feel like it," she said, and skipped over a couple of cracks in the sidewalk.

We had a little snow on the ground — just a few inches, but John had the heat cranked up in the store so high the windows were starting to fog up. The place felt like a Turkish bath. "Okay, Hope," I said nonchalantly as we walked in. "One treat for you and one treat for me, got it?"

"Okay! Thanks, Uncle Joe," she said and happily skipped over to the candy aisle.

"Hey Joe," McGuffey said. "I see you're on babysitting duty today, huh?"

"I'm not a baby," Hope called from the back of the store. "I'm almost eight." You could definitely hear a conversation at the register if you were in the candy aisle. McGuffey had a pretty clear view of the store from behind the counter, but I had to turn around to see Hope. If you were standing in the candy aisle watching someone cash in a lottery ticket, it wouldn't be hard to stay out of their line of vision.

I gave McGuffey a "Kids — what are you gonna do?" kind of shrug and a smile and leaned on the counter to make small talk about football while Hope picked out her candy.

"What kind of candy do you like, Uncle Joe?" "Pabst Blue Ribbon," McGuffey said and laughed at his own bad joke.

"Necco Wafers."

"I like those too. Can I have some and I'll give you some of my Tootsie Roll?"

"Sure."

Hope brought the candy over to the counter, and I took my time getting out my wallet.

"I haven't seen you since you were in with your grandma. It's been a while," McGuffey said to Hope.

"My grandma's been in the hospital, so it would be kind of hard for her to come in and buy lottery tickets," she replied. John glanced over at me like he was waiting for me to say something. Normally a child who was being rude would get a scolding from me, but I was still annoyed enough with McGuffey that I let it go. And I had other things on my mind, because the ridiculousness of what we were doing started to sink in right about then. I guess maybe I thought we could hang around McGuffey's and the chubby guy with the birthmark would just miraculously show up.

Then Hope announced, "My dad has to go the hospital too. He's having a birthmark removed because they think it might be cancer, but I'm pretty sure it's not."

"Wow, that's sounds kind of scary," John said.

I had seen Phil that very morning and knew he had no such birthmark. I gave Hope a quick look, and she smiled back at me with that little angel face and kept right on going.

"The doctor said that if you have a big birthmark, you should get it removed so they can see if it has cancer in it. *Nobody* wants to have *cancer*. But my dad's lucky, because it's on his leg. *Imagine* if you had a big birthmark on your face. Then you'd definitely want to have it removed."

"I'll keep that in mind," John said to Hope. He rang up the candy, put my money in the cash register, and handed the change to Hope. "Here you are, young lady. Twenty-four cents change."

"Thank you," Hope said. "Twenty-four is a nice number." She looked at the change in her hand for a moment and then looked up at McGuffey. "Do you know anyone with a birthmark on their face?"

He looked her dead in the eye and said, "No, I can't say that I do."

The most I've ever been able to say about John McGuffey is that he doesn't gouge you on the staples like milk and bread and eggs. When you want a little snack, though, like a bag of Doritos or some cookies, you'll pay through the nose. McGuffey knows that nobody is going to drive four miles over to Sparkle just for a bag of potato chips. I never thought of him as a dishonest businessman until he lied to my great-niece's face. Don't ask me how I knew he was lying. Maybe it's because he didn't look at me at all, only at Hope. Adults lie to children all the time. Between Santa Claus, the Easter Bunny, and the Tooth Fairy, it's practically a national pastime. But that doesn't make it the right thing to do, not when there's something important at stake.

I didn't bother saying anything else to McGuffey, just led Hope out of the store and headed home. She walked with her head down, eyes on the sidewalk. "Now what do we do?" she asked me finally. From the expression on her face, I realized she must have expected we'd be halfway to tracking down these guys by now. My fault. I should have realized even a fool's errand would get her riled up.

"Maybe we can go look around for them sometime," I said, trying to make her feel better.

Immediately her enthusiasm was back in action. "When? Can we go now?"

"No, no, we're going to go out to the rehab center to see your grandma and I'll hand you off to your parents. Grandma should be all settled in by now."

"Daddy said that those guys said they were from the Water Department. Maybe we should ask somebody from there."

"I think they were lying about being from the Water Department."

"Oh, right." She walked quietly for a minute, deftly skipping and stepping over all the iced-over cracks in the sidewalk.

"Step on a crack, break your mother's back," I chanted.

She stopped and looked genuinely upset. "I'm trying not to. I stepped on one once in kindergarten and that's when Mommy hurt her back."

"Oh Hope, you didn't hurt your Mom. She slipped on the ice on your driveway and twisted her back. It wasn't your fault."

"How do you know?"

"I don't know for sure, but I've been on this planet for nearly seventy years and I've never known anyone to have their back broken because their child stepped on a crack in the sidewalk."

"I know what I can do," she replied and went back to skipping over and around the cracks.

Children get all up in arms about the darndest things. You just have to nod and play along.

III

We met the rest of the family at the rehab center later in the afternoon. It's over on the South Side, not really close to where we live. Truth be told, it's a better neighborhood. The rehab center is called Fairemeade and it's nice. The hospital recommended it, and you figure they ought to know. Dolores had her own little room on the second floor with a view of some trees and benches down below. Better than looking at the parking lot.

She still wasn't herself. I don't know how to describe it. Dolores hasn't always been the easiest person to get along with. She's polite — our mother raised us to act like a lady and a gentleman — but she'll always tell you exactly what she's thinking. The old Dolores would have driven the entire staff of the rehab center bonkers within three

Dolores Nagy did drive the staff of Fairemeade Assisted Nursing Facility crazy, but only because she made them do every little thing for her. Adjust the pillows? She rang the bell. Change the channel on the television? She rang the bell and claimed she didn't know how the remote control worked. I've watched Dolores on and off for most of her life. At first I thought she was just taking advantage of the one time in her life people were there to pick up after her instead of the other way around. After a few days, I agreed with Joe. She was different.

days because she'd tell them all that they were cleaning wrong or how to make the food better. Ever since the surgery, though, she'd been kind of loopy, like she wasn't really paying attention to what was going on around her. That wasn't like her.

Hope helped me pick out a few of her favorite books before we left. Dolores has always been a fan of old potboiler mysteries. I thought maybe reading would help her pass the time when the therapist wasn't working on getting her hip back in shape. The therapist looked like she was still in high school but she seemed to know what she was doing.

Ruthie and her family left around six o'clock. I stayed and chatted with Dolores while she ate her dinner. She didn't say much back. At six twenty-eight, I asked if she wanted to turn on the TV to watch them draw the daily number. She looked at me like she didn't know what I was talking about. "Why do they give every day a number? Why don't they just look at the calendar?" she asked.

"It's not the date, it's the Daily Number. People pick a number and if they pick right, they win money."

"Ohhh ... that." I turned on the television and we watched them pick the number, nine-three-two. "I'm glad we didn't buy a ticket for that," Dolores said. "It doesn't have a double number."

I didn't have the heart to try and explain that the double numbers were just a Hope thing, and that she would have won if she had bought a ticket with nine-three-two today. As much as I griped about her and Hope going down to McGuffey's all the time, it had been fun for them. That was another thing that got my goat about the guys who robbed Dolores. They didn't just hurt her. They didn't just take her money. They took one of the few things that really seemed to give my sister pleasure, one of the few things she did for fun. And now it looked like they might have taken the best part of her mind too.

I left when visiting hours ended at eight o'clock and took the long way home, thinking about the robbery. I know when something like that happens, you're supposed to thank God nobody got killed. I know it could have been worse, but if the man upstairs arranged it so Dolores wasn't killed, just hurt, why should I thank him for that? And look what happened after they fixed her hip.

Some of those Holy Rollers came by the house last summer to talk about my personal relationship with God. I told them I don't talk about my personal relationships with strangers and closed the door. Church stopped being a moving experience for me long, long ago. I still go, more out of habit than anything else. It's a chance to catch up with the neighbors, and it keeps Dolores from crabbing at me. Plus, sometimes I pick up extra work for myself or Javorsik's garage.

Usually Dolores is the one who nudges me off to church with her, but the next morning I went on my own, no nudging required. I went partly out of curiosity because Father Troha, our pastor, was supposed to finally announce that he was leaving to go to El Salvador and do missionary work. Dolores and the other old biddies in the parish had been buzzing about this for a month at least. It was the worst-kept secret in the history of Saints Cyril and Methodius Church. But if he was really going to announce it, I figured I ought to be there so I could give Dolores a blow-by-blow account later. If she even cared anymore.

When we go to church at St. Cyril, Dolores always sits in the second row in the left transept, over by the confessional. That's been our family's pew for years, even when there's just the two of us. I sat there thinking I'd be all by myself when Ruthie and her family and Peggy, my other niece, showed up. Suddenly the pew was pleasantly crowded.

Dolores and I grew up in the parish, and all four of her kids went through St. Cyril. When Eddie and his three kids lived with us, his kids went there too, so we can say

When her oldest daughter moved sixty-five miles away to Cleveland, Dolores threatened to stay in her room for forty days and forty nights. I have to give Peggy credit — she was twenty years old with her first real job offer and she went. Her first home in Cleveland was a residential hotel called the Catholic Young Women's Hall. I can't vouch for whether every resident was Catholic, or young, or even female, but the name made Dolores feel a little better. And it wasn't forty days and forty nights. She came out of her room after five hours because Eddie and Ruthie were still in high school and needed dinner.

we've had three generations there. I like that kind of continuity. Ruthie and her family live across town and Hope goes to St. Christine's, but they come to church with us once or twice a month. Phil isn't even Catholic, but he still shows up out of loyalty to his wife.

It was nice to see Peggy with them. I don't get to see her very often anymore, what with her living in Cleveland with her husband and their flock of kids. Louis Jr. left home early for his job with the phone company and travels quite a bit. Peggy was always the sensible older sister when Ruthie and Eddie got up to some hijinks.

During Communion, I spotted Ralph Krasniak slowly making his way down the main aisle with his two older kids walking behind him and his wife bringing up the rear to catch any stragglers. Ralph's Polish, but he goes to St. Cyril with us Slovaks because there isn't a Polish parish in the Hollow and he's too lazy to go across town just for church. The Communion line sometimes moves so slowly you can practically have a conversation as someone goes by you. Peggy was next to me on the kneeler, head bowed, praying away. Ruthie was on my other side, hunched over, head buried in her hands. She always looks to me like prayer is something painful for her. Phil's job was to keep Hope quiet and occupied.

While the rest of the family was praying, I was thinking about how to find the low-lifes who robbed Dolores. Smoky Hollow is small enough that everybody knows everybody else, so it couldn't have been someone from the neighborhood. Dolores would have recognized them. With so many people out of work in the city, it could have been anybody. And speaking of people who are out of work, there was Ralph in all his unemployed glory. He lives near McGuffey's and might have noticed somebody from outside the neighborhood hanging around.

I tried to catch Ralph's eye, but he had his head down, hands lightly folded in front of him in that kind of halfway-to-prayer stance most of us adopt after the age of nine. His two boys were right behind him and doing pretty much the same thing he was, so I guess his semi-reverent example didn't go to waste, but it made it hard to get his attention.

The choir and about twelve people were singing the Communion hymn, so I took the liberty of stage-whispering Ralph's name. Ruthie and Peggy both looked at me like I had just stood up and started singing *The Star-Spangled Banner*. Hope giggled.

Ralph nodded and smiled, but immediately focused his attention back to the spot on the ground in front of him. I knew he was just putting on the prayerful front because his wife and kids were there, but it made me look bad in front of my nieces.

Right before the final benediction, Father Troha formally announced that he was leaving Saints Cyril and Methodius in the spring to do mission work in El Salvador. Everybody in the church gasped as though they all hadn't been talking about this for the past month. He's a popular priest, and on top of the closing of the Campbell Works, having Father Troha leave gave everybody one more reason to believe the sky was falling.

After mass was over, Ruthie and Peggy and the rest got in line to see Father Troha. I went looking for Ralph. His

wife and kids were standing in the long line to talk to Father
Troha too, so I knew that Ralph and a cigarette would be
just outside the front doors.

The front of the church looks like it has a big concrete
front porch with stairs on both sides and a brick and stone
railing. It's the place where brides and kids making their
First Communion wait outside before making their grand
entrance and where pallbearers worry about tripping on the
steps after funerals. There's always a bunch of guys hanging around off the stairs to the left, near the sidewalk. If
they were on the other side, folks going to the parking lot
would see them. Sure enough, Ralph was out there with a
bunch of other guys from the neighborhood, huddled together against the cold, having their after-church smoke
and talking about football. We're smack dab in between
Cleveland and Pittsburgh, so everybody kind of roots for
either the Browns or the Steelers or sometimes both. The
prospect of getting home before game time was the only
reason anybody ever made it to early mass.

"Hey, Joe," Ralph said as I walked down the stairs.
"Waddya know?"

"Hi fellas. Pretty big news about Father Troha, eh?"

"I'll say, going to work in El Salvador? Isn't that all
jungle?"

"Mostly jungle," one of the other guys said. "But a few
piss holes too."

The other guys laughed and went back to talking football. I took the opportunity to talk to Ralph one-on-one.

"How's the Charger running, Ralph?"

"It's running great, thanks. Of course, now I don't have
a job to go to, but the Charger she's a-runnin'."

"Well, you've got a good attitude," I said. "You'll find
something else." Ralph is the most happy-go-lucky Pole
I've ever met. Any other guy in his situation would be mop-
ing around and complaining about his bad luck, but Ralph

just keeps joking away. I took a couple of steps back up the stairs, to kind of draw him away from the other guys without seeming impolite. It seemed like he wanted to talk to me in private too. We leaned on the stone railing and looked out over the parking lot and neighborhood beyond, our backs to the front door of the church.

"Are you still working over at Javorsik's?" Ralph asked in a quiet voice, like he was placing a bet and didn't want anybody to hear.

"Just one or two days a week. He calls me when he needs me."

"Do you know if he's hiring anybody?"

"Sorry, but I don't think so. It's been slow," I replied. I didn't bother to mention that if Ralph were a good enough mechanic for someone to hire, I wouldn't have to work on his Charger all the time.

"Yeah, it's been slower than the Browns' offensive line. But I figure something will turn up."

"Of course it will," I said. "Anybody you know from the Sheet & Tube find work yet?"

"A couple of guys, but they were all higher up, management types or had some college."

"Well, it's only been a couple months."

"Oh yeah, sure. Nobody's desperate yet, although I think Santa's gonna have a quiet Christmas this year," he said with a sad half-smile. "So how are yunz doin'?"

"No complaints."

"I was just wondering because I heard about the house getting robbed. Glad Dolores is gonna be okay. Broken hips are serious business."

"She seems to be healing all right. Thanks for asking." We're a pretty tight-knit neighborhood in the Hollow, so I knew people had heard about the robbery. I don't like gossip, but when you live close by to people, sometimes that's what you get.

"Cops have any idea who did it?" Ralph asked.

"Nope. They said it sounded like a Gypsy scam."

"I heard a couple other old … older, you know, retired people got robbed about a month ago. Some lady up on the North Side and some old guy down in Struthers."

"Really? Where'd you hear that?"

"Some guys were talking about it over at the Tip Top Lounge last night. Not a scam, just your garden-variety break in when the people were out of the house. It's getting rough out there. Robberies and people getting hurt and all these fires … ."

"Call them what they are — arson for insurance money," I said.

"Yeah. You know, we're close to where the university was trying to buy up people's houses. If they made us an offer, I'd take it … ." Ralph's eyes got a little misty looking, like he was looking at something too far away to see clearly. "Except we don't have anywhere else to go."

You people always think about leaving, about moving on. You have some cockamamie idea that the grass grows greener in some other city. Didn't you learn anything from *The Wizard of Oz*? You want to find your heart's desire? You don't need to look any farther than Federal Plaza. I'll tell you this now: No other city will ever take you in and hold you the way I do. No matter how far away you go, I'll be with you. You might as well just stay here.

"Hi, Uncle Joe!"

I was startled to see Hope standing next to me. "Hope, you snuck up on me like an Indian."

"I'm not an Indian. I'm a spy," she said with a raise of her little eyebrows.

"What are you doing here?"

"I got bored waiting to talk to Father Troha so I decided to come out and talk to you."

"Well, that's nice of you. Ralph, you know my great-niece, Hope, right?"

"Sure, you helped your uncle fix my car a few months ago."

"Yep, that was me," Hope said. "How's it running?"

Ralph chuckled. I don't think his kids are as charming as Hope is. "It's running just fine, thank you. Yunz did a good job."

"Thanks."

"Do you think you'll grow up to be a lady mechanic?"

"No, I'm going to be an astronaut," Hope said very matter of factly.

"A lady astronaut?" Ralph kind of laughed. "I don't think we've had one of those."

"I'm not going to be a *lady* astronaut. Just an astronaut." Hope said the word "lady" like it was some other kind of four-letter word. Then she stared up at me and at Ralph like she was waiting for me to say something. I guess I was quiet too long for her tastes because then, she just blurted out to Ralph, "Do you know a fat guy with a birthmark on his cheek?"

Ralph burst out laughing, which I could see annoyed Hope to no end. I've always tried to treat children like rational beings. Why not? They're raw human material that just needs shaping. Why not shape them into thinkers? Laughing at them doesn't do them any good. "Dolores said that one of the guys who robbed her was kind of chubby and had a birthmark on his cheek," I explained.

Hope just stood there glaring at Ralph until he said, "Oh sorry, sweetie. I wasn't laughing at you. Something your uncle said before just struck me as funny."

"Well do you?" Hope said.

"There's no need to be rude," I said to her gently and added to Ralph, "We're still a little upset by the whole thing."

"Well sure, somebody strolls into your house and steals all your money and breaks your Grandma's hip. You have every right to be mad, Hope."

She looked satisfied with that, but you could see she was still waiting around for an answer, so I said, "You live near McGuffey's. You see anybody who fits that description hanging around, somebody who might have seen Dolores with some cash?"

"Oh, I see what you're saying." Ralph thought for a minute. "No, I haven't seen anybody but the usual neighborhood rug rats lately. I did used to work with a guy in the blast furnace a couple years ago who had kind of a good-sized birthmark on his cheek, but I haven't seen him since before they closed the mill."

"What was his name?" Hope asked.

"Um, Bob. Bobby. What the hell was his last name? It'll come to me."

"Was he fat?" Hope asked, like she was some short Kojak.

Ralph gave another little chuckle. "Naw, nobody could get fat in the blast furnace. All you did was sweat all day. Anyway, he was a good guy. Not some low-life scum."

Just then, all the little Krasniaks and Ralph's wife, Doris, came out. He has two boys who both look older than Hope and a girl a little bit younger. Hope and the youngest Krasniak looked at each other like two cute little dogs sniffing each other and trying to decide if they want to play or not.

"Hi," Hope said.

"Hi," the little one said back.

"Hope, this is my daughter, Sally," Ralph said.

"Can we go now?" said the oldest Krasniak. Doris hushed him.

"How old are you?" Hope asked.

"Five."

"Almost five," Doris said. "December first. Another week and a half."

"I was born in December too," Hope said.

"It's the best month," Sally said.

Then Doris said to Ralph that they needed to get home because they were going to her parents for lunch. Ralph kind of rolled his eyes and muttered to me, "Hey, it's a free meal." Guess he didn't say it quietly enough because Doris just said, "Yes, it is. With leftovers."

"Have fun being five," Hope said to Sally. "It's a good number."

"Thanks," Sally said over her shoulder as Doris hustled her away. Then it was

Doris Swirski used to walk around Ursuline High School like a runway model. She was voted "Best Looking" in her graduating class and bought her prom dress with money she earned being a model in advertising circulars for Strouss' Department Store. Ralph Krasniak told her all the time she ought to move to New York and be a model because she was pretty enough to. He was lying, not about the being pretty enough to be a model part, just the part where she should move to New York. Doris went. For seven months she worked as a waitress in a pizza shop on 44th Street and waited for her big break. Ralph wrote her a letter a week the entire time. Her stint in New York taught Doris two things: 1) she wasn't the only pretty girl in the world, 2) being the only pretty girl for a nice guy with a steady job who adored her didn't seem like such a bad way to go through life. I got Doris Swirski Krasniak back. Too bad, you Big Sour Apple.

just me and Hope out there on the front steps of St. Cyril. The other guys had finished their cigarettes and gone back inside or home or wherever they were going to go. I was starting to freeze my tail off, so I shooed Hope inside the front doors to get her out of the cold.

"Hope, I think when we're being detectives we should try to be a little more subtle when we're questioning people," I said.

57

"What does 'subtle' mean?"

"It means you don't go around asking people if they know a fat guy with a birthmark." I guess I might have sounded angrier than I was because Hope looked really upset, like she might cry. I forget sometimes how easily little girls can cry. "I just mean, we're a team, right? We're working on this case together. Let's make sure we plan our next moves together, okay?"

She nodded and said okay, and then we went in to find the rest of the family. They were still waiting in line to talk to Father Troha, who was standing in the rear vestibule of the church talking to parishioners on their way out. Normally people file out quickly, with just a wave or maybe a quick handshake, but today everybody wanted to talk to Father Troha and tell him how much he meant to them, even though he won't be leaving for six months. Since our pew is near the front of the church, the family was stuck near the end of the line to talk to the good father. The last shall be first and the first shall be last and all that.

Hope and I cut into line next to Peg, Ruthie, and Phil.

"Hi, Mommy! Hi, Daddy" Hope gave Ruthie a big hug that almost sent her poor mother to the ground. Ruthie made an "Ugh!" sound as though Hope knocked the wind out of her.

"Sorry," Hope said.

"It's okay," Ruthie said. "I'm fine." "What are you and Uncle Joe up to?"

"We were with some of Uncle Joe's friends, just chatting."

Hope is one of those kids who can say things like that and the adults around her just think she's being precocious. "Are you going to wish Father Troha good luck?" Ruthie asked.

"Yes, but he's not going anywhere until after Easter. I heard him. He's going to be here for First Communion."

"She's got a point, dear," Phil said, and I could see he was trying to hide how bored he was. "It's not as though today is the last time you'll ever see him."

"He announced that he's leaving today, so it's polite that we tell him today how much we admire his decision. Mission work in El Salvador is difficult and dangerous." Ruthie said this and then shifted her pocketbook in her hands, staring ahead of her, patiently waiting her turn.

"The Great Oz has spoken," Peggy said. Usually she's the only one in the family who could get away with making a joke like that without getting on Ruthie's bad side, but she must have hit a nerve because Ruthie played her trump card.

"If Mom were able to be here, she'd agree with me." The rest of us couldn't do anything but agree with her.

We finally had our turn to talk to Father Troha and everybody shook the poor guy's hand, even though he'd probably shaken a hundred and fifty hands already that morning. I have to say that the good father is a good guy because the first words out of his mouth were "How is your mother doing?" to Ruthie and Peggy.

"She's recovering," Ruthie replied.

"I'm glad to hear it. Please tell her I'll come and visit her this week."

"That's very kind of you. I know you must be busy wrapping up your affairs here."

"Well, I'm not leaving yet," Father Troha said. "You're stuck with me for a few more months. The last mass I celebrate at Saint Cyril will be the First Communion mass for the second graders on May seventh."

Hope turned and looked at her mother."Aww ... they're lucky!"

"Hope is making her First Communion this year," Phil explained.

"Are you?" Father Troha said. "I remember when you were just a wee little babe."

"I grew." This got a laugh, even though I could see Hope was completely serious.

"Hope," Peggy said, "your mom told me that you make your First Communion the week before, on April thirtieth. It's on my calendar. You can go to Father Troha's last mass *and* take communion like one of the big kids."

Hope's face exploded into a smile and then she seemed perfectly content to listen to her mother and aunt chat with Father Troha a little more. Phil was the one who finally had to remind them that people were still waiting behind us to talk to the good father and maybe we should move along.

Usually after mass, Ruthie and Eddie and their families come to our house for Sunday lunch, but since Thanksgiving was just a few days away, we gave each other a break from all the togetherness. And without Dolores there, it just wouldn't have been the same. Instead, when I got home, I didn't even go inside but walked down the street to the Tip Top Lounge.

I used to think the same thing, but one night I watched Rabisi scold the young guy working in the kitchen for using lukewarm water to wash the glasses and dishes. The guy said it made too much steam when it was really hot. Angelo told him to really clean the dishes the water needed to be scalding, like you were standing next to Jenny, one of the blast furnaces at the Brier Hill Works. He actually said, and I quote "When you're washing the dishes, it should feel like you're putting your hand into Jenny's pussy. That's why I give yunz gloves." After that, I didn't worry about hygiene at the Tip Top. And believe you me, I have enough to worry about.

I'm not a big drinker, but it's a man's prerogative to tipple his share once in a while, and besides, I had some investigating to do. The Tip Top is only a block away from the house. It's kind of a shot and a beer place with cheap food — nothing fancy and nothing dangerous. Sometimes nothing clean, but after living with Dolores all these years, a little bit of dirt can be a welcome sight. Dirty though it may be, the Tip Top is run well. It's owned by a fellow named Angelo Rabisi, and he doesn't put up with any shenanigans. If you wouldn't do it in front of your grandmother, you don't do it in front of Angelo.

I wasn't sure what or who I was looking for. Sometimes, if you just sit quietly long enough, you'll hear what you need to know. So I went into the Tip Top, made the obligatory small talk with Angelo, and ordered a beer. The two television sets behind the bar were playing the Browns-Giants game. I didn't have to pretend to be interested in that, but I did keep an ear open. I wasn't sure for what.

I eavesdropped on a lot of conversations, but none of them told me anything about some guy who might be named Bobby or Gypsy scams or anything else that would tell me who had robbed my sister and broken her hip. It was just plain dumb luck that Ralph had heard somebody talking about a robbery. It wasn't ours. And so what if he used to work with a guy named Bobby who had a big birthmark on his cheek? Plenty of people have birthmarks on their face. The guys weren't from the neighborhood and the Tip Top wasn't their bar.

Anyplace where you have a lot of men working together, you'll find a lot of bars. We men have our habits. We'll keep going to the same bar over and over even if we don't work near it anymore, even if our favorite bartender leaves, even if they change all the songs on the jukebox from big band to disco. We'll keep going back. All I had to do was find their bar and I could find them.

IV

onday night, I went to the Mahoning Valley Restaurant. MVR is a popular place, a landmark really. It isn't fancy, but my guess is it's still too nice a place for guys who would rob an old lady and knock her down. Tuesday, I stopped in two different bars downtown, but those were pretty much filled with white collar types, folks who work nearby and aren't petty thieves. At first, I kidded myself that I could somehow systematically check every bar in a five-mile radius. I even pulled out my street map, a pencil, and a compass and drew a bunch of concentric circles radiating from our house even though I knew those guys weren't from our neighborhood. If anything, I'd lay even money that one or both of them had worked at the mill. Men will do stupid things when they're out of work and need money. I erased the circles and drew a new set of concentric circles radiating from the Campbell Works. Most fellows like a bar that's close to work because it's convenient. If they're married, it gives them a little time to sober up on the way home. Realistically, I knew I'd never be able to visit every single bar around the mill, but a man needs a hobby.

The Campbell Works used to have five thousand guys working there in three shifts. It's too big to know everybody. People tend to mix with people they know, the ones they work with. For instance, the fellows in the rolling mill usually stuck together and didn't mix much with fellows from the blast furnace. All I had to go on was a guy with a birthmark and a fellow who might have an accent. Ralph said he knew one guy with a birthmark on his face from his blast furnace days. You don't need to be all that smart or to speak good English to shovel slag. That's where a lot of immigrants start out. Could be that's where the fellow with the accent worked. Ralph and one or two other guys from the neighborhood had worked in the blast furnace. The next step would be to find out what bars the blast furnace guys went to.

I had other responsibilities too. I still visited Dolores every day, spending a couple hours with her to help her pass the time. We didn't talk about the robbery. We didn't talk about much of anything. Sometimes I'd just sit with her in her room while she read one of her potboiler mysteries and I did a crossword. The mental side of things didn't seem to be improving. The people at the rehab center kept saying "Oh, that's just how she is," even though I tried to tell them that wasn't how she is, that my sister wasn't some loopy old lady. They must have gotten sick of me because finally one of the nurses took me aside and said that this might be who my sister was now. "We see this a lot," she said. "After a big physical trauma and surgery, some older patients don't fully recover their mental faculties."

Maybe they saw this kind of thing every day and were used to it by now. But this was my kid sister, and I sure didn't like the idea of her never being herself again. Neither did her children. We all just went on for a while pretending everything was okay.

That Thursday was Thanksgiving. Everybody used to come to our place for the holiday but, as Dolores has gotten older, it's gotten harder for her to cook for that many people, plus the family has gotten bigger, so we need more room than the little house on Audubon has. Ruthie and Phil have hosted Thanksgiving for the past few years, even though Dolores usually brings half the food across town anyway.

The rehab center said we could bring Thanksgiving to Dolores, so Ruthie still did the cooking, but then we had to cart everything over to Fairmeade. Ruthie is a competent cook. She knows how to cook a turkey. But she's spent so many years relying on her mother for advice that sometimes it seems like she doesn't trust herself. I like a family that sticks together, but too much togetherness can cripple you.

I got to Fairmeade around ten o'clock, so Dolores wouldn't be left alone all morning. I enjoy being with my sister. The only problem is, once I get there, after half an hour of talking, I'm itching to get up and fix something or walk somewhere or do something. When we're at the house, there's always something to do. Dolores and I share a house, but that's about it. We have our separate lives, our separate interests. On Thanksgiving morning, she almost seemed like herself, asking about the house, the weather outside, whether I'd cleaned the gutters before the first snow (even though she had seen me do it), what time I thought Eddie and his kids would be coming (even though I told her three times one o'clock), if I thought Peggy and her whole family would come and visit or just herself. After a while, we just put on the Ma-

Peggy was always one of my favorites. I can't see her when she's in Cleveland, but as soon as she comes to me, I know it. People who love you change the air around you. Peggy loves me. Her husband, Jack, is one of mine, too, from up Briar Hill way. He always makes their crew visit his family when they're in town, then if there's time they might squeeze in a visit to her family. It's always his people first, then hers. I'd take Peggy back in a heartbeat, but Cleveland can keep her husband.

cy's Thanksgiving Day Parade on the television in her room and watched that.

God only knows what time Ruthie started cooking that turkey, but she, Phil, and Hope showed up at one o'clock with a covered platter of turkey and stuffing and a covered dish of sweet potatoes. And God bless him, Eddie and his three young ones showed up fifteen minutes later with a dish of green beans and some cranberry sauce. The fact that he got all three kids, himself, and food to Fairmeade on time got a "Holy Jupiter!" from his mother, canned cranberry sauce be damned.

I wheeled Dolores down to the dining hall where a number of residents were celebrating Thanksgiving with their families. The rehab center was very nice about giving us real china plates and silverware and glasses. We commandeered two of the round tables and put the kids at one and the adults at the other. Of course, fifteen minutes later the kids were done eating and saying they were bored. Kids seem to get as bored with their parents as often they do with an old toy. I decided to give the parents a break. Out with the old, in with the new, here comes Great Uncle Joe to play.

Hope had a Thanksgiving coloring book and some crayons, so I set all four of them to coloring, even though Eddie's oldest, Edie, is twelve going on thirteen. Edie resembles her mother, much to my sister's consternation. At first, I thought Edie was supposed to be named for her father, but Eddie's former wife told me it was for some actress. Eddie's former wife named all their kids — Edie, Lou and Nico. When they got tired of coloring, they drew outlines of each of their hands to draw a flock of turkeys, and Hope and Nico walked around the dining room saying, "Gobble gobble gobble" and annoying everybody. It seemed like time to take evasive measures.

"Come on," I said. "We're going exploring." I figured Dolores wouldn't want the whole crew messing around in her room, so we headed in the direction of the lounge area down the hall, where I knew there was a big television.

We walked down the hall past open doors. Most of the rooms were empty, but I heard a woman's voice say, "It's the Thanksgiving Day Parade!" as we walked by, so I made the kids stop. The woman was all alone. I guess she had a daughter somewhere who couldn't make it back to Youngstown for the holiday, so the kids dragged her out to meet their parents and grandmother and they fixed her a big plate of food and everything was as it should be, with good cheer and kindness and all that.

After a bit, the good cheer and noise got to be a little more than I could stand, so I went back down the hallway and this time, I made it to the lounge. The only person in there was some fellow who probably wasn't much older than I am but looked like he'd been through the wringer. I noticed a walker next to him. I nodded. He nodded back. He had the television tuned to Channel 43, the UHF station out of Cleveland. They show *King Kong* every Thanksgiving Day. The relationship between *King Kong* and Thanksgiving has never seemed very clear to me, but they show it anyway.

Saying that Joe Steiner was sweet on Julia Winetsky is like saying it gets a little warm in a blast furnace. He was crazy about her. They went together for two years. Everybody figured they'd end up getting married. Old Grandma and Grandpa Steiner, Joe and Dolores's parents, liked her, and Julia wasn't even Slovak. Like most foolish young men, he got scared and messed the whole thing up.

I still remember when the movie came out. I was twenty-four years old and working for a fellow named Ernie Davenport, who had a garage downtown. I took a young lady I was sweet on at the time to see it. The special effects weren't like they have today with *Star Wars* and all that, but the first time I saw that gorilla, I was terrified, and my date was so scared that she held my hand the whole time. It was great.

The movie was just starting, so I happily sat down on one of the three aqua blue loveseats that ringed the television on the far end of the lounge. The screen was bigger than the one in Dolores's room or at our house. Plus it got pretty good reception. The other old fella and I watched for a few minutes when Hope wandered in. I guess she got bored out in the dining room.

"Hi, Uncle Joe. Whatcha doing?" she asked as she plopped herself down.

"Just watching a little TV with my buddy here."

She gave a little wave to the guy with the walker on the opposite loveseat. "Hi. May I watch TV with you?"

"Absolutely, young lady," the other fellow replied.

"Do you want some turkey?"

"Thank you, no. My family is coming to see me in a little bit."

"Okay." She settled in for a second and then asked, "What's this?"

"*King Kong*," I replied. "It's an old movie."

"Is the parade still on?" she asked.

"Nope, sorry. It's over."

"Next year can we go downtown and watch it?"

"I don't think so. The parade is in New York City and we're in Youngstown."

"Why don't we have a parade on Thanksgiving?"

"Because we aren't a big city like New York. They have eight million people. We have maybe a hundred twenty-five thousand."

"That's still enough people for a parade," she said,

I am not without parades. There's a parade down Federal Street the day after Thanksgiving. Some people are just too lazy to mention it because they don't feel like taking their great-nieces downtown.

sounding as condescending as a seven-year-old girl can sound, which is pretty condescending. Fortunately for me and the fellow with the walker, she settled in and started watching the movie. I had a hunch Hope would like it and she did. Little kids always like *King Kong* for the same reason they like dinosaurs. When you're that small, it's nice to think there's something bigger than your parents.

She made me tell her the name of every actor in the picture. At first all I could remember was Fay Wray — all that peroxide hair and all that screaming. But then I remembered Robert Armstrong and Bruce Cabot, character actors who I saw in plenty of films. They're kind of like the guys you see every day walking into a factory or an office, the ones you never really notice until they're gone. After we talked about the actors, Hope asked me if King Kong was real.

"It's not like there's really a gorilla that big, right?" she asked, and I could hear just a hair of worry in her voice, as though she thought a fifty-foot gorilla was going to make its way down Belmont Avenue that very afternoon. The guy with the walker chuckled a little bit at this.

I told her "No," and explained how they used a model of King Kong that they moved a little tiny bit every frame and how long it takes to make a movie like that.

"What's a frame?" she asked.

"It's like a little picture. And there are hundreds of thousands of them in a motion picture."

"I don't get how King Kong moves if he's just a doll. How come you don't see their hands when they move King Kong?"

"Excuse me," I said to the fellow with the walker. "Do you know if there's a scratch pad and a pencil around here?

"Don't think so," he replied. "Sorry."

"I have a pad of paper and pencil in my bag with the coloring books!" Hope exclaimed. "Let me go get it." She hopped up and ran out of the room. I apologized in advance to the fellow with the walker for the noise. As I suspected,

Hope came back carrying a little canvas bookbag with flowers on it and with her cousins in tow.

"King Kong!" Lou exclaimed and jumped onto the one unoccupied loveseat. Nico, who's only about two years older than Hope, piled in next to him.

"I've seen that movie," Edie said, and wandered out of the lounge.

"Well, I'll be seeing you," the fellow with the walker said as he slowly stood up. "My family will be here soon."

"Need a hand?" I asked.

"No, thanks. My knee needs to learn to work on its on again." He managed to get himself upright and underway. He shuffled out of the room to a chorus of "Happy Thanksgivings" from the kids.

Hope pulled a little notepad and a pencil out of her bookbag and handed it to me. "This is the pad where Mommy always had me write down the lottery number for her and Grandma."

My hand stopped in mid-air. "Can I use it?" I asked.

"Sure," she replied. "I don't need it anymore."

I took the scratch pad and pencil and carefully started drawing a little stick figure on the first page. On the next page, I made the stick figure lift one leg, just a little bit. I went on and on like this until I had a little stick figure on each page. Hope kept looking over my shoulder, trying to see what I was drawing.

"Why do you keep drawing the same thing over and over?" she asked. "That's boring."

"It's not the same thing. See? Every drawing is a little bit different. Now look." I took the scratch pad and flipped through it, making the little stick figure look like it was running across the page.

Hope squealed so loud that Lou and Nico looked up from the movie. She held up the scratch pad, saying "Look! Look!" like it was the greatest thing she had ever seen.

During the commercials, she made each of her cousins flip through the scratch pad and watch the little stick figure run across the page a few times, then she settled down.

Hope flipped through the scratch pad once in a while to watch the little stick man run while we watched the movie. I decided my babysitting stint would be over when the movie was over. A man has the right to do nothing but eat his fill and watch football on Thanksgiving, and I like exercising my rights.

Hope was leaning on me the way little kids sometimes use adults as La-Z-Boy recliners. I don't mind too much. It's a nice feeling when a little one leans on you like that; it's like having a dog or a cat cuddle up next to you. It means you're trusted. There was a time, long ago, when I thought I might marry a certain young lady and start a family with her, but it didn't work out. Instead, I've been the stand-in father and granddad for my nieces and nephews, and that's worked out just fine.

Like I said, he's got no one to blame for that but himself. Julia Winetsky went and married a lawyer and moved to Warren. If Joe Steiner hadn't been such a coward, she'd probably still be here and there would be more kids on those aqua blue loveseats.

When King Kong started climbing the Empire State Building, Hope sat straight up. "Why are the airplanes attacking him?" she said.

"They think he's dangerous."

"They have to save the city," Lou added as though Hope ought to know this.

"But he's just trying to save the girl because he loves her. It's like they're both trying to do what they think is right."

"Yeah, it's tough, isn't it?" I said.

"Is he going to be okay, Uncle Joe?" she asked.

Lou piped up "I know what happens!"

"Shh ... don't spoil it!" Nico said.

Nico didn't seem to be too upset by the whole thing, but she's kind of a tough girl, and Lou had that little boy fascination with fights and airplanes. I kept an eye on Hope. When King Kong finally lost his grip and started to fall off the top of the Empire State Building, Hope gave little gasp and then the picture on the television changed to another channel, even though the remote was sitting way over on the empty loveseat where the guy with the walker had been. None of us were even close enough to touch the television, but the channel still changed. We didn't get to see Kong lying on the ground or hear the last line about beauty being the one who killed the beast. Instead we were looking at some soap opera.

"Awww! What'd you do that for?" Lou asked.

'It was mean of them to take him away from his island," Hope said.

"So? You don't have to change the channel."

Hope gave Lou a dirty look, and Nico hit him and said, "Shut up."

I tried to explain to the three of them that Hope couldn't have changed the channel because none of us had touched the remote or the television.

"Then how did it happen?" Lou asked. All three of them looked at me like I was the village idiot about to explain Einstein's Theory of Relativity. Like they knew something I didn't. Frankly, I didn't know how it happened. There wasn't any earthly reason why the channel would just change all on its own.

"I'll bet this does things like that all the time," I said. "I'll bet the remote in somebody's room affects this TV." It wasn't anything close to a reasonable explanation, but at least it was an explanation.

"Naw-uh. Sometimes Hope ... ."

"Shut up!" Nico and Hope said at the same time. I heard Nico whisper something about grown-ups to Lou.

They all three looked guilty of something, I just wasn't sure what of.

"What's going on?" I asked.

All three of them said, "Nothing," in a little chorus. Then Nico said, "Poor King Kong" and jumped up and ran down the hall back to the dining room, with Hope and Lou close behind. I sat there for a minute, wondering how on earth the channel had changed all on its own. I took that as my cue to grab a plate of leftovers and go home so I could drink a beer and watch a football game or two in peace.

All through Thanksgiving weekend, I kept thinking about the guy with the birthmark who had stolen Dolores's money and broken her hip and how he *could* be the same Bobby with the birthmark that Ralph Krasniak used to work with in the blast furnace and who *might* be the same guy Hope saw in McGuffey's. Those were too many "coulds" and "mights" for my taste, but it's all I had to go on.

I kept trying to look at the whole thing from a rational standpoint. When you're trying to fix something, you need to take it step by step. You make your first hypothesis about what might be wrong and see if that's what's causing the problem. If that first try doesn't fix it, then you think of what else it could be. If not A, then B. If not B, then C. And you keep fiddling with it until you fix it. That's how I've always fixed things. Not just cars and engines but clocks and radios and furnaces and squeaky doors and you name it. When Dolores's children were little, they used to think I could do magic because I was always fixing their bicycles or roller skates. When Ruthie was a little girl, she always said "Uncle Joe can fix anything." I tried to explain to her that it wasn't that I can fix anything, it's that just about anything can be fixed. Every problem has a root cause. If you can figure out the root cause, you can fix anything.

Almost.

There used to be a guy named Pete who lived on Emerald Avenue around the corner from us. He fancied himself a dog trainer and always said that you have to break a dog's spirit in order to train it. I say that's a load of hooey. Breaking somebody's spirit — even a dog's — is the worst thing you can do. It kills something inside that I don't think you can ever really fix. Pete always had two or three dogs and the poor things always looked miserable and terrified. That's no way to go through life, even a dog's life. The doctors had fixed Dolores's broken hip, but they couldn't fix her spirit. The police had already given up on the robbery as a Gypsy scam and said there was nothing they could do. The only person looking for these guys was me. Me and the Heebie-Jeebie Girl.

V

Christmas was only a few weeks away, so the following weekend, I told Ruthie I would take Hope downtown to Strouss' department store to see Santa and help her do her Christmas shopping and just have a fun Uncle-Niece Day. She bought it because mothers always need a break.

I picked Hope up bright and early on Saturday. I like where Ruthie and Phil live. Their neighborhood is the suburbs the way I think the suburbs were supposed to be. Most of the houses are just little ranch homes like theirs, but they know their neighbors, they have block parties, and everybody has a nice yard for their kids to play in. Hope has a bunch of little friends on the street or around the corner. In fact, I'm pretty sure she's going to marry the little boy next door. His name is Michael and he's a hoot. Every time I see him, he calls me Great Uncle Joe and shows me how he's learned to whistle through his teeth or snap his fingers or something, and I give him a quarter.

I pulled into the drive and knocked on the side door near the garage. Nobody in our family ever uses front doors. I think Eddie's kids never even realized the house on Audubon Street *had* a front door until they lived there. Ruthie let me in and said, "Well, Hope is in a bit of a mood today. You don't have to take her if you don't want to."

"What kind of mood?" I asked. "Good? Bad? Crazy?"

"Seven going on fifteen."

We were standing in the eat-in part of their little eat-in kitchen when Hope opened the door to her room and walked down the hall to us. She was wearing a little pink fairy outfit with a big ruffled tutu and lots of shiny little sequins and big fairy wings and not much else.

"Hey there, Fairy Queen. Wasn't that your Halloween costume?"

"Yes," she said.

"You're getting your holidays mixed up. It's almost Christmas." I said.

"I want to show my outfit to Santa Claus."

"I told you already that it's too cold for you to wear that. You need tights, at least. And a sweater," Ruthie said. She and Hope butt heads on a regular basis, and I got the feeling they had had this conversation a few times already this morning.

"You never let me do what I want to do!"

"It's cold out!"

"If I put a sweater on, nobody will be able to see my wings!"

"I have an idea," I said. "What if you put on a few layers underneath, like a long-sleeved shirt and some tights?"

Ruthie upped the ante right off the bat. "A turtleneck and two pairs of tights. And an undershirt."

"What about my wings?"

Then I suggested that Hope put the wings on over her winter coat so they wouldn't get crushed. "It's going to be very cold today. But not much snow, so your wings shouldn't get wet," I added.

"Okay." I never know what I like better — getting Hope to do something when her mother can't or helping Ruthie out when her kid is being stubborn. Maybe both.

We finally got Hope put together, even though she was mad that she couldn't wear the wings in the car because they'd get crushed. Then, as soon as we got inside the department store, she handed me her winter coat so she could put on her wings again. I timed it just right, because when we got in the Santa line at ten thirty in the morning, there was almost no one there. Little kids are fidget machines, so I didn't want to waste a lot of time waiting around for Santa. While we were waiting, Hope asked me what kind of sleigh Santa drives.

"What kind of sleigh? You mean like Chevrolet or General Motors?"

"Yes. What kind of sleigh is it?" It's always flattering when a child thinks you know unknowable facts like this. If she was asking, I guess she still believed in Santa Claus. "I believe Santa's sleigh is specially made by the elves. It's a one-of-a-kind, customized roadster edition with a prototype four-forty Hemi short-block engine with a four-and-a-quarter-inch stroke and three hundred fifty horsepower."

"Wow."

"Hey, four-four-zero is a good number. Should we play it?"

"No. I don't pick lottery numbers anymore."

"Because of what happened to your Grandma?"

"I don't want to talk about it."

That seemed pretty final, so I went back to talking about Santa Claus. When it was finally Hope's turn to talk to Santa, she twirled around for him and his helper elves a few times.

The guy playing Santa was a good sport, because he said, "Well I'll be, it's a genuine fairy right here in Strouss'."

Hope hopped onto his lap and crossed her legs at the ankles like a little lady. She and Santa started with the usual small talk — "Have you been a good girl this year?" "Have you been listening to your parents?"

"Yes," Hope replied. "And I just made my First Confession a few weeks ago, and since that erases all your sins, it's almost like I haven't done anything wrong at all this year."

Even through the fake white beard, I could see Santa give her a funny look. He probably figured a comment like that meant Hope was spoiled, but she's not. "Well if you haven't done anything wrong this year, I suppose you have a long list of things you want."

"Not really. I'd like Princess Leia and Chewbacca action figures and some more Legos, please. And that's all, but if you could help find the guys who robbed my grandma's house, that'd be great too."

Santa kind of coughed back his surprise and said he'd see what he could do on that front. Then one of the elves took a picture of Hope and Santa. Hope said goodbye, and I thanked him. As we were walking out, I heard Santa mutter to one of the elves, "Yeah, you'd only hear that in Youngstown."

Some cities might hear that and think it's an insult, but some cities have thin skin. I know my people. That's pride.

After we were done with Santa, we noodled around Strouss' for a little while and then walked over to Woolworth so Hope could pick out some Christmas presents for her parents and aunts and uncles and cousins and her future husband (although I'd never call little Michael that in front of Hope). It was getting near lunch time, so I asked if she wanted to go out to lunch.

"Yeah! Can we eat at the counter at Woolworth. And then can we get a chocolate malt?"

"We could," I said carefully. "Or we could have lunch *and* work on our investigation."

"That! That! I wanna do that! Let's go!" she said and started running toward the exit before I could even say anything else.

"Whoa! Hold your horses there, Hope," I said. She stopped, and I caught up with her. "Now look, we're going to some new places. You're going to have to listen to me, okay? Your mom and dad would kill me if anything happened to you."

"Sor-ree ... " she said with a sigh. "I promise I'll listen to you and stay right next to you the whole time. Where are we going?"

"We're going to try and find where this Bobby fellow hangs out."

"Where? Where is that?"

"Well, I'm not exactly sure," I said as I helped her take off the wings and put her coat back on. "But my guess is that it's somewhere near the Sheet & Tube."

"I thought it wasn't there anymore?"

"Well, the mill is closed but the buildings and everything are still there. And there are a lot of bars and taverns around there where the men who worked in the mill used to go. I thought we could stick our heads into a couple places and just see if we see a guy who looks like him."

"What's a tavern?" Hope asked. We were out on the sidewalk by now and walking fast because it was so cold. I hadn't believed all those predictions for a long, hard winter but I was starting to.

"It's kind of like a bar that also serves food. Like the Tip Top Lounge. You've been there, right?"

"No. Mommy wouldn't let me. But when Edie, Lou, and Nico lived with you and Grandma, they used to go there all the time. They told me."

"Your cousins are a little bit older than you are."

"Nico was my age when they lived with you, and she went there. Can we go to the Tip Top? Please?"

"Not today. Besides, the Tip Top is in our neighborhood, and we know those guys don't hang around there."

She gave an exaggerated sigh of resignation as she walked. "I guess that makes sense."

We got back to the car, and I headed out of downtown and over to Wilson Avenue. Even though the Campbell Works had only closed a few months before, you could already see the effects, with a closed storefront here or there and almost no cars or people on the street. The mill used to run twenty-four-hours a day, seven days a week. Not anymore. There were still a few bars and diners hanging on among the convenience stores and such, but already the area was getting that ghost town feel — not enough happening, not enough meaningful things for people to do, and not enough people working to keep places in business.

So what if I'm not as good-looking as I used to be? I'll bet you aren't either, but somebody still thinks you're worth something.

We passed by a place called The Croatian House. The second-generation Croats around here usually give their kids Old Country names. A Croatian named Bobby didn't seem to fit. We drove by a place called Anthony's. "He could be Italian ... " I muttered.

"I'm not Italian," Hope piped up. "I'm Irish."

"That's right, your dad is Irish. And you're Slovak and Polish and German on your mother's side. But mostly Slovak."

"And Gypsy. Grandma always says that your and her grandpa was a Gypsy."

"So the story goes ... " I said. I was driving slowly up and down McCartney and some of the other side streets off Wilson Avenue. I just felt like if I looked hard enough, I'd find the right place. I don't pray much; God and I have a live-and-let-live kind of relationship, but I will confess that I said a little prayer to find this mystery Bobby's hangout. It wasn't much to go on, but it was all we had.

"Is that true? Was he really a Gypsy? Did your grandpa wear a big gold earring? My friend Elizabeth's older sister dressed up like a Gypsy for Halloween and she wore big gold earrings and said that all Gypsies wear them. Do you know if your grandpa wore one?"

"Probably not. The men in our family aren't partial to jewelry."

"Did he tell fortunes?"

"I don't think so."

"Where's Gypsyland?"

"Where's what?"

"Where do Gypsies live? Where do they come from?"

"Bohemia. Except there is no place called Bohemia anymore, so the Gypsies are scattered."

"What happened to Bohemia?"

We went back and forth for a while, me trying to explain wars and refugees to a child without all the gory parts and Hope firing question after question at me. After a while, we were both getting pretty testy. I knew I was taking us both on a wild goose chase, but there was something in me that just wouldn't or couldn't quit looking. Hope said something else, and I confess that I didn't really listen. It seemed like all I had to do was keep looking and I'd see some paunchy young man with a birthmark on his cheek walking down the street.

"Uncle Joe, I'm hungry," Hope whined. "When are we going to eat lunch?"

"Soon, soon ... " I said. I kept driving, scanning the storefronts. There were so many possibilities, even in a semi-ghost town. How was I ever going to find this fellow?

"Uncle Joe!" I looked over at Hope in the passenger seat. She was almost in tears. "I'm hungry." She looked worn out. I forget sometimes that she's just a young kid.

"Okay, we'll stop and get something to eat now." I did a U-turn and cut back over to McCartney Avenue, where we had seen Anthony's. I've spent enough time around kids to know that they all like macaroni.

Anthony's was a long, low building made out of wood and cinderblock painted in the colors of the Italian flag. I'm proud to be Slovak and all, but I always wonder when people get so excited about their ancestors. We're all Americans now.

The parking lot was so empty for a second there I wasn't sure if they were open. I parked near the door, and as Hope was getting out of the car she screamed. I went running over to the other side of the car.

"What's wrong? Did you slip?"

"No, look!" Hope held up a small, fluffy white feather. "Look what I found."

"Wow, that's a pretty nice feather."

"Isn't it? Who do you think it's from?"

I put one hand on her shoulder to try and lead her inside the restaurant. Standing around in the cold talking about feathers wasn't getting us any closer to lunch. "I'm guessing a bird. Now let's get ourselves inside and get something to eat."

"Uncle Joe, you aren't listening!"

I wasn't sure what I was supposed to be listening to. It was just a feather. But to be kind, I stopped and gave Hope my full attention. "What's so special about this feather?"

"Mom says whenever you find a white feather, it's a little note from an angel. Especially if you find it in an unusual place, like in the middle of winter and with no birds around. This feather is definitely from somebody we know."

I'm no angel, but I like making little kids happy.

"You're right. That is a pretty special feather. Maybe it's from your grandpa."

"Your dad?"

"Yes."

She looked up and gave me a huge smile. "Maybe." Hope put the feather in her coat pocket, and we went inside. Anthony's went in for traditional Italian restaurant decorating. Along the tops of the walls were murals of people in rustic clothing dancing and stomping grapes. It was all done up in reds and greens and tans. If it weren't for the rotting hulk of the steel mill a few blocks away, you'd think you had wandered into some little country tavern somewhere in Tuscany.

All the tables had red and white checkered table-cloths, which Hope declared were "quite pretty." Booths made from dark walnut ran along both sides of the dining room, and Hope was able to take her pick of them. Three guys in the booth on the end were having a late lunch. Other than that, the place was empty. Once the waitress, an old girl who looked almost as worn out as Hope, had brought us some water and bread and butter, we both perked up. Pretty soon Hope was playing with the salt and pepper shakers, making them walk around the table and talk to the silverware and the water glasses. She still had the fairy dress on over her tights and turtleneck. Her coat, with the fairy wings still attached, was hanging from a little coat hook in between the booths. It looked like she was just taking a little break from flitting around and doing whatever it is that fairies do.

"Hello there," the pepper shaker said to her fork. "How are you today?"

"I'm fine," the fork said. "I just went to see Santa Claus."

"Wow. I'd love to go see Santa but me and the salt shaker had to stay here and work."

"Work, work, work. That's all we do," said the salt shaker. "And I have to do the most work because everybody likes me the best."

"No, they like me the best," the pepper shaker said.

I grabbed the big shaker of grated parmesan cheese and said in a silly voice, "No, everybody likes me best."

"Stop it, Uncle Joe," Hope said. "Here, you can be this knife and this spoon."

Hope took the cheese shaker from me and started playing with it. "How come this is crooked?" she asked.

"It's shaped to look like the Leaning Tower of Pisa," I answered.

"Tower of *Pizza*?"

"Pisa. It's the name of the city where the tower is."

"Oh." She was quiet for a moment, looking at the cheese shaker, and then asked why it doesn't fall over.

"It's not leaning that much. And they've done their best to fix it so it doesn't fall over. Now it's a big tourist attraction."

Hope stopped playing with the cheese shaker and just gazed at it, turning it around in her little hands. "I hope they don't fix it all the way," she said. "I like it crooked. Things are prettier when they're a little different."

I thought that was a rather astute observation, and I told Hope so. Then I had to explain what "astute" meant, and then the waitress came to take our order.

"May I have the cheese ravioli, please?" Hope asked, and for a second, she just looked like the sweetest kid on the planet. You could tell it made the waitress's day.

"I'll have the angel hair macaroni" I said.

"Looks like you already have the angel," she said, with a tilt of the head to Hope. "Is this your granddaughter?"

"Great-niece."

"My name is Hope," Hope said politely. I was impressed by how tactfully she made her way back into the conversation. Most kids can't do that.

"Well I'm pleased to meet you, Hope," the waitress said. "My name is Bernie."

"Hello."

"Kind of quiet in here today," I remarked.

"Yep, even for a Saturday afternoon." Bernie scanned the near-empty dining room, with its rows of empty booths and tables. Looking at her face, it was as if she could still see the place packed full of guys starving after a long shift or maybe families out for a treat and all the couples who had a first date or celebrated an anniversary there. And now there was almost no one. "Time was when we'd be busy even in the middle of a Saturday afternoon. When the mill was running three shifts, we were always packed. Not anymore."

She turned her focus back to us, just a little turn of her face, but it looked like a big effort for her to smile again. "Let me go put your order in," she said.

I thanked her, and Hope went back to playing with the silverware. We were alone and quiet for a moment, then Hope asked, "Uncle Joe, do you think the waitress knows Bobby with the birthmark on his cheek?"

"I don't know."

"Why don't we ask her?"

"Hope, you don't just go around asking strangers if they know somebody. We don't even know if this is the same guy."

"I thought we were supposed to be looking for him? Why did we go here instead of eating at Woolworth if we aren't going to look for him?" she asked.

"I don't know," I replied. I tried not to sound too mean or grumpy when I said it, but I guess I did a poor job of it because Hope's face wrinkled into that about-to-cry expression again. "What's the matter?" I asked.

"You're getting mad at me and I didn't do anything wrong."

I took a deep breath. "You're right. You didn't do anything wrong. I'm mad at a lot of things right now, but you aren't one of them."

Hope was silent for a moment and tilted her head as though she was listening to something.

"Do you hear the waitress coming with our lunch?" I joked.

Hope just shook her head but didn't say anything until Bernie showed up with our lunch. I expected Hope to dig right into her lunch, but she didn't. She said a polite "Thank you" to Bernie when she placed a huge plate of ravioli in front of her and then just sat and looked at the plate for a second.

"Everything okay?" Bernie asked.

"Yes, thank you," Hope replied. Then she looked up at Bernie the Waitress and said, "We're looking for a guy named Bobby. He's kind of fat and has a birthmark on his cheek. Do you know him?"

"Hope, stop," I said. I looked at Bernie. "It's a game we were playing."

My great-niece couldn't have looked more angry at me if I had strung up her Malibu Barbie by its ears. "No, it is not a game. He's a real person and we have to find him. How else are we going to find him if we don't ask people?"

At that point, I was so tired of looking that I wasn't even sure I cared about anything anymore And Hope had a point. We would never find those guys if we didn't look. The question was certainly better coming from her than me. "Fine," I said. "Ask away."

"We're looking for a guy named Bobby who has a birthmark on his cheek and is kind of chubby and he worked at the Sheeting Tube."

"You mean the Sheet & Tube, sweetie?"

"Yeah."

Bernie looked sympathetic. This was probably the most action she'd seen all day. "I'm so sorry, honey. But so many people come into the restaurant that it's impossible for me to know them all by name or even remember what they all look like." She thought for a second. "He might have come in here, but a lot of people have birthmarks. I wish I could help you." Bernie looked from Hope to me with a little half-smile. "Does this guy owe you money or something?" she joked.

"Kind of," I replied.

"He stole from my grandma. At least we *think* he did."

"Whoa, that's pretty serious." I noticed Bernie was talking to me now, not Hope, and she wasn't using that extra cheerful voice some people do when they're talking to children. She had nice eyes, and for a second I wondered if she liked older men.

"It's a bit of a wild goose chase," I said.

"Uncle Joe and I can find him, because we're good detectives."

"I'm sure you are," Bernie said with a smile. "Now you let me know if you need anything else."

Hope didn't seem to want to let Bernie leave, because she jumped out of the booth and grabbed Bernie's hand.

"Hope, leave her alone."

Bernie seemed unflustered, which I thought was the mark of a woman of superior character. "It's okay. What's the matter, honey?"

Hope put a hand on Bernie's shoulder to pull her down to her level and whispered something in Bernie's ear. I heard Bernie say quietly, "What is that?" Hope whispered something else to her, to which Bernie replied, "Oh, I see."

Joe couldn't hear her, but I could. Hope said, "771."

"But you have to do it today," Hope said. "It'll work."

"I will, sweetie. I promise," Bernie replied. I had no idea what Bernie was promising, but I got the feeling she'd be true to her word. The guys at the only other occupied booth in the place were looking over at us and one waved to get Bernie's attention. "I have to go back to work now. Why don't you eat your lunch before it gets cold?"

"Okay." With that, Hope plopped back down in her seat and went to town on that cheese ravioli.

After Bernie had walked away, I asked, "What was all that about?"

"Nothing," Hope replied in between inhaling the ravioli.

"What did you need to tell her?"

"It's a secret." Hope paused, and then she said, "Girl stuff." She just gave me one of those little angel-child smiles and went back to her lunch. By this time, I think we were both kind of talked out. The rest of the lunch was quiet, with me thinking about frustration and injustice and Hope thinking about whatever it is that inquisitive seven-year-old girls think about.

Bernie came by to check on us more times than she had to, but since we were pretty much the only people in the place, I guess she didn't have anything else to do. When she brought the check, I noticed that she had written "Thank you! Bernie" on it and underneath her name was a phone number. Maybe she did like older men.

"How much was it?" Hope asked.

"Why? Are you paying?"

"No, just curious."

"It was thirteen dollars and thirty-one cents," I said, as I folded the check in half and put it in my pocket. "Can you tell me something unusual about thirteen thirty-one?"

"No."

"One-three-three-one. It's the same backwards and forwards. That's called a palindrome."

Hope considered this for a second and shook her head. "No, it isn't. It's thirteen and it's thirty-one. Those are two separate numbers." With that, she hopped out of the booth and started to put on her coat.

"Whatever you say."

We had to monkey around a bit with Hope's wings and her coat, but finally we got her all situated. An older couple, husband and wife, had come in and Bernie was taking their order, so I just left the money for the meal on the table. I'm not a rich man, but I made sure to give her as big a tip as I could afford. I don't know how anybody could make a living with no customers.

It was getting on near three o'clock and we still had to drive across town to get Hope home and somehow I had to sneak in a visit to Dolores. There is nothing more gray than a northeast Ohio afternoon in December. The sky and the asphalt and the buildings all seem to meld into one. There wasn't much snow yet, but you knew it was going to dump a load of the white stuff on us any minute. And it was freezing. I got Hope in the car and the engine started as quickly as possible.

"Why can't I go with you to see Grandma?" she asked as she settled into the passenger seat next to me.

"Because that wasn't the plan. It's getting late. And your mom and dad are expecting you at home."

"Okay." Hope leaned back and settled into the corner between the seat and the door. She was curled up in her winter coat, the fairy wings lying on the seat in between us. "I think I'm going to close my eyes for a little bit," she said.

"I understand. We've had a busy day."

I meant to drive directly to Ruthie and Phil's, but something compelled me to drive by the Sheet & Tube. When we were driving through the neighborhood earlier, I confess I had avoided it. But we were there, and it was there, so even though it was getting late, I felt the need to drive by and see what once was.

I turned onto the Central Avenue Bridge and slowly drove over the Mahoning River, over the tracks and furnaces. I remembered driving over that same bridge late at night when there was no one on the street but the mill was running. Even in the middle of the night, you knew the third-shift workers were in there, sweating and slaving away, making steel, making somebody other than themselves rich. The mill ran so hot that flames and the heat would almost encase the bridge. It was like driving through hell itself.

You people are so afraid of things that burn. Fire is nothing to fear. I can always be rebuilt. Your flesh and bone? Probably not. I've seen that *Six Million Dollar Man* show. It's fiction. You ought to have more faith in concrete, steel, and brick.

Once we were over the bridge, I slowed down. I couldn't get too close. There was still a blocked-off drive and a vast, empty parking lot surrounding this side of the mill. But even from a hundred yards away, you could see how massive the whole structure was. And in the dead calm of a winter afternoon, it looked lonely, the huge, hulking building, the four dead blast furnaces, the smoke stacks, the empty train tracks. Deserted. When the mill was running, the iron ore dust on the furnaces was a light brown. It was already starting to turn a dark, rusty color from disuse. I pulled over by the side of the road and just stared.

Hope must have been really tired, because she was already sound asleep in the front seat. Funny that the perfect angel child snores a bit. I figured she'd be all right if I got out of the car for a moment. I just needed a few minutes alone here. I hadn't set foot in a steel mill in decades, but I still felt connected to them. I guess everyone from these parts is carrying around some soot and garbage from the mill inside them.

I turned off the car, got out, walked over to the passenger side, and leaned against the hood of my old Hornet to soak up some extra heat. It was a lousy car, but I didn't have the heart to get rid of it. That's always the curse of a mechanic — you know how to keep even the bad cars running. After a while, it becomes a personal challenge. The afternoon temperature was dropping, but I didn't even feel it, and it wasn't because that old Hornet always ran hot. I was angry.

I had a lot to be angry about. Two low-lifes gave my sister a broken hip and were walking around with her life savings while she was getting worse by the day. If she died, it would be their fault. I felt like a chump going through life tied to some quaint idea about how the world works and how a man should behave while everything around me seemed to be going to hell.

It seemed like the mill, the massive hulking mass of the mill, was at the bottom of everything. We made the mistake of building everything in the city around it. Even people who didn't work there lived for it, lived because of it. I generally try to keep the conversation polite. I may not always be a perfect gentleman, but with nobody out there except me and what was left of the Sheet & Tube, I was free to tell that old mill to fuck off.

I yelled it, and once I started yelling, I couldn't stop. I called the mill every curse word I've ever heard and then some. When yelling wasn't enough, I started throwing snowballs. We were too far away for the snowballs to even come close, but that didn't matter. I didn't have my gloves on, but in my rage, I couldn't even feel the cold. I threw and yelled with everything I had, and then I heard the car door open and a quiet voice ask, "Uncle Joe, what are you doing?"

She got me in mid-throw. I stopped. Suddenly I could feel again — could feel how cold I was from packing snow with my bare hands, how out of breath I was, and I felt the foolishness of being an old man yelling at an empty mill, yelling at higher-ups in suits who only visited the mill twice a year and didn't care squat about me or anyone like me. I dropped the snowball to the ground and shoved my hands in my coat pockets to warm them up. "Honestly, Hope? I'm not even sure."

Hope got out of the car and closed the door behind her. She stared at the mill for a moment. "What is this place?" she asked.

"That's the steel mill they closed in September."

"It's big."

"Yes, it was. Almost five thousand people worked there."

"Where are all those people now?" she asked, although she said it so quietly I almost couldn't hear her.

"Looking for new jobs, I guess." I didn't add, 'Or robbing people.'

"Do you think Bobby with the birthmark is looking for a job?" she asked.

"I don't know. I guess so."

90

"I wish we could find him. I want to get Grandma's money back."

"Me too," I said after a moment, "but I don't think that's going to happen. Sometimes bad things happen that you can't fix."

"Is Grandma going to get better?"

"Honestly? I don't think so, sweetie."

We were quiet for a moment, soaking the December cold into our bones and watching our breath leave our bodies and evaporate into nothing. What could you say about a ghost factory and scum who hurt little old ladies? Then Hope said, "Uncle Joe, remember on Thanksgiving when we watched *King Kong*?"

"Sure."

"This reminds me of the end of the movie, where King Kong falls off the building."

I smiled and tried to make her laugh. "Why? Do you see a fifty-foot gorilla somewhere?"

Hope didn't giggle. "No, that's not what I meant," she said in a voice so pained I thought she was about to cry. "Because it's big and it's dead and it shouldn't be dead ... ." She looked around and then she really did start crying. Not in the screaming, whining way little kids do when they don't get their way or when they're tired. She was just ... crying, as though she was so full of emotion that she couldn't contain it all.

"I think I understand," I said, and put my arm around her narrow little shoulders to guard her against the cold. It was all I could do.

Youngstown

People are judged by the company they keep. So are cities, except I don't have a say in the matter. You're born to me or come to me — somehow you show up. I have no choice but to take you in no matter who you are or what you do.

You people are strange beings. You do stupid, cruel things with one hand and build beautiful things with the other. Build up, tear down. I wonder if you see any difference. Sometimes I think you're just interested in action, in doing something, even stupid things and cruel things. No matter what you do, somehow, it's always my fault. You steal, you kill, you rape, you lie, you destroy, and I'm the one who ends up with the bad reputation while you creep back into my woodwork. I'm stained with your sin.

Some cities will chew you up and spit you out. Not me. I don't have people to waste. I have no other choice but to put up with you, all of you. Despite my better instincts, I still care about you.

Bobby
October 1977

Robbing people isn't my idea of fun. When I first mentioned it to Salazar, it was right after they shut down the Sheet & Tube. Things you say in a bar when you just lost your job don't count as real ideas. Everybody knows that. But Salazar is part Gypsy, or at least that's what he says. He's definitely not from around here. If you say something to him, he takes it real serious and considers it like it's a real idea. He doesn't get that you're just shooting the breeze.

People had been talking about them closing the mill all summer long. Some of the guys said, "Yeah, it's just a matter of time," but they was older guys who had a lot of years in the union and decent pensions built up. They'd be okay. For somebody like me, who'd only been at the mill six years and wasn't vested or nothing, you kind of started to worry. For the last couple of months, every day without a pink slip felt like a good day. Even so, the morning they padlocked the gates, it was still kind of a surprise. I had to make my way through a huge crowd of people just to see it for myself.

The first couple of days, most of us waited it out. I think a few guys went right to the unemployment office, but almost everybody figured the mill would reopen. I mean, the Sheet & Tube was huge. Who just shuts down a steel

> I have a word for the guys who shut it down, but I'm too much of a lady to say it.

mill and lays off five thousand people all at once?

After a couple weeks, when everybody realized that they weren't going to re-open the mill — that none of us had a job anymore — everybody kind of panicked. Guys started applying for all sorts of jobs they never would have thought about before, like the drug store or the grocery store. These were older guys with families who had twenty or thirty years in at the mill and they were ready to go pack groceries at Sparkle. You'd go to the unemployment office and there'd be a line of guys out the door, and you'd recognize most of them. Even if you didn't know their names, they were guys you had maybe seen in the parking lot or the commissary and you were both part of the same family because you both worked for the Sheet & Tube. Seeing each other in the unemployment office was just sad. Nobody wants to be part of that family.

It was about a month or so after they closed the mill that I got the idea. Me and Salazar was in Barlock's, trying to see how long we could make one beer last, when I said I was worried about how me and Denise were going to pay for the wedding.

> Piko Salazar showed up sometime in 1968 with a wife whose hair was darker than iron ore without a single strand of gray. At least that's how he always described her to the men in the blast furnace. Everything he did before he came to me is a mystery. What I do know about him: He'd do anything for his kids, and he has a bunch of them. I told you I've heard most of you making love with your sweetie. Salazar and his wife are re-peat customers, if you catch my drift.

Salazar has these bushy black eyebrows that I swear are almost as long as the hair on his head. He raised those big wooly bear eyebrows at me. "A man does not pay for his own wedding. Where is her dowry?"

"This is America, Salazar. We don't have dowries."

"My understanding is that the bride's family must pay for the wedding, no?"

"Yeah, that's what usually happens, but Denise's family doesn't have a lot of money — her dad is on disability, so we're paying for it ourselves."

"Robert, I worry sometimes that you are not enough of a man."

Salazar is the only person who calls me Robert. My mom and the nuns at St. Columba used to call me Robert when I was in trouble, but I've been Bobby to the rest of the world my whole life. Salazar is like that. He can call you by your full name and you know he's doing it on account of that's how he was raised, not because he's being a smart aleck. It's like how he can say that he worries that I'm not enough of a man. I know he isn't trying to insult me or call me a faggot. That's just how he is.

"I'm paying my own way instead of riding along on somebody else's coattails. Doesn't that make me a man?"

Salazar thought about this for a second, then he agreed with me. "And I must add, my friend, that your bride is worth it. I know of families who had to pay a young man a large dowry in order to take an ugly daughter off their hands."

"Denise is not ugly."

"No, she is very beautiful," Salazar said.

That's one thing I got going for me — the love of a good woman who's good-looking to boot. I'm not sure how it happened, because I'm not much to look at, mainly on account of my birthmark. It's on my left cheek and kind of bean-shaped. It isn't huge, but it's there. A lot of women won't even look at you if your face isn't perfect. But Denise did.

Her brother, Andy, used to work with me in the blast furnace. One day he said that his sister had broken up with this guy because he cheated on her and now she needed a date for a friend's wedding and would I go with her?

Apparently the girl whose wedding it was had gone to Ursuline High School with Denise. It was one of those situations where a girl is friends with her worst enemy. I never understood that. I guess this girl had always been the type to show off and put other girls down if they didn't have the right clothes or the right boyfriend. Andy said Denise didn't want to go to the wedding without a date because it would be like a failure. First I said that this other girl sounded like a real piece of work and why would his sister want to go to her wedding in the first place? Andy said it was something about Denise's pride, something that she couldn't let go of, even though she graduated high school three years ago. I can understand about pride, and I figured weddings always have an open bar, so I said, sure, I'd go with her.

Andy arranged for me and Denise to meet at Anthony's, which is this Italian restaurant near the mill. It's a nice place, and cheap enough that you can get a good meal without breaking the bank. Me and some other guys used to go there once in a while. I figured me and Denise could just have something to eat and get to know each other a little bit before we went to this wedding together. We went in there one Wednesday night after work. Andy and I sat at the bar to wait for Denise. I made sure the seat on my right was free for her — I figured things might go better if she didn't have to look at my birthmark all night.

Denise came in, and she was this knockout girl with blond hair and big brown eyes and a killer body. She made me want to go home and put on nicer clothes. I was kind of speechless, because Andy is a nice guy and all, but to look at him, you'd never think that his parents had enough left in the tank to make a kid who looked like her. I remembered my manners and shook her hand and bought her a drink. We moved to a booth and got something to eat. Then she talked and I just kind of sat there and stared at her all night. Andy split after a while and then it was just the two of us. When we talked, I could see her eyes looking at my eyes, they weren't moving down to stare at the birthmark. It felt good. She made me feel good.

The wedding was the next week. I only own one suit, but I made sure to get it cleaned for the first time in probably ever, and I got a haircut too. I picked her up on time and just tried to be the perfect date for her — opening the car door and things like that. I wanted everything to be perfect so maybe she'd want to see me again.

The wedding was this big shindig. I swear Youngstown Italians put on the splashiest weddings in the world, even the ones who aren't Mafia. Everything was decked out in eight shades of pink and the waiters actually served you at the table instead of it being a buffet. It was quite a spread.

I will admit that my parades are small, but nobody can throw a wedding like my people.

The bride, her name was Anne, I think, was floating around to all the tables with her new husband, soaking up the compliments and adoration from everybody. The guy she married was one of those tall, skinny Italian guys who always look like they need a shave. He had big, sleepy puppy dog eyes. I guess most women would think he's good looking, plus he was wearing a tux. You could put a monkey in a tuxedo and he'd look good — look at Lancelot Link.

So Anne comes by our table, dragging her sleepy new husband behind her, and when she meets me, I can tell she's not impressed by the way she just kind of sticks her hand out a little bit, like I'm too plain to shake her hand. I stood up when they came over, and I could see that Anne's new husband was a couple inches taller than me, but I had broader shoulders. He looked bored and didn't say anything while Anne and Denise chatted for a couple minutes, both of them saying how pretty the other one looked and how beautiful the wedding had been and stuff like that. Anne didn't ask anything about me, like had we been dating long or anything. She just kind of ignored me for a couple of minutes and made a big show about how she had so many people to talk to because she was the bride. Through the whole thing, Denise was smiling, but as soon as Anne and the bored new husband had moved away from the table, Denise said she needed some air.

She didn't say she wanted to be alone, so I followed her outside. It was a June wedding because somebody like Anne couldn't get married in any other month but June. The weather outside was really nice. It was a pretty evening.

When Denise stepped outside the door of the party center, she flung her arms out for a second and took a deep breath. "Ah, that's better," she said. "It was awfully stuffy in there. Too many people, and too much cigarette smoke."

You'd think after all these years I'd be used to hearing you people lie. You lie to each other, you lie to yourselves. You know who doesn't lie? Me. I'm exactly as you see me. You can map me, track every alley, every tree, every crumbling curb — you can document it all. I still have some secrets, but I always tell the truth.

I noticed the night Andy introduced me to her that Denise didn't smoke, so I didn't light up either. Since the night I met her, I'd been trying to quit. I didn't even have any with me at the wedding because I didn't want to be tempted. When we walked by the bar area, I caught a good whiff of cigarette smoke and it kind of made me itchy for one. "Yeah," I said. "You know, I used to smoke, but I quit. And I, I feel a lot better now."

Denise turned to face me and kind of smiled. "Good for you. I'm glad you quit. You'll live longer," she added, and I hoped maybe that meant she liked me enough to want me to live a long time, maybe even with her. She glanced back at the glass double doors to the party center where an older couple was just coming out. We said "Good night" to them as they shuffled by and then just stood there looking at each other for a moment until the old couple was gone. Denise looked kind of sheepish. "We don't have to stay if you don't want to. I really appreciate you coming with me and all, but I'm sure you're bored stiff by now."

I've been turned down by enough women to realize she wasn't trying to ditch me. She honestly thought I didn't want to be there. "No, I'm having a great time," I replied.

"It wasn't fair of me to drag you to this. You don't know anyone here. You barely know me."

I've never been the sort of guy who could put the moves on a woman. I've had dates and a couple of girlfriends, but I'm no Casanova. But the way Denise said that and the way she looked at me as she said it just flipped on a little switch in my brain and it was like I knew exactly what to say and do. I took a couple of steps toward her, until I was standing right in front of her, just a little bit closer to her than you would normally stand. And then it was like I heard somebody whispering the right words to me, because I said, "I can't think of anything else I'd rather do than get to know you."

And then I kind of reached out and held her chin with my right hand and gave her this gentle kiss on the cheek. I made sure to maneuver it just right so that if she didn't close her eyes, she was looking at my good cheek and not my birthmark.

After the kiss, everything felt different. Touching her was like sticking my finger in a live outlet. I felt like every part of me was alive. It was great. I wasn't sure if she felt the same way, so I changed the subject. "Besides," I said, "we can't leave without a piece of wedding cake. And we haven't even danced yet."

"You dance," she said, not like a question but more like she was surprised and wanted to make sure she had heard me right.

"A little, yeah," I said.

They signed him up because Bobby Wayland was a fat little boy who was lousy at sports. His father gave up trying to teach the kid how to throw a ball when Bobby was eight, so his mother and grandmother took matters into their own hands and put him in the only exercise they could afford — dance lessons. It didn't help much. The only thing that ever made Bobby lose weight was the blast furnace. Nobody can be fat in the blast furnace.

Actually, I dance pretty good. My mom and grandma used to make me take dancing lessons because they thought it would build up my confidence. When it got around St. Columba that I was taking dancing lessons, I got teased and beat up a couple of times, so I don't know how confident that made me. Every time I complained about taking dancing lessons, my grandma told me that one, every girl loves to dance and two, a man who knows how to dance will be popular wherever he goes. I guess Grandma was right, because every time I've gone to a wedding or something, I've had my pick of dance partners, that's for sure. All you have to do is find one girl to dance with you. Once the rest of the girls see that there's a guy who can dance and even kind of likes it, they'll all dance with you.

Denise and I went back inside. The DJ was playing that Paul McCartney and Wings number, "Silly Love Songs," which is a pretty good song. There were some couples on the dance floor — mostly older folks who had probably been dancing together for forty years — and a bunch of women dancing in a circle. I saw Anne and the new husband trying to dance. He was trying some half-assed version of the Lindy Hop like you see the kids on *Happy Days* do, just holding onto her hands and kind of stepping from side to side, and he didn't look too good doing it.

"Come on. Let's dance," I said, and for the first time, I took Denise's hand. Touching her hand gave me that same electric, tingling feeling up my arm. I suppose I could have started off easy, just to see if Denise knew how to dance, but I didn't. You know how you hear women say they were swept off their feet by some guy they met? I wanted to be the guy who swept Denise Skernicki off her feet.

I twirled Denise onto the dance floor, right by Anne and her sleepy-looking husband, and danced like there was no tomorrow, like it would make me shift supervisor. And all of a sudden, Denise was laughing and smiling, really smiling, not just being polite. She was finally having a good time at this wedding, and it was because of me. Out of the corner of my eye, I could see quite a few people checking out our moves, including Anne and the new husband.

The next song the DJ played was "Baby, I Love Your Way." I've always been too shy or embarrassed to slow dance to a love song with a girl I hardly know. Maybe it was something about Denise or maybe it was Peter Frampton that made me confident. When the song started, Denise stopped moving, and for a second it looked like she was gonna go sit down like just about everybody else. Slow songs are for couples. I wanted us to be a couple, if she'd have me.

"Would you like to keep dancing?" I asked.

She looked me straight in the eye and smiled. "Yeah."

I held her close and we danced and I think I made Denise fall in love with me right then and there on the dance floor at Anne's wedding. Ever since then, every time "Baby I Love Your Way" comes on the radio, I think of her. There have been times when the song came on the radio and we've called each other and just held the phone up to the speaker, not saying a word. We never had to talk about it, but something clicked for both of us right then. We became a couple.

That was a year and a half ago, when I was still working at the Sheet & Tube, and things looked pretty good. She still loves me. Except now we're engaged and I don't have a job and I don't know how I'm going to pay for our wedding and that's how I ended up joking to Salazar one night near the end of October, "Maybe we should rob a bank or something."

Salazar looked at me kind of thoughtfully. Those bushy eyebrows of his went up when he said, "A bank? No, a bank is too difficult. Too dangerous. I do not like to rob a bank."

"I don't like to either," I said. "Hell, I don't *want* to rob a bank. I was just joking around."

"A store, perhaps. Stores are easy to rob. I would help you."

It took me a second to realize that Salazar was serious. I mean, my buddies and I shoplifted some candy or baseball cards from the drugstore a few times when we were kids — mostly on a dare. When I was sixteen, I pinched a package of pork chops from the meat section for my mom's birthday, but that's by far the most expensive thing I've ever stolen.

Amazing how a young man can forget about the three baseballs he stole from the sporting goods store over three successive springs and the full set of hubcaps he took with two other boys.

"A store?" I said. "What kind of store?"

"A small store. What I think you call a convenience store. They are very easy to rob. I have done so before."

"What? Shhh! You don't say things like that in public." Barlocks is a little bar downtown, close to where Salazar lives. It's kind of a dive, and I wouldn't be surprised if half the people in there had a police record, but it still seemed kind of stupid to talk about robbing a store in the middle of a public place, and I told Salazar so.

"No, this is a fine place to talk about robbing someone. People are so sure that everyone is listening to what they're saying. People think they are so important, but no one is important except for President Carter. No one is listening to us."

I took a quick glance around the bar. There were people all around us — at the bar, at the little round tables scattered around. Three guys were shooting pool on the beat-up table with felt so worn you could almost see the wood underneath. Some girls were dancing to KC and the Sunshine Band on the jukebox. Everybody was talking and off in their own little world. I looked at all the people around us and realized Salazar was right. We all think that the little world we're in is the only game in town, but really, we're all just background noise for everybody else. Even though nobody was listening to us, I still lowered my voice. "I'm not so sure about this. I'll find a job."

"The mill has been closed for a month, Robert."

"I know, I'll find another job doing, you know, something."

"Robert, when I first came to this country, I could not find a job. Each day I would go out looking for work, and each night I came home with nothing. A man must give his family a place to live and food to eat. I did what I needed to do so that my children could eat, and I will do it again."

When somebody says something like that, you shouldn't make them spell it out. I knew what Salazar was saying: He stole. I've known people who lifted something here or there — everybody does that, but I had never known anyone who made a living and supported their family by stealing. That was a whole new can of worms.

"Wow," I said. I didn't know what else to say, really. We just kind of sat there for the rest of the night, watching the television over the bar and pretending that we hadn't just talked about robbing convenience stores.

II

When I got home that night, the house was quiet. My younger sister, Cathy, is studying to be a nurse at Youngstown State. My mother is a nurse too. She works in the maternity ward because she says she likes to be around new beginnings. Our father died when Cathy and I were kids, so my grandmother lived with us and took care of us when my mother was at work. Then Grandma died when I was a senior at Wilson, but by that time Cathy and I could take care of ourselves.

When I started working at the mill after high school, I said to myself that I'd only live at home until Cathy was out of high school. Then Cathy got into college, and I met Denise and my whole world kind of changed, you know? It's like I realized that everything I had been planning for was backwards and instead of planning to get an apartment and seeing how much beer I could drink and how many cigarettes I could smoke, I should be planning on how I could buy a house and start a life with the most wonderful girl I'd ever met.

I think I started saving for the house and the wedding even before I asked Denise to marry me. You know how people say that when they met the love of their life they just knew? That's how it was for me. One look at Denise and "Boom!" I knew.

Ever since I lost my job, my mother's been telling me to keep a regular schedule, but it's hard. Somehow the night seems more attractive. And if I sleep late, then that's less of the next day that I have to spend wondering about the future.

You people throw the word "love" around so easily. You say you love me, your car, your dog, your spouse, and whatever it is you're currently eating. Your car will rust and break and you'll get a new one. Your dog will eventually run off or die. So will your spouse. Whatever it is you're eating that you love so much will turn to literal shit. You know what's left, don't you? Me.

I told everybody I quit smoking, but I still keep an emergency pack in the garage. Once in a while, you need a cigarette to help you think. And I had a lot to think about that night. I was standing on the little porch just outside the back door, smoking what I swore to myself was going to be my last cigarette even though it never is, when I heard footsteps in the kitchen. I turned around and saw my sister through the screen door.

"Hey, Stinky," Cathy said.

"Hi, Cootie Face," I replied. "Mom asleep?"

"It's eleven o'clock on a Tuesday night. Yes, Mom's asleep."

"Don't you have class in the morning? You ought to be in bed too."

"I was studying. Got an organic chemistry test tomorrow."

I took chemistry in high school, but I got a C. I thought we were going to blow things up and do some mad scientist-type stuff. The lab part was fun but not the rest of it. I don't know what all Cathy's organic chemistry test was about, but I knew I couldn't do it. She's always been a better student than me. I was getting tired of talking to her through the screen door, and it looked like we were in for a real conversation, so I flicked the cigarette onto the driveway and walked inside.

"Close the door," Cathy said. "It's cold out there."

As I locked the back door, I remembered that I needed to take the screen out of the door and put in the glass storm panel before the really cold weather set in. Cathy pulled out a chair, but instead of sitting on it like a normal person, she sat down on the kitchen table and put her feet on the chair. With her big glasses and that new feathered hairdo, she looked like a little owl perched on top of our crappy old kitchen table. Our mom always tells Cathy not to put her feet on the chairs, but they're these old orange plastic and metal things that came out of a school cafeteria. Cathy's feet aren't doing any damage to those chairs that hasn't already been done.

"I thought you quit smoking. What's eating you?" she asked.

"The usual," I said.

"You know, I was reading about that campaign to re-open the mill. I hear there's going to be a rally ... " she started to say, but I just looked at her. We both knew that nobody was going to get the mill to reopen and nobody was going to transfer me to the Briar Hill Works or anywhere else. "Well, you'll find something. I know you will."

It was nice of Cathy to try and be encouraging, but I'd been looking at the want ads in *The Vindicator* every day and there wasn't much of anything for a guy like me. If there was, another five hundred guys were applying for the same job. My chances of getting a new job were pretty much slim and none, and slim had a one-way ticket out of town. All I said to her was, "Yeah, maybe. If I'm lucky."

Cathy fiddled with a stray piece of fuzz on her sweater, not looking at me. I walked over to the sink to get a drink of water. After enough beers, I always feel kind of dried out. Behind my back, I could hear Cathy's voice kind of quietly say, "Maybe you could go to school too."

She said it like she figured I'd think it was a dumb idea, but I had kind of been thinking the same thing. Cathy was trying to make something of herself by going to nursing school. That's a really great thing. Why couldn't I go to school too?

I took a gulp of water. "I don't think I'm cut out for college, but I've been thinking about trade school."

Cathy spun around to face me. The kitchen table squeaked as she did so. I ought to try and fix that thing. It's gonna collapse during dinner some night. "Electricians make a good living," she said.

"Yeah, they're all union guys."

"And you're good at that kind of thing. You could do it."

"Actually, I've been thinking about computers. Have you ever seen those commercials for Control Data Institute? I get the feeling that computers are going to be big. That might be something to get into."

"That's a great idea too!" She was so enthusiastic about me wanting to go to school that I realized she and our mother must have had another talk about me. We talked a little bit more about school, with Cathy giving me all sorts of ideas and suggestions about how to get started with applying and when I went to bed that night, I felt almost as hopeful and enthusiastic as she did.

Of course, the next morning I woke up and I still didn't have a job. Or the money to pay for any sort of school. Or the money to pay for the wedding. I barely had enough cash for a couple of beers and a pack of cigarettes. Mom was already at work and Cathy was at school, so I had the house to myself and another day of doing nothing in front of me. I figured I could always change out the screen door in the kitchen and maybe do some other stuff to get the house ready for winter. But I just lay there in bed for a while, thinking.

Tuition takes money, more than unemployment pays. When I was working, I put away a little something every month, thinking I'd use it to buy me and Denise a house someday. But the furnace in Mom's house went kaput last winter, so most of what I had saved went to buy a new one. I still had a job back then, so I figured I'd just start saving again. You always think there's going to be more time, you know? You figure you have years and years to go to work and save your money and live your life. Then you show up for work one day and there's a padlock on the gate and there's no more time.

I took a glance outside. It looked like one of those crappy, cold, kind of rainy fall days where anybody with any sense would just stay in bed. When I worked at the Sheet & Tube, I didn't mind days like this because the blast furnace was so hot that the cooler weather made things a little more bearable.

I rolled over and moved the blankets around so they were kind of covering my head but left an air hole so I could breathe. When I was about three or four, my mom started working nights at the hospital and my dad used to bundle me up in the back seat of the car and tell me to take a nap while he went into the bar and tied one on. He'd always put a bunch of sweaters on me and wrap me in this rough old Army blanket. He'd leave a Slinky and maybe a little toy or a picture book in there in case I got bored. I guess he figured it was late and I ought to be asleep anyway, so what did it matter whether I was sleeping in my bed at home or in the back seat of his Dodge? He'd always wrap the Army blanket around my head, saying he didn't want me to get cold, but I think he didn't want anybody to see that there was a little kid in the back of the car. As soon as he'd go in the bar, I'd pull the blanket down. I don't like having my face covered.

Once Cathy was born, he stopped doing that. He could get pretty plastered, but he wasn't so bad that he would leave a baby alone in a car. By the time I was ten and Cathy was six, he was dead because his liver was corroded. I missed him sometimes, but he wasn't really the cuddly Andy Griffith kind of dad. He was the kind of dad who wandered in after work and listened to you tell him about school for about two minutes and then sent you off to play outside while he read the newspaper and had a drink.

He worked at the Sheet & Tube for a while but got fired. Then he worked at the ice cream factory over in Brier Hill, but I guess he got let go from there too. I'm not sure why he kept getting fired. It's hard to know all the facts when you're a kid. All I knew was after a while, he didn't go to work at all.

When I started at the Sheet & Tube, there were a few older guys around who had worked with my father. I always felt like I had to work extra hard to show them I wasn't like him and that our family was full of good people. I tried to pay attention to little things, you know — first one to clock in and the last one to leave, not taking too many cigarette breaks, not mouthing off to people. As close to the ideal employee as I could get. I think everybody there liked me, for whatever that matters now.

When I was working, my salary went for the bills and the mortgage so my mom could help Cathy pay for school. It worked pretty well when I had a job. My unemployment

Francis Wayland had his heart set on being an architect. That's what he told his classmates and teachers. That's what he whispered to the Indiana limestone of Stambaugh Auditorium while he waited in the wings to march across the stage when he graduated from Rayen High School. He and the auditorium came into the world the same year, 1926, and Francis seemed to think that connected them somehow. He said he was going to build something just as beautiful, just as permanent. He was going to make me breathtaking. The week after graduation, he enlisted in the Army and spent three years as a winch operator in North Africa where he started dreaming of neat shots of whiskey in a quiet corner and never dreamt of Indiana limestone again.

wasn't going very far — we were kind of making ends meet, but I had maybe ten bucks saved for the wedding.

"I need more time," I said outloud, just to sort of test my voice. There wasn't anybody else in the house to talk to. There wasn't anything else alive in the house except me. We used to have a dog when I was a kid, but it died my junior year in high school. A pet takes a lot of extra money and time, so we never got another one.

It's kind of stupid to say you need more time when you're unemployed, because pretty much all you have is time. But Cathy was a senior — only one year of tuition left to pay. And the wedding was Saturday, May fourteenth, so I had about eight months left to scare up enough to finish paying for the hall and the caterer and everything.

The more I thought about it, the more Salazar's idea of robbing a convenience store didn't sound so crazy. What if we just knocked over one or two? I only needed a couple grand. Just enough for a really small wedding, some to help Mom with Cathy's tuition, and a little for some kind of trade school for me. That's all. Once I was done with the trade school, I could get another job and nobody would ever know. I just needed enough money to buy some time.

Nobody ever says, "I want to be a crook when I grow up." Well, maybe somebody does, but not me. I kept thinking about what Salazar said, about a man needing to feed his children. I don't know any guy who doesn't believe that. My grandma always said that it didn't matter what you did for a living, as long as it was honest work you were doing something noble and good. I guess there's something noble in doing whatever it takes to feed your family, even if it's something dishonest.

Once I decided to do this, somehow getting out of bed seemed easier. I even took a shower and put on clean clothes and threw a load of dirty stuff into the washing machine. And I put the storm panel into the screen door to keep out the draft and put all the clean dishes away that my mom had washed that morning. After all that was done, I felt ready to call Salazar.

One of his kids answered the phone. He has a whole flock of kids. Even though his wife is pushing forty, she's still cranking them out. I asked Salazar about this once, and he said, "A man and a woman's love is not like a country. Passion does not have borders." I took that to mean that he and the missus go at it whenever they get the chance and to hell with birth control.

I can independently verify that this is true.

"Hey, Salazar," I said when he finally got on the phone. "Um, I've been thinking about what you and me were talking about yesterday ... ."

"Ah, the robbery plan," Salazar said real casual, like I had just reminded him that the Indians fired Frank Robinson last summer. I wanted to shush him, even though there wasn't anybody in my house to overhear. I guess no one in his house cared about things like breaking the law.

"Yeah ... that," I said. I arranged to meet him later that night. I didn't like the idea of going to Barlocks again, in case anybody had overheard our conversation the night before. Salazar said I worry too much, but he agreed to meet me at a place called the Tip Top. It's just far enough away that nobody there knows me or Salazar. Plus I hear they serve up a great macaroni dinner for a dollar with ten-cent meatballs. My mom is a great cook and all, but she's never mastered Italian cooking.

All that day, I had a ton of energy. Besides doing the screen door, I checked the furnace and tried to clean up the basement a bit. I found some old caulk down there so I went around the house and checked all the window and door frames. Anyplace I felt a draft, I caulked up the cracks. It's not a big house, but it's old. Anything you can do to keep the cold air from getting in is a good thing. Maybe it'd save us a couple bucks on the gas bill.

My mom was on a long shift and wouldn't be home until after eight o'clock, but Cathy was due home sometime before dinner. I didn't want to see her. I didn't want any part of her or my mom or Denise touching any part of this plan. Or maybe I didn't want the plan touching them. Anyhow, even though it was hours before I was supposed to meet Salazar, I left.

We live over in Arlington. The Tip Top is a few miles away in Smoky Hollow. I parked on the street near the bar, and since I had a lot of time to kill, I took a walk. Walking through Smoky Hollow, I realized that we're doing okay. It's not like we have a lot of money, but the houses in Arlington are a little nicer than the ones in Smoky Hollow. You can tell these are three-up, three-down set-ups with one bathroom. Real simple. Our house is a little bigger, maybe a little nicer. I headed north

> You're not going to make me choose between Arlington and Smoky Hollow. That would be like me asking if you prefer your left hand or your right knee. Who has a favorite limb? Who has a favorite part of them? Not me.

and ended up on Wick Avenue, not really thinking about where I was going, just trying to keep moving and keep warm. It was only the end of October, but you could already feel all that cold air coming in from Canada, making everybody down here freeze their asses off.

The farther north you go into Wick Park, the bigger the houses get. All the lawns are wide and neat and look like the people living there have professional gardeners take care of them. I don't bother daydreaming about having a big house like that. I don't need a big house, just four walls and a roof that doesn't leak for me and Denise. Even one of those little houses in the Hollow would be okay if it was mine. I just want a life.

Growing up, it seemed like everything I did was getting me ready to be a man. Like going to school and learning to read and write and do math and watching all the dads go to work and even learning how to dance was all part of this big plan to teach me how to be an adult, you know? To turn me into a man who could stand up and take his place with the other men, so I could help build things and fix things and keep the world turning.

I had that for a while, working in the mill. There's something about steel that's permanent and solid. It makes you feel like you're part of something. I had this teacher at Wilson, Mr. Woolf, who said steel was the foundation of civilization. He said steel let us build cities and railroads and bridges and ships and airplanes; otherwise, we'd just be cavemen cutting things with stone knives. And I got to be part of that. Youngstown has a bunch of steel mills, but I always wanted to work at the Youngstown Sheet & Tube because it was named for the city. It was based here, not like Republic Steel or some of the other ones.

In high school, before I started working there, I'd just drive by or park near the coke plant or the blast furnace, just to look. The whole place was so huge that you could be two football fields away from the buildings and still feel the heat and see the smoke. There was this glow around the whole place. It was like the Wizard of Oz lived in there.

I started out working the Bessemer converter in the blast furnace. This guy named Ralph Krasniak showed me around on my first day. Ralph's the kind of guy who's always making jokes and stuff. Just about every day he'd start singing that old song "Besame Mucho," but he'd sing "Bessemer Mucho." For some reason, that always made me crack up.

The converter gets loaded with pig iron, and then the oxygen in the converter blows out all the impurities and converts them into slag and refines the iron into steel. Cathy could tell you all about the chemistry and what happens, but it always seemed like we were doing some sort of magic in there. There's a thing called the teeming ladle that holds molten steel. There's a pouring mechanism in the bottom to fill ingot molds. The teeming ladle was taller than I am, taller than the biggest guy at the mill. That thing could hold one hundred seventy-five tons of molten steel. And when it went up — when I was the guy at the control making that ladle go up and moving tons of glowing hot steel — it was the biggest rush I ever had. Who'd want to be one of those poor slobs sitting behind a desk pushing around paper clips when you could be pushing around one hundred seventy-five tons of molten steel? When you could be turning ore into steel? Sometimes you felt like you were brushing a little too close to death for comfort, but that's when you knew you were alive.

What did I tell you about magic? This isn't fake alchemy. It's its own sort of magic, and I have it in spades.

I walked around Wick Park for over an hour, until my legs started to hurt and I was so hungry it felt like my stomach was turning inside out. I used to stand up for a nine-hour shift and not even feel it, but I haven't been doing much of anything since the mill closed except sitting around watching TV and gaining weight. It kind of felt good to be moving.

I must have covered about five miles but it was still only six fifteen by the time I walked into the Tip Top. Salazar was supposed to meet me there at seven o'clock. I could make one beer and a plate of macaroni last that long. The Tip Top is kind of dark. It's the kind of place you could imagine somebody like Keith Richards and the rest of the Rolling Stones hanging out in, not causing trouble, just drinking and smoking and minding their own business.

The Tip Top is long and narrow — guess that's why it's so dark. I sat at the far end of the bar, near the kitchen. It's a little noisier and busier down there, so I figured people would be less likely to overhear me and Salazar talking.

The bartender was near the middle of the bar, making change for somebody. "Hey, son. Whatcha need?" he said to me.

"A Bud and a plate of macaroni," I replied. You don't generally say "please" in a place like this.

"Meatballs?"

"Yeah, three. No wait, four," I added, noticing a quarter on the floor near my bar stool. I picked it up when bartender went back into the kitchen. I don't think anybody saw me. Nobody wants to be the guy picking up spare change for his dinner, even though anybody else in there would have done the same thing.

It was a Wednesday, so there wasn't any football on. One of the TVs above the bar was tuned to the six o'clock news and the other was tuned to the UHF station, which was showing some old cowboy movie. I was in front of the TV with the cowboy movie. When the bartender brought out my food, it was hard not to wolf down the whole thing in two seconds. Back in the mill, you'd bring your lunch or your dinner in a grocery bag. I've always been on the chubby side, but once I started at the Sheet & Tube, it was hard to keep weight on. You were just sweating and moving all the time. Not anymore. Now I look like I did in high school.

Even though I tried to eat slow, I was done by the time Salazar wandered in a little after seven. Everybody always notices Salazar because he's tall and thin and has this wild bushy hair. He's one of those guys who walks into a place like he secretly owns it.

"Robert! Good evening," he said and sat down next to me at the bar. He raised one hand to the bartender. "A gin and tonic," he said, although coming out of his mouth it sounds like "Geen and tawnik." This surprised me because Salazar had been sticking to cheap drinks since the mill closed, just like everybody else. "And what would you like?"

he said to me. "Beer? Are you hungry? Let me buy you some dinner."

You don't have to ask me twice if I want free food or free booze. I ordered another plate of macaroni and two more meatballs — I didn't want to break Salazar's bank. He ordered food for himself too — a gigantic burger with a pile of chips and a pickle the size of a baby's arm. I wanted to ask how come he was spending like he was flush but it didn't seem like the right time. It was only after about half an hour, when the Tip Top was busier and noisier, that I asked him what was up.

Salazar looked at me from behind those big bushy eyebrows. "Robert," he said quietly, "I have work for us."

"Really? You found us jobs?" I said. For a second, it was like somebody had pulled open the curtains in a big dusty room and I could see daylight. I took a deep breath. Salazar had found us jobs. Everything was going to be all right.

"It is not a traditional job," he said. "But I know a man who has some work that needs to be done and he cannot do himself."

Under-the-table work was fine by me because I could keep getting unemployment checks. Salazar said we'd go see this guy after dinner. I ate that second plate of macaroni feeling like a new man. I even had time for a couple more beers, because Salazar said we weren't meeting this guy until nine o'clock.

At about eight forty-five, Salazar paid the bill. He didn't even notice that he was paying for my first plate of food, or if he did, he didn't say anything. This guy we were meeting must be loaded. He must have given Salazar some kind of advance. I didn't ask if I'd get a cut of the advance, because I hadn't done anything so far.

We walked down Audubon and cut on over to Andrews Avenue. It was a hell of a lot colder than it had been a few hours before. I asked Salazar if we should drive but he said it was very close. He didn't talk much, just said that this man had some work that needed to be done and that he would pay well.

When Salazar walked into a little convenience store, I thought he needed cigarettes or was still maybe thinking about the robbery idea. But then he said, "Good evening, John" to the man behind the counter, so I figured this must be the guy who was going to hire us.

"Salazar, thanks for coming by. This your friend?" he said, nodding to me.

"Yes. I can vouch for him," Salazar said.

I tried to act polite because I wasn't sure if this was a job interview or what. "Hi. Bobby Wayland," I said and walked over to shake his hand.

"John McGuffey." The sign in front of the store had read "McGuffey's" so I realized this guy must be the owner. He was probably Salazar's age, but a lot shorter. Smaller than I am and scrawny like a twelve-year-old kid.

McGuffey's family has been keeping shop for three generations. He's a distant relation to the McGuffey who wrote all those primers, like the ones Laura Ingalls read back on the prairie. That skinny little link to fame always seemed to make John McGuffey think he had one up on everybody else. He's not my favorite, but you know what they say about choosey beggars.

Guy like that would melt down to nothing in the blast furnace, and he probably wouldn't last long in the rolling mill either. I made sure to look him in the eye when we shook hands, like you're supposed to. His eyes went down to my birthmark. Everybody's eyes do that when they first meet me, except Denise's. "Just let me close up and we can go in the back and talk," he said.

McGuffey turned out the lights and locked the front door. Then he led us through a door in the back of the store that led to a stock room and a tiny little office with a desk and a chair and some filing cabinets but no window. Salazar and I huddled into the office, and McGuffey sat down behind his desk like he was some big captain of industry.

"Thanks for coming by, Salazar," he said. "And thanks for bringing Bobby." Salazar just nodded. "Here's the deal. I own a few properties around town that are no longer pulling their weight. One used to be a small storage facility, and the other two are rental houses. Both empty for a long time," he added.

When McGuffey started talking about his properties, I was thinking maybe he needed somebody to do maintenance on them or maybe needed a super for the rentals. I could take care of the two houses and maybe even get a place for me and Denise to live rent free. But McGuffey said he was having trouble with the mortgages on all three places because he didn't have any tenants and the buildings had problems with the plumbing and electric and other stuff that would cost more to fix than the houses were worth. Then he said that he needed us to help him make one of the properties "go away." And that's when I realized this wasn't just an under-the-table job.

"You have a third up front and the remainder when I get the insurance money," McGuffey said. "If you get caught, I don't know you. If the fire department or the cops find any evidence that this was deliberate, I don't get paid. And if I don't get paid, you don't get paid."

"I understand," Salazar said. "I have some experience in these matters. We will take care of it."

When Salazar said, "we" it kind of dawned on me that I was actually going to have to help him set a place on fire and burn it down. McGuffey gave us the address of a house on Logangate, which is up in Liberty.

It turns out that Salazar had parked near McGuffey's and walked over to the Tip Top, so we got in his car. That made me glad, because I didn't want my car anywhere near the scene of a fire. I said, "How are we gonna do this?" as we trudged down around the corner to the side street where Salazar had parked.

"I am prepared," Salazar said. I wondered how long this plan had been in the works. If he had come up to me with this idea yesterday, or if he said this was something we were gonna do next week, or even tomorrow, I would have had time to think about it. I would have had time to say "No." But I didn't.

III

By the time we got to Salazar's car, I was freezing my tail off and it was starting to snow. Salazar drives this big Mercury Marquis. That thing is so long, he probably spends most of the winter fishtailing on the ice. I guess he needs a station wagon to haul all those kids around, but it sure felt like we were launching the Queen Mary.

"Do you have cigarettes with you, Robert?" Salazar asked. He knows that I didn't exactly quit smoking, and sometimes I bring my emergency pack along when I'm going be drinking. I like a smoke or two with a beer.

"Yeah. You want one?" I said and pulled a pack of Marlboro Reds out of my inside coat pocket. Just about every guy in the blast furnace smoked Camels, but I started smoking the Marlboro Reds, hard pack, because that's what I remember my old man smoking. Kind of a stupid reason to do something, but I guess sometimes I'm kind of stupid.

"No, but it is good that you have them." Salazar didn't say much else on the ride up to the house on Logangate. It was just this two-lane road with no sidewalks and about four houses that kind of connected a decent neighborhood with a nice development. This stretch of road looked like it just fell out of the backwoods of Appalachia or something. By this time, it was close to eleven on a weeknight, so none of the houses had lights on. Even so, Salazar drove around the block and killed the headlights as we approached the street the second time, so it was like we were just sliding along the road like a big beige cat or something. Across the street from the house was an empty parking lot and a building that used to be a chair factory. Salazar pulled in there and parked behind the empty factory. Then he killed the engine, and we just sat there for a minute.

My stomach started hurting, and I know it wasn't because of those two plates of macaroni and all those beers. Salazar reached behind my seat and grabbed a big paper bag that looked like it was from a grocery store. I thought I heard some bottles clinking in there when he picked it up.

The chair factory employed two generations of Liberty Township residents, including one of Bobby's uncles and two second cousins on his mother's side. Once she became a Wayland, Annabelle Shifton didn't spend much time with her family. The Shiftons were a pretty smart bunch. They had Francis Wayland's number early on. Once they realized Annabelle had married a lush and wasn't going to listen to reason, they kept a polite distance.

"Come on," he said, and his voice sounded so nice and kind of fatherly that I didn't think twice. I got out of the car and followed him across the street.

There was a streetlight on the corner, about fifty feet away, and another one farther down the road, but nothing near us. There was maybe half a moon that night, so it was pretty dark. Even so, I didn't like that we went up to the house from the front. It seemed too obvious. As we got closer, I could see that the house wasn't in that bad of shape. It just needed some TLC and a good paint job. The porch was sagging and needed to be replaced, and I wouldn't have been surprised if it needed a new roof, but that's all stuff that could have been fixed. The plumbing and the electric too. Or it could have been fixed up if there was somebody to rent it and live in it, which there wasn't.

The drive wasn't paved — just gravel and dirt leading to a slouchy-looking single-car garage set far back from the house. We walked down the driveway to the back door, which had a little porch and an overhang from a balcony on the second floor. You could tell that there used to be a pillar or something holding up the balcony because it looked like it was going to collapse right on top of our heads.

There wasn't any screen door, just a solid wood back door that was unlocked. I guess McGuffey had been hoping somebody would come and burn it down without him having to pay them.

Salazar slipped in the door silently and easily, like a shadow, but I felt like an ox. My feet didn't want to move at first. I fumbled with the door when I tried to close it and stepped on Salazar's foot.

Instead of saying "Ow!" or getting mad, he just stayed real calm.

"Shh," he said gently. "Follow me." He flicked on his Zippo lighter for just a second and looked around. We were standing in a little mud room area. Three steps up to my left led to an empty kitchen. A set of old wooden stairs down led to the basement. "Nine steps down," Salazar said and snapped the lighter shut.

I could hear his footsteps slowly start down the basement stairs. I had a lighter in my pocket, too, but the house was supposed to be empty, so I figured the less light, the better. I felt around for a railing, and thank God there was one, or my fat ass would have fallen right down those steps. I counted the steps to myself. When I got to nine, I put my foot out real carefully looking for solid ground to make sure Salazar had counted the steps right.

He had.

Salazar lit his Zippo again and we took a quick look around the basement. There was an old wooden tool bench and a cheap aluminum shelf against one wall. Some half-empty paint cans and a rusty container of turpentine were on the middle shelf. I remember McGuffey saying something about the turpentine. So we

Here are the nice things I can tell you about Piko Salazar. He's not exactly what you would call honest, but he doesn't tell lies to his friends. He has good instincts, and I've never seen him hurt anyone. And he can count very quickly.

had something flammable. Even as I was thinking "We can use the turpentine to start a fire," I was wondering how I could ever do something like this. I'm no Boy Scout, but I'm no criminal either.

"Salazar, are we really gonna do this?" I said. "I mean, arson is a big deal."

Salazar held the lit Zippo up and away from his body so he could see me. From that angle, I could just make out maybe half of his face and the outline of his bushy hair. He looked like something out of a ghost story. "McGuffey owns this house. We are not doing anything that the owner of this house does not want us to do. No one is living here. We are hurting no one. There is no crime." He flicked the lighter closed and we were in darkness again.

I didn't have much to say to that. Technically, he was right. McGuffey didn't want the house anymore. Obviously, he couldn't sell it. Hell, people were losing their houses left and right because they couldn't pay the mortgage. We were just doing what the owner of the house asked us to do.

"Okay. So what should we do?" I said. "Maybe throw the turpentine around, light it, and run?"

Salazar's voice came out of the darkness. "That is for amateurs."

I remembered that I had my lighter with me and pulled it out so I could have a little light too. I heard the clinking of bottles and went over to where Salazar was squatting on the basement floor in front of the bag. He took a squished bit of an old candle out of his pocket and lit it, let a few drops of hot wax drip onto the floor and stuck the lit candle in it. Then he took a six-pack of Coke, a thing of lighter fluid, and a big bag of potato chips out of the bag. As he took two liquor bottles out, he added, "Rum and whiskey."

"Looks like we're having a party," I said.

"That is exactly the point."

Salazar's idea was to make it look like some kids or a couple of bums broke into the house, had an early Halloween party, accidentally started a fire, and left. One corner of the basement had a drain, and you could see the hookups near it where the washer and dryer used to be. I went and dumped out half of the Cokes in the drain. While I was doing that, I realized all those beers I had at the Tip Top were starting to back up on me.

"Salazar? Is there a bathroom down here?" I said.

Salazar was doing something with the bottle of whiskey. "I do not know."

I figured if a bunch of kids snuck into an empty house for a party, they wouldn't bother using the bathroom, so I unzipped and took a piss against the wall by the drain. The basement smelled damp to begin with, but the smell of urine made it feel lonely, like a bus stop nobody uses. I've used the bushes outside a few times in an emergency, but my mother didn't raise me to be a screaming

> Blah blah blah, he pissed on me. It says a whole lot more about him than it does about me. Once I'm washed, you'll never know what's happened to me. I'm my concrete, my steel and brick and wood. That's what I *am*. But people? You're all made of the same flesh, more alike than any two cities could ever be. What you're made of isn't who you are. You are what you do.

banshee or whatever. I'm not an animal. But I have to tell you that once I pissed against the wall, I felt like I could do anything. It made me feel like a cowboy or a pirate. It made me feel like Dirty Harry, G.I. Joe, and a Hell's Angel all rolled into one.

I zipped back up and turned around. "Let's start a fire," I said.

"Do not enjoy yourself too much," Salazar said. "We are still working. We must be careful."

I knew what we were doing was illegal, but when I looked at it as work, it didn't seem like a crime. It just seemed like our job was to set a fire and that's what we were doing. Like a bonfire or something. I didn't ask Salazar too many questions about whether he'd done this sort of thing before or not, but boy, was he prepared. We poured some rum into each of the Cokes and spilled half of the bottle on the wooden tool bench and made sure to wipe our fingerprints off the bottles and cups. Salazar put the turpentine and the whiskey bottle on the bench, too, and spilled a lot of each of those too. The bench was sure to go up in flames. If we did it right, the fire would spread to the wooden beams and collapse the whole house.

He handed the bag of chips to me. "Here, eat these."

"I'm not hungry."

"Eat. You do not need to eat all, but most. It must look like there was a party. The fire must look like an accident or McGuffey will not get the insurance money." The part he didn't have to say was that we wouldn't get paid if McGuffey didn't get the insurance.

He sent me upstairs to the kitchen with what was left of the bottle of rum and some of the Coke. I started in on the chips, just shoving handfuls into my mouth and chewing without even tasting it. Then I got thirsty from all the salt, so I drank some of the rum and Coke, making sure to spill a lot of rum on the floor. There was a wide doorway leading to the living room. Through the dim moonlight coming in the front windows, I could see half of the ceiling had fallen in.

Once I had made a mess of the kitchen and spilled all of the rum on the floor, I went back downstairs. When we were almost done, Salazar put the open lighter fluid container on the tool bench and then knocked it to the floor. It fell a foot or two away, the lighter fluid making a little pool on the floor close to the lit candle

"Give me your cigarettes," he said. I lit up a cigarette and Salazar lit two and smoked them both halfway down at the same time, really fast, and then dropped them near the drain, still burning. We left one of the rum and Cokes on the aluminum shelf, one on the tool bench, and one on the steps. Salazar told me to hold the fourth one and leave it in the kitchen when we went upstairs. I quickly smoked another half a cigarette and half stamped it out. Then Salazar made us both light another one.

"Go upstairs and smoke by the back door," he said.

By this time, I was pretty much three sheets to the wind and felt near about to burst with all the booze and food I'd had that night, but I did what he said. The last cup of rum and Coke spilled when I tried to put it on the kitchen counter, but at this point, that didn't matter. Salazar followed me to the top of the stairs, holding a lit cigarette and the rest of the bottle of whiskey. He sloshed a little bit of whiskey on the top step and made a whiskey trail into the kitchen. Then he dropped both of our cigarettes on the whiskey. They smoldered a little bit in the alcohol.

"Get ready," Salazar said and pulled out his Zippo lighter. He put on one of his gloves and wiped all the fingerprints off the lighter. Then he lit it using his gloved hand. He walked down a couple steps and gently tossed the lit Zippo into the puddle of lighter fluid.

It took.

"Leave," he said.

We left through the back door as fast and quiet as possible. It had to be at least two o'clock in the morning. After the dank basement, the cold night air was like a smack across the face. I felt more awake than I had in weeks, even with all the booze. There was a part of me that felt bad for the old house. I couldn't stop thinking about all the people who had lived in it over the years and called it *their house*. We were the last people to eat or drink in that house, to talk in that house, to warm up in that house. Hell, I was the last person to take a piss in that house and I did it on the wall. It just seemed like a real undignified ending.

The last people to live in that house were the Gallaghers, a family of seven: Sean and Gracie, then Malcolm, Maggie, Noreen, Rosie, and Seamus. Rosie was actually born in the house during a snowstorm in 1967. Sean couldn't get the car out of the drive to take his wife to St. Elizabeth, so Rosie was delivered in the big bedroom on the second floor by two firemen from the fire station down the road. The Gallaghers rented from John McGuffey for nine years while Sean worked at the chair factory across the street and he and Gracie skimped and saved to try and buy the house their children called home. McGuffey never would agree to a price they could pay. When the chair factory got sold to a company from South Carolina, all the work moved south. So did the Gallaghers.

We hurried across the road and through the parking lot of the old chair factory. I stopped and turned around to look at the house one more time. If you looked at the basement windows, it looked like maybe someone had left a light on down there, but I knew it was the beginning of the fire. I had never seen that house before in my life, had never even seen it in the daylight, but I felt bad for it now. I felt bad that we were the ones ending its life.

Salazar pulled my arm. "We do not stop and admire our work." We got to the car and Salazar drove away without turning on the headlights. I didn't realize there was a fire station maybe half a mile down Logangate. The building wasn't totally dark — guess they have to have somebody up all night to keep an eye on things, but it didn't look like anybody was getting ready to go out on a call either. If we lit the fire right, it would probably be another ten or fifteen minutes before anybody bothered calling the fire department. By that time, we'd be back at the Tip Top. We didn't see another car until we passed Hubbard Road.

I don't remember much about how I got home that night. Salazar took a winding route back to the Tip Top so I could get my car. When he dropped me off, he just said, "Go home and go to sleep, Robert." He didn't have to say anything else. I got in my car and kind of went on autopilot. I was lucky it was a week night, so the cops weren't out checking for drunk drivers like they do on weekends.

The house was all locked up when I got home. My mother had left the light on above the stove for me, with a note saying she hoped I'd had a good day and telling me that Denise had called. Tired as I was, it made me feel kind of guilty because I've been avoiding my mother lately, and Denise and I were supposed to go out to some Halloween party on Saturday night.

I knew I probably stank like cheap booze and lighter fluid, but I didn't even bother taking a shower. I was too tired. I spent most of the next day in bed, sleeping off the hangover, but when my mother got home from work, I made myself presentable and had dinner with her and Cathy. And I called Denise back and we talked for a while. We were supposed to go to a party that some friends of hers were having. Things like parties are hard when you don't have a job, because when you meet a new person, what's the first thing they ask you? What do you do for a living, right? I didn't have anything to say to that, but I thought we could go out for a nice meal beforehand. It'd be something for Denise to tell her friends at the party so they wouldn't look at me like I was a complete waste.

On Saturday afternoon, I went over to McGuffey's. With the money Salzar was spending the other night, he must have gotten the advance from McGuffey, but he hadn't given me anything. And my unemployment check wouldn't come in the mail until the end of the month. I looked in the *Vindicator* on Thursday, Friday, and Saturday morning to see if there was anything about a house fire on Logangate. Since the mill closed, it seemed like Youngstown was starting to have more fires. It's not like breaking the law is anybody's first choice. It was only when people started running out of options that they started setting buildings on fire. McGuffey was one of the first to go that route. The idea of John McGuffey as a trend setter was kind of funny to me, so I was smiling when I walked into his store.

"Hi, John," I said real casual, like I was just a regular customer coming in to buy something. He was waiting on a hunched-over old lady and a little girl who didn't even bother looking at me. At first, I thought they were buying lottery tickets, but it turned out they were cashing them in. This lady had eight or nine winning tickets from the daily number. I kind of kept one eye on them while I stood in the snack aisle. After I grabbed a bag of Fritos, I browsed around just like I was a regular customer. I heard McGuffey say something to the old lady about her winning big again. She just said, "Oh, I just have my good luck charm with me," and patted the kid on the head. The little girl was probably seven or eight — somewhere around there. She had blond hair and big brown eyes and reminded me a bit of pictures I've seen of Denise when she was a little girl. This kid would probably grow up to be quite a looker. And now she had a rich grandma to boot.

The grandma was busy with McGuffey and her lottery tickets, so the little kid started wandering around the store. She eventually got to the snack aisle, where I was standing and said "Hello" to me.

"Hi," I said back. "Is your grandma gonna buy you some candy with all that money she won?" I asked her.

"No. I asked her if we could get Oreos, but she said no because she made cookies yesterday," the kid said.

"Well at least you got cookies," I replied.

"It's not the same," the kid said like I should know better and wandered back to the front of the store. Then the grandma hustled her out of there without even looking at me. I guess she didn't want her grandkid talking to strangers.

McGuffey and I were alone in the store. "Hey, John," I said again as I walked up to the register. "Did uh ... everything go all right? I mean, I hope you were satisfied with me and Salazar's work."

"I'm not sure."

I waited for him to say something else. Nobody else came into the store so I said, "You gave Salazar an advance, right?"

"What of it?"

"Well, I did half the work... ."

"You want half the advance, take it up with Salazar."

"I can't get in touch with him, and I could really use the money." I didn't want to add that last part, but I had five bucks in my pocket, an empty gas tank, a date, and another week before I'd get my unemployment check, and most of that was going to my mother.

The bell to the front door rang. A good-looking housewife came in and went right over to the cooler along the back wall where the milk was.

McGuffey looked annoyed, like he wanted me out of there. "What are you getting?" he asked.

"Just the Fritos," I replied and put them on the counter.

"Okay. Thirty-five cents," he said.

I handed him a dollar, but McGuffey gave me change for a twenty. I looked down at the money in my hand —

nineteen bucks and change wasn't a lot, but it would definitely get me through.

"This is great. Thank you so much," I said. I must have sounded happier than you might think a guy buying a bag of chips ought to be because the housewife said, "I guess you must really like Fritos." She was standing in line behind me with a gallon of milk. I just said, "Yeah" to her and walked out the door.

That good-looking housewife was Doris Krasniak, who poured milk down her children's gullets like she was filling up the gas tank on an old Lincoln Continental. She hoped it would make their teeth strong because the family didn't have dental insurance anymore.

When I drove to Denise's house that night, it was nice to have a full tank of gas and a little bit of money in my pocket. Denise works as a bank teller, but she's still living with her parents because she's trying to save a little money and take a couple classes at Youngstown State on the side. And since her dad is on disability, it helps her parents out too. I was just wearing jeans, but I had put on a button-down shirt because I wanted to look good for our date. She answered the door wearing this frilly, ruffly dress that was kind of off-the-shoulder. It made her neck and shoulders look gorgeous, but she frowned at me as I walked in the front door.

"Sweetie, where's your costume?" she asked

"What costume?"

"I told you this is a costume party." She kind of held her hands up to herself and moved them up and down like she was Carol Merrill on *Let's Make a Deal* but showcasing herself instead of some car or refrigerator. "I'm Scarlett O'Hara. And you would be ... ?"

"I don't know," I replied. "I'm not a big fan of costume parties. I mean, I like parties and all, but you know that me and costumes don't really mix well."

"This time you said you would wear a costume."

131

"I did?"

"Yes, when we talked about it a couple weeks ago. You said you'd come up with a costume that wasn't really a costume." I opened my coat to show her my clean jeans and white shirt, hoping maybe she'd think of something I didn't. With everything going on this week, I totally forgot this was a costume party. "What are you supposed to be?" she asked.

"I don't know. I'm sorry. I kind of forgot."

Denise sighed and gave me a cute little "What am I gonna do with you?" smile. "I have an idea. Go in and say hi to my dad and I'll be right back."

She ran out of the vestibule and up the stairs, so I went into the living to talk to her father. Mr. Skernicki used to work construction, but he took a bad fall on the job a few years back and has to use a walker to get around now. I've only ever known him as this kind of frail-looking guy who spends most of his time sitting in the living room, but there are pictures of him from before the accident. He looked like a rough and tumble kind of guy. Denise said he used to be really strong and was a great softball player and used to hold these big barbecues in their backyard. It's too bad he can't do any of that stuff anymore.

"Hey, Mr. Skernicki," I said. He can't get up easily, but he kind of half-stood anyway to shake my hand. The first time I met him he kind of blustered and puffed himself up, like he was trying to make me afraid so I'd respect his daughter and treat her right. He didn't know that I fell for Denise hook, line, and sinker the first time I laid eyes on her. I'd sooner eat dirt and root for the Yankees than hurt Denise Skernicki.

I sat down on the end of the sofa and Mr. Skernicki looked me up and down and asked "Well, where's the costume?"

"Come on, Mr. Skernicki. Not you too."

"A woman invites you to a costume party and tells you she's dressing up as Scarlett O'Hara, if you don't show up dressed like Rhett Butler, there's a problem."

"Yeah, I know. I messed up. I already apologized to Denise. It's been kind of a busy week."

Mr. Skernicki gave me a skeptical look. "Job hunting?"

"Yes, sir. Every day," I said. I didn't like lying but I did *think* about finding a new job every day, even if I wasn't applying for a new job every day. It's kind of the same thing.

"That's good, that's good. Andy found something and you will too." Andy was one of the guys who took the first thing he could find, and now he was working the night shift as a security guard at one of the office buildings downtown.

Denise called down that stairs that she'd be right there. I stood up. "Well, I'd better go and see what she's cooked up for me."

"You have my condolences," Mr. Skernicki said. He lowered his voice. "I was never a fan of that *Gone With the Wind* movie."

"Me neither," I whispered. He gave me a big smile and said to have fun. Denise came running downstairs holding a thick piece of ribbon, a can of hair pomade, and an old-fashioned black suit coat that I guess must have belonged to her dad way back when. She made me put on the jacket and tied the ribbon like an old-fashioned tie around my neck. The jacket was a little tight around the waist, but I figured I didn't need to button it. "Who am I supposed to be?"

"You're a poor woman's Rhett Butler," Denise giggled. "Now hold still." She pulled a little makeup pencil out of the jacket pocket and drew a pencil-thin moustache on me. She put some pomade on my hair to slick it down too. I could hear Mr. Skernicki laughing at me while he watched from his spot in the living room. When Denise was done, I took a look at myself in the mirror they have hanging in the vestibule by the front door. I looked stupid. No stupider than usual.

I walked the couple of steps to the living room door and leaned my head in the door, saying "Mr. Skernicki, if you still weren't sure that I'm crazy about your daughter, just remember what she's making me wear tonight and that I'm still going out in public with her."

He kind of laughed and told us to have fun. And we did. The party was full of Denise's friends from the bank and people she went to high school with and is still friends with. I don't see much of the people I went to school with. A couple of guys, like Johnny Parrento and Brendan Flannery, ended up at the Sheet & Tube with me, so we stayed in touch. But other than that, if I hang out with anybody, it's guys from work or it's Denise. Ever since I met her, it's always been Denise.

Denise's friend, Sally, from the bank was having the party. She lives with her sister in a house on Gypsy Lane that I guess used to belong to her grandparents, so they have a nice set-up for two young girls. You could tell that just about everybody at that party had really put in some time on their costumes, even the guys. There was one guy dressed up like General Custer who had stuck all these arrows to his clothes to make it look like he'd been shot up by Indians. That was the best one. Another guy was a gangster and had a real-life zoot suit that must have once belonged to his dad.

Denise and I went into the little kitchen to get drinks and I whispered to her "Geez, you'd think these guys have nothing else to do all day than make their Halloween costumes."

Personally, I've always thought Denise could do worse than hitching her wagon to Gary Biddulph. But some people choose to adore. Some people choose to be adored. Denise Skernicki chose the latter.

"Gary's a loan officer at the bank and is taking night classes in accounting," Denise said as she plopped a few cubes of ice into two cups. She didn't look at me when she said this. Gary was the General Custer guy, and I wondered if Denise maybe liked him a little. He had a job and was going to school to get a leg up in the world. And I had to admit that his costume was kind of funny, so he was probably a smart guy to boot.

We made ourselves a couple of vodka and cranberries and joined the mass of people in the living room. I put my arm around Denise's waist and whispered in her ear that she looked great. She said thanks and led me over to a group of people sitting on a low sectional sofa that looked like it might have been inherited from Sally's grandparents too. Gary was over there, and I was glad to see that all the arrows sticking out of his costume made it hard for him to get too close to anybody else. Denise introduced me to everybody and I said hello. And then General Custer had to ask, "So what do *you* do, Bobby?"

"I cater to Denise's every whim," I said because I knew it'd get a laugh, and it did.

Gary kind of chuckled and said, "Well, of course you do *that*. I mean *besides* catering to Denise's every whim." As soon as he said this, I knew he liked Denise, knew he thought I wasn't good enough for her, knew he'd try to muscle in if he had half the chance.

"Bobby was at the Sheet & Tube," Denise said, which is really all anybody needed to say. You say that, and you know a person used to have a good job and doesn't have one anymore.

"I'm picking up some part-time work here and there," I said. Burning down houses for John McGuffey *was* part-time and if he was going to pay me, then it was work, too, so I wasn't really lying. "But I'm going to go study computer programming."

Denise turned to me and her face went from shocked to happy. She gave me one of those smiles that makes me feel like I could conquer the world. She took my hand and said, "Yeah, now Bobby's going to study computer programming."

I couldn't help but give Gary a little smile. *Sorry chump, go try and steal somebody else's girlfriend.*

With both of us living at home, Denise and I don't get to spend much time in private. After a couple more vodka and cranberries, when we were kind of in-between conversations and not standing near anybody, I leaned in real close and whispered in her ear, "Hey, don't Rhett Butler and Scarlett O'Hara get it on at some point?" Denise giggled and said, that, yeah, they do. There was a short hallway off the living room that led to a little den where a bunch of people were drinking and watching some old horror movie on TV. I figured there had to be a bedroom down there somewhere. There was a bathroom at the end of the hall with two doors to the left of it and one door to the right. I picked the door closest to the bathroom, but it turned out to be a linen closet. Denise and I were giggling by the time I pulled her into one of the two bedrooms.

"Will Sally mind?" I said, kissing her neck.

"Actually, I think this is her sister's room. Maybe we should get out of here."

"We won't hurt anything," I replied, and ran my tongue around the edge of her ear. I don't know how I figured out that gets Denise going, but it does.

Denise and I had only had sex a few times. At first, it was because she wanted to take it slow, and after we got engaged because there's no place for us to do it. I wasn't going to pass up the chance of an empty bedroom and nobody bothering us. At one point, somebody opened the door and then closed it real quick, and we heard a voice say, "There's already somebody in there." I think knowing that other couples were trying to do exactly what we were doing made Denise relax a bit. Even though I was really excited and just wanted to be inside her, I did my best to take my time and make it good for her.

Afterwards I just wanted to lie there next to her, but I think Denise was kind of embarrassed because we'd been away from the party for so long. We got dressed as fast as possible, even though I had trouble zipping up her fancy Scarlett O'Hara dress. Then we slipped out of the bedroom. A guy and a girl who were both dressed like mice were sitting in the hallway making out, and I think they might have gone into the bedroom after us. When we walked past the den, we saw Gary and another guy dressed like a mouse watching the original *Frankenstein* movie. Neither of them looked very happy. The guy dressed like a mouse was wearing sunglasses on top of his head, and I heard him say to Gary, "We were supposed to be the *three* blind mice ... ."

"Good" is a relative term when it comes to young men and sex. You might not think that a city knows anything about sex, but I know that "good" isn't a train speeding through a tunnel, and "taking your time" isn't a giant backhoe making hard, clumsy swipes at the earth. "Good" is a steel beam that fits tight and square against the one below it. "Good" is a cornerstone that bears the weight of whatever moves on top of it. 'Taking your time' is the speed of a rowboat pulled by two strong arms gliding smoothly along the river that runs through my center. That's what a city knows about sex.

I kind of felt bad for that guy, and I made sure to say good night to Gary.

IV

After I dropped off Denise at her house, I went home and just lay awake on my bed for a while. I kept thinking about Denise's body, about how it good it felt to kiss her and how amazing it was to have her naked in my hands. Usually after a date, I have to go home and finish off whatever we started because we don't have any privacy, but tonight I could just kind of bask in the afterglow. I didn't think about houses burning down or tuition money or the padlocks on the gates at the Sheet & Tube or how my mom would pay the bills without me in the house. I just coasted on memories until morning.

The next day, I ate dinner with my mom and Cathy. I'd been kind of avoiding them, but I was feeling pretty good, so I made sure to be home. Mom made breaded chicken, which is my favorite meal. I guess she did it on purpose because after we had said grace and started eating, Mom said, "A little bird told me that you've decided to go computer school. I'm so proud of you, Bobby."

I glanced over at Cathy, who just kind of shrugged and said, "Tweet tweet."

I hadn't done anything about signing up or even looking into how much classes cost or anything, but it seemed like every woman in my life already had me enrolled. My mother looked so happy — happier than I've seen her in a long time, happy enough to realize that she'd been doing a lot of worrying about me. There was no way I could say anything but, "Yep, that's what I'm going to do."

Mom gushed a bit more while we ate, and I let her. It isn't often I give her the opportunity to be proud of me.

That night, I stayed up late watching TV, and when the commercial for Control Data Institute came on, I wrote down the phone number and called them the next day. They said they'd mail me some information. They also said that a year of classes cost six hundred dollars. Between that and the four hundred fifty dollars in tuition Cathy had to pay for her last two quarters, plus all the wedding stuff, I needed maybe two grand to make everything square. When I saw Salazar later that week and told him how much money I needed, he shook his head.

"I am sorry, Robert, but our first attempt was not successful. We are going to have to go back to work."

We were sitting at Barlocks again. Salazar likes to go there because it's close to his house and I guess people leave him alone. It was a Tuesday afternoon, so the place was pretty empty. Even so, I'm glad he said, "our first attempt was not successful" instead of "the house didn't burn down," which is what he meant. The house wasn't a total loss. McGuffey was only going to get enough insurance money to make repairs to the basement and part of the kitchen, because those were the only things that had actually gotten damaged.

"The house is a mile from the fire station," Salazar said quietly. "We cannot blame the fire department for doing their job well."

"Will McGuffey hire us again?"

"He said he might give us another try, but not for several months."

That made sense to

John McGuffey is so cheap he'd hire the same amateurs to do the same job after they screwed it up the first time.

139

me. If you have a fire on one of your properties, the insurance company will probably ignore it. If you have a second one right after the first one, they'll know something's up.

"Where does that leave us?" I asked.

"Zee same place where we started."

I knew Salazar meant we were back to the original idea of robbing somebody or someplace. Frankly, the idea of going into a store or a gas station and scaring somebody enough so that they'd give me all the money in the cash register just didn't seem like something I could do. And if you get caught robbing someplace with a gun? Forget it, you're going away for a long time. I wasn't sure I had that in me.

"Maybe I should just start playing the lottery," I said.

"Gambling?" Salazar looked at me like I was crazy. "Nobody makes money gambling."

"I don't know about that. I saw this old lady at McGuffey's the other day cashing in a bunch of daily number tickets. She must have had five or six winning tickets. And it sounded like she wins a lot. So it can be done."

"She must have a system," Salazar said. I always like how he says "system" like "sees-stem."

"Little old lady like that? Naw, no system. Some people are just lucky I guess."

Salazar and I started talking about other stuff. I told him I wanted to study computers. He told me half of his kids had outgrown their winter boots from last year and the other half needed new coats. You don't talk about finding a job when you know there isn't one to find. But the whole idea about the lottery got me thinking. Maybe the old lady did have a system.

On Saturday afternoon, I went back to McGuffey's around the same time I had been there the weekend before. McGuffey didn't look all that pleased to see me, but there were a couple of customers in the store, so he couldn't say anything until after they left.

He didn't say hello or anything. He just said, "I expect you've talked to Salazar."

"Yeah, I did." Even though there wasn't anybody else in the store, it still didn't seem right to come right out and talk about the fire that wasn't a fire. "Sorry that ... things didn't work out like they were supposed to," I said.

"I should have expected as much." The way McGuffey said this kind of ticked me off. Like he thought we were idiots or something because we didn't commit a crime the right way.

"Look. We did the best we could. I'm a hard worker, and I don't cause trouble. I'd rather do something legit, like working in your store instead of that other thing."

"I don't have any openings," McGuffey said.

"I wasn't asking, I was just saying." I turned away from him and walked over to the snack aisle. For a second, I thought about just taking a bag of Fritos, saying "I figure you owe me this much," and walking out of the store. My hand was just reaching out to the Fritos bag when the store door opened and in walked the old lady and the little girl I had seen the week before. The old lady had some more daily number tickets to cash in with McGuffey. She never even looked at the back of the store where I was standing. From the sound of it, she had another bunch of winning tickets. Those things are worth a hundred bucks each. I stayed where I was, kind of hidden, listening to them make small talk about Halloween and things like that. The little girl looked bored and started doing that kid

There are moments when you wonder how the world would unfold if someone turned around and memorized a stranger's face or walked into a place two minutes earlier or two minutes later. I don't control what happens. It's all up to you. I'm the space where you make all your mistakes, but your mistakes aren't my fault.

thing where they start bouncing around and touching everything in sight.

McGuffey said, "That's quite a lucky streak you're on, Dolores."

The old lady just shrugged him off by saying something like "Oh, I just pray about the numbers."

"Grandma, that's not how we get the numbers," the little girl started saying.

"Hope, I need a quart of milk," the old lady said. "Could you get it for me?"

"Can I get some Necco Wafers for me and Uncle Joe?"

The old lady sighed and said okay. I guess this was enough to shut the kid up, because she skipped on over to the snack aisle.

I was still standing in front of the chips and watched her as she gave the candy section the once-over. "Is your grandma gonna buy you some candy with all the money she won?" I asked.

The kid gave me a look like she was a teacher and I was a kindergartener who didn't know how to tie his shoes. "She's going to buy me candy, but I don't know if it's from the lottery tickets or from her Social Security check."

There's nothing like getting put down by a seven-year-old. I just said, "Well, okay then," and watched the kid grab a roll of Necco Wafers and a quart of milk and prance back to the counter. Her grandma said something to her about needing to get home because her mom was going to pick her up. She didn't seem like a bad kid. The grandma didn't seem all that bad either. But for some reason, right then, I hated them. Why did they deserve to win all that money? Why them and not me?

I waited until the old lady and the little girl walked out of McGuffey's. Some teenage kids came in after them, so John was busy watching them and kind of forgot about me. I put the bag of Fritos back on the rack and walked out of the store without saying another word to McGuffey. I walked down the block to my car and started it but didn't put it into drive right away. I didn't realize I was waiting to see which way the old lady and the little girl went until they got to the end of block and took a left.

I turned the car around in a driveway and drove to the corner. I could see them slowly walking down Andrews. They didn't notice my car idling at the stop sign way behind them. I stayed there until I watched them turn down Audubon two blocks down. I counted to twenty and then really slowly, I crawled down Andrews. When I got to Audubon, I could see them still walking. They were near the Tip Top. I drove down a ways and parked across from the bar. I took my time getting out of the car and locking it. As I crossed the street to go to the Tip Top, I saw the old lady and the little girl walk into a little house with dark gray shingles on the corner of Audubon and Adams. I memorized the address: 602. I walked into the Tip Top and had a quick beer, thinking about a plan. I called Salazar from the pay phone and told him to meet me at Barlocks in an hour. I figured it was safer for us to plan this at Barlocks, because it isn't anywhere near Smoky Hollow. With a tight neighborhood like that, where everybody knows everybody else, it wouldn't pay to talk about robbing somebody who lived right down the street.

The old lady was winning on a regular basis. I could tell that from the way McGuffey talked to her. Plus, I had seen her cashing in tickets twice. The kid already told me she got Social Security, so it's not like she was living off her lottery winnings. My old grandma used to sock money away for a rainy day in an old coffee can that she hid behind the washing machine. A lot of these old folks do the same thing. They all lived through the Depression and none of them trust the bank. I was positive she had the money in the house somewhere.

I wasn't about to go and mug an old lady, but there had to be a way to get a share of whatever she'd won. She could just go and win some more, so it wasn't like we'd be hurting her by taking some of her winnings. Somehow it all seemed fair. I didn't have a real plan — just an idea. I thought somehow we could get into the house, get the money, and get out without hurting anybody and without getting caught. I didn't want to scare her or hurt her. I'm not a mean guy. I know we were talking about robbing somebody — a hunched-over little old lady somebody. Maybe that sounds mean, but you know how they say "desperate times call for desperate measures?" That phrase started making sense.

Salazar thought we could pull it off.

I got the idea to pretend to be from the Water Department, which would get us into the house, no questions asked. But once we were inside, I didn't know how we'd find the money. Salazar had an idea to say that the lady had overpaid but that we didn't have exact change to give her a refund. It was kind of scary how fast he came up with the idea, like maybe he had done this sort of thing before. It made me wonder if he really was part Gypsy, because scamming people seemed to come natural to him.

It took us a couple of weeks to find matching gray workshirts, but Salazar came up with two shirts that even had nametags sewn on the front. Mine was "Rory." Salazar got the one with "Dominic," I guess because he could pass for Italian. The shirts made us look kind of official. Salazar said his wife found them at Goodwill, but I don't know if I believe that.

Whenever you people get a stupid idea, I always wait for you to think better of it. You never do. I have all the time in the world. I keep hoping one of you will surprise me.

We planned the whole thing for a Tuesday morning, because we figured the old lady would be home but the grandkid wouldn't be around. Salazar was really cool and calm when we talked about this, like it was nothing. I'd get a little nervous when we talked about it, but it was easy to pretend that it was still just an idea, not a plan. It wasn't until the night before that it started to sink in what we were going to do. I couldn't sleep that night. My stomach hurt, and I kept wondering if maybe this wasn't a good idea. I mean, I knew it wasn't a *good* idea, the way the nuns at St. Columba had talked about good and evil. I knew what we were going to do was illegal, I just wasn't sure if it was evil or not.

There were all sorts of thoughts going through my head. How would you feel if it was your grandma who got robbed? If somebody wins money gambling, is it really theirs? If somebody is using the daily number like a bank machine, how much would it really hurt them to take some of the money — wouldn't they just win more? If I'm going to use the money for something good, like Cathy's tuition or a wedding, doesn't that make stealing it less wrong?

I couldn't talk to Salazar about any of this because I knew he didn't have a problem with taking things that didn't exactly belong to him. There was nobody else to talk to, so I just shut up and did it.

Salazar picked me up at my house in a white van. He said he borrowed it from a friend. We were both supposed to wear navy blue pants with the gray workshirts, to try and make it look more like a uniform. The only navy pants I have go with the one suit I own, the one I wore to the wedding with Denise on our first official date. The suit pants were too small now, but I found an old pair of black pants from high school. It was close enough. Without a belt, they looked enough like a uniform.

Salazar and me didn't talk much in the car. We had agreed that I should be the one to do most of the talking with the old lady because of Salazar's accent. The drive over there was worse than when we went to burn down the house, because this time I knew what I had to do. I had seen this lady, and it was broad daylight and I had to talk to her. We weren't hiding in the darkness this time. And it was all my idea.

> Let me put this into terms you might be able to understand. If I have a brain, a nerve center, if you will, it would be downtown. But Smoky Hollow is my heart, and my heart isn't sad. Not usually.

Audubon Street is like the rest of Smoky Hollow — kind of a run-down. Obviously if the Tip Top Tavern is one of your neighbors, you aren't living at The Ritz. The houses are all as neat and tidy as people with no money can make them, but still, it's a pretty sad neighborhood.

Salazar parked on the street in front of the house. It was early enough that the Tip Top was closed, and there wasn't anybody on the street. We had a clipboard with a bunch of papers on it to make us look more official. My whole body was trembling so hard I could barely pick up the clipboard. Salazar must have noticed because he said, "Robert, do not worry. We are not here to harm anyone. The woman, she has won all this money. She did not have it last month, and she was all right, yes? And she will be fine if she does not have the money next month." I didn't know if that was true or not. Maybe the lottery money was the only thing keeping this old lady from having to eat dog food.

Once, in high school, we did *The Music Man* and I was in the chorus because they needed more guys and because I really liked this girl named Maria Santiani, who was one of the Pick-a-Little ladies. The director always said that we had to pretend to be somebody else, to really believe that we were these individual people who lived in River City, Iowa, and who were worried about their kids hanging out in pool halls. I decided to do the same thing now. I decided that Rory — the guy from the Water Department that I was pretending to be — had just gotten married and his wife was expecting their first kid. I pretended I had gone to Ursuline High School and that I went to church every Sunday and my wife didn't even have to nag me about it. I pretended I was a nice guy whose job it was to give a refund to one of the Water Department's customers. When we knocked on the door and the same hunched-over old lady I had seen in McGuffey's answered the door, that's who I was. And she believed me.

The whole thing was easier and faster than I ever thought it would be. If you act like you're telling the truth, people will believe what you tell them. And if you don't have an accent and talk the way they talk, people really believe you. When I told the old lady that we were there to give her a refund and to check the water meter and the pipes because she had been overcharged, she let us into her house. And once she thought we were there to give her a refund, she didn't hesitate to go right to this little box up in one of the bedrooms and pull out change for a fifty-dollar bill. Salazar watched her as she went up the dark, narrow staircase. She took a left at the top of the stairs. That told us what room she kept her money in.

I called upstairs and said real politely, "Ma'am, my colleague needs to turn on the water in the bathroom while I go to the basement and check the meter." Salazar told me later that when he went upstairs, he looked in the door of the bedroom to the left and saw a wardrobe with one of the doors open. That's where he found the money after he turned on the water in the bathroom. I went downstairs to the basement and pretended like I was "Rory, the Water Department Guy," checking the water meter. The basement had a concrete floor and two wooden pillars. The floor was so clean you could probably eat off it. There was a short clothes line running from the wall to one of the pillars, and I saw a couple of men's shirts hanging on it. I had thought the old lady was a widow and figured we were lucky no one else happened to be around.

I called upstairs and asked the old lady to come down for a minute. My job was to keep her in the basement so Salazar could search the bedroom for the money. I looked at the meter and tried to make up something about how to read the meter and why it overcharged her. I started looking at all the pipes and saying things like "Have you noticed any leaks?" and "How's your water pressure?" I kept trying to be Rory, the good guy, instead of Bobby, the guy who was robbing her.

At one point, the old lady asked where my co-worker was and said she wanted to go back upstairs. She headed up the basement steps but I reached out and grabbed her arm to stop her. It wasn't hard or mean. I just took her arm like I was trying to help her cross the street, like a Boy Scout. Except Boy Scouts aren't supposed to rob people. I couldn't stop thinking that everything I was doing was wrong. I've never thought of myself as a bad person, but I was doing a really good job of being bad.

When I put my hand on her arm, I thought maybe she knew something was wrong, that we were lying. I didn't know if Salazar had found the money yet or not, but I said, "Okay, well, everything looks okay down here." And everything would have been okay except right at that moment, Salazar yelled for me. He didn't say my name. And he didn't call me Rory. He just yelled something that sounded like "Ah-va!" I don't know why he yelled like that. He's always the one who's cool and calm, like when we tried burning the house down, I was a nervous wreck, but he knew exactly what to do. He told me later that he yelled when he found the money because there was so much of it. When he yelled, it startled me and I kind of jumped, and I knocked the old lady over.

The next thing I knew, she was lying at the bottom of the basement steps kind of moaning. I didn't mean to hurt her, but she got hurt, I guess. I mean, she only fell maybe two or three steps, but she was pretty old. I saw her lying there

This isn't the way things are supposed to be. This isn't the way people are supposed to act. Not my people.

and got really scared and ran out of the basement.

Salazar wasn't in the kitchen. I figured he must still be upstairs. The stairs to the second floor were right across from the back door where we had come in, in between the kitchen and the dining room. I went to the bottom of the staircase and it was like I couldn't move my legs to go any farther. I wanted to, but I couldn't. I kept seeing the old lady lying on her basement floor. She was moaning, so I guess she was alive, and there wasn't any blood. If I closed my eyes, all I saw was the old lady on the floor, so instead I stood there looking down at the stairs. They were wood and not carpeted, and they had those thin rubber strips along the edge so you don't slip. I only ever saw that on outdoor stairs or in a school or something, not in somebody's house. If I kept my eyes open and just looked at the thin rubber strips on the stairs, I could breathe, but I couldn't make my legs move to go up so I just said really loud "We gotta go."

A few seconds later, Salazar came trotting down those wooden steps, his brown work boots stepping on each one of those thin rubber strips. I turned around and walked out the back door with him right behind me. Salazar is smart enough not to ask why we needed to go when we did. We walked out of the house and got in the van like we were done with one customer and on our way to the next one, like we hadn't done anything wrong.

He started the van and pulled away — not too fast, but he didn't waste any time either. It wasn't until we had gone a couple of blocks and were on Wick Avenue that Salazar said, "What happened to the old woman?"

"She fell."

"Fell?" He almost sounded concerned but he didn't slow the van or turn around or nothing.

"Yeah, when you yelled I kind of panicked and bumped into her and she fell over. I didn't do it on purpose, it was an accident."

"Where?"

"On the basement stairs. She only fell down a few steps."

"Is the woman dead?" he asked. I couldn't figure out if Salazar was worried or just trying to find out what happened. I could see a little bit of white on his knuckles where he was gripping the black steering wheel.

There's a certain point where you turn off a television show or put down a book you've started reading or walk out of a movie because the story is too painful, too cruel. There's a certain point where you stop watching. I do the same thing when I'm watching you. This is when I stopped watching Bobby Wayland and Piko Salazar for a while.

"No, she was awake and breathing and everything." Every time I talked about or thought about the old lady, the sight of her lying at the foot of her own basement steps kept coming back into my head. I figured we ought to change the subject. "Did you find the money?"

You've got to really know Salazar to get when he's joking and when he's serious, or when he's not feeling anything and when he's happy. I know him well enough to spot the tiny little smile before he said. "Robert, I expect to be invited to your wedding."

"Sure, you're invited, Salazar," I said.

"Good, because with this much money, I expect you to throw a party fit for a king." I didn't quite get what Salazar was talking about until he started emptying his pockets and tossing wads of money on the bench seat in between us. At a stop sign, he had to reach down into his pants and pull out another wad of money. I didn't really want to think about where those twenties had just been, but I couldn't believe how much money there was.

"I will drive for a while. You count," he said as we pulled onto the freeway.

The money was mostly in tens and twenties, so we were halfway to Cleveland before I finished counting. Each time I counted out another hundred bucks, I'd shake my head, maybe glance over at Salazar. It was crazy. I knew that old lady had been on a lucky streak with the daily number, but I couldn't believe she had this much money. I mean, who the hell keeps nine thousand eight hundred and forty dollars in their *house*? That's how much money there was — almost ten thousand bucks. In cash. Tax-free. The sight of all that money on my lap, on the seat of the van, even on the floor of the van, was enough to make me stop thinking about what we had just done and drove the image of the old lady on the floor out of my mind.

We split the money straight down the middle. I offered to give Salazar a little more because he had gotten the workshirts and the van and everything, but he said no, I was the one who found the target. The word "target" made me stop for a second, like we had been out shooting at something. I didn't like thinking about that hump-backed old lady as a target, but I couldn't think about her as a real person with feelings and stuff. Whenever I did, I started thinking about my grandmother or even what my mom might look like in another twenty years and my stomach started to hurt.

I took my share of the money and put it into piles on my lap, murmuring to myself "This is Cathy's tuition. This is for me to go to computer school. This is for the wedding." I looked up at Salazar and said, "Let's go out and celebrate."

"That is the last thing we should do, Robert. Do not flaunt this money. Use it a leetle bit at a time." This was one of the only times I ever heard Salazar sound like he was a little angry.

He's probably one of those dads who almost never gets mad and scares the crap out of his kids the few times he does.

It only took me half a second to realize he was right. If everybody knows that you don't have a job and suddenly you start spending money like a drunken sailor, people are gonna know something's up. I had another idea. "You know, I think I'll tell my mom and Cathy and Denise that I got a job. Not a real job — I'll say I know a guy who runs a moving company and needs an extra guy sometimes off the books."

"That is a fine idea. My wife will not question where the money came from. We will use it where we need it. You, you have large bills to pay, yes? It is wise to tell people that you have a job."

"And if I tell them that I'm getting paid under the table, they won't wonder why I only have cash."

"Yes."

It all seemed to make perfect sense, like everything was clicking into place. Salazar dropped me off, and I walked into my house with three huge wads of cash in my pockets. Cathy was at school and my mother was at work. I found a couple of envelopes and an empty margarine container that my mom used to keep extra buttons in and divided the money into separate little packets. Then I hid some of the money in my room and some in the basement. I had to find places where the ladies of the house wouldn't look. Sometimes my mother gets on these cleaning kicks and goes through old paint cans and stuff in the basement or wherever. But she isn't much for home improvement projects — she leaves that to me — so I hid one envelope at the back of a drawer in my father's old tool bench and folded up another envelope and tucked it into one of the eight million jars of nails and screws we have down there. When Cathy and Mom got home, I told them I had a job. And I called Denise that night and told her the same thing. And just like the hump-backed old lady in the house on Audubon Street, they believed what I said.

V

It was a good feeling to go through Thanksgiving and Christmas with a little bit of money in my pocket. I tried not to spend too much at once, but it was hard not to. And it was hard to lie. The more I told people I had a job but got paid in the cash, the bigger the lie became. Denise or somebody would ask me about the guys I worked with, and I had to make up names for them. I didn't make up big elaborate stories, but you can't say "I don't know" if somebody asks you the name of the guys on the moving truck with you. They have to have names. And you can't say "Nothing much," every single time somebody asks what happened at work. Once in a while, something — good or bad or funny or stupid — something happens to you. Or at least it does if you're actually going out to a job and seeing other people and doing something. Nothing much only happens when you're sitting at home all day watching TV or taking long walks in Mill Creek Park or hiding in the library. Because that was the other problem.

Now that I was supposed to be going to work, I had to leave the house and stay out of sight for a while before I could come home. I told everybody that the moving company didn't need me every day — just a few days a week. But I had to remember if I said I was working on a certain day or not so I could remember to leave the house and pre-

Bobby Wayland was better at this whole lying business than I thought he'd be. I once heard one of you tell your wife that a good liar has to have a good memory. You were carrying on an affair behind her back at the time, so I suppose you knew what you were talking about. Now I can't seem to remember which one of you it was who said this. Was it you? Do you have a good memory? Are you a good liar?

tend to go to work. It got confusing sometimes. The public library was a pretty good place to hang out, but I went to the one in Struthers or Liberty because I figured I wouldn't see anyone I knew there. I read some old Horatio Hornblower books about the sea and stuff. Those were pretty good. Sometimes I'd leave when Cathy and Mom left but come home an hour later. Then when they got home, I pretended I'd been gone all day and just got home before they did.

The other thing I did was start taking a little bit of cash — maybe thirty bucks or so — to the bank every week, like I had a job and was trying to bank some of what I earned. Back when I worked at the Sheet & Tube, I'd sometimes go into the Dollar Savings and Trust to cash my paycheck. Before I met Denise, there was this one bank teller there named Alice who was really cute, and I used to go and try and talk her up. Some of the bank tellers recognized me, so I had to tell them the whole lie about finding a new job and getting paid in cash and listen to them all say, "Good for you, I'm glad you found something."

It got to the point where I told the lie so often that I could almost believe it. But when I didn't have anything else to think about or anyone else to talk to, the image of that old lady lying by her basement steps kept coming back to me. I tried to keep busy so that wouldn't happen.

I paid cash for all my Christmas presents. My present for my sister was paying her tuition. I couldn't just give her the money outright. If I gave her four hundred in cash, she'd think I robbed a bank, which was too close to the truth for me to think about. She needed to finish school — nobody is gonna hire a nurse who didn't finish school. The tuition for her next quarter had to get paid before January seventh. A few days before Christmas, I went down to Youngstown State, found the bursar's office, and paid her tuition bill in cash. The ladies in the bursar's office looked at me kind of funny, like maybe they thought I was a bagman for the Mob or something. Even so, they were happy to take the cash. People are always happy to take money from you. They gave me a receipt showing that her tuition was paid, and I put that in a card for her to open on Christmas morning.

Finding something for my mother was harder. The only thing she really needed was money to pay bills, but I couldn't just give her a wad of cash. My parents bought this house in 1953, the year I was born. The mortgage is through Dollar Savings and Trust, so I went in one day and paid two hundred dollars on the principal. I also went to Strouss' and got her a really nice outfit so she'd have something to open on Christmas morning and pretended like that was the whole gift. My plan was to put a few hundred dollars on the mortgage a couple more times before I moved out after the wedding in May. All that extra money on the principal would be enough so that by this time next year, the house could be paid off. Then she could do whatever she wanted, and I could move out with Denise and not feel like I was leaving my mother in a lurch.

Denise and I had already agreed that we'd just do small gifts for each other. It made sense to save our money, except now that I had some money to spend, I wanted to spend it on her. I didn't go crazy. I got her the *Frampton Comes Alive* album, because it had "Baby, I Love Your Way" on it, plus it's a great album. And then, because I knew she didn't have her own turntable, I got her one, plus some really great speakers.

I brought it to her house on Christmas morning. It was a really big package, and at first Denise kind of freaked out and said I spent too much. Her brother Andy pointed out that the stereo would be going into our new apartment in six months, so it was almost like I bought it for myself. That's not entirely true, but it made Denise forget a little about how much the whole setup cost.

What I'm saying is it was hard not to spend all that money right away. There was stuff we needed. Not just tuition and the mortgage and the wedding, but things for the house and groceries and bills. And yeah, I went a little crazy because it was Christmas and I wanted to do some nice things for my family. But I couldn't enjoy myself, not really.

For two weeks after we robbed the humped-back old lady, I'd look through every page of *The Vindicator* to see if there was any story about an old woman falling down the basement stairs during a robbery and dying. There wasn't anything, which made me think that maybe she was okay, or at least alive. Knowing that didn't make me feel any better.

That was because Joe Steiner didn't want to publicize that the house had been robbed. Would you want everyone to know that your sister had made a terrible mistake and lost all of her money?

My mom, Cathy, and I all spent Christmas Day at the Skernickis, and we got home late, full of food and happy. Mom and Cathy went up to bed right away, but I hung around downstairs, drinking one last beer and watching *White Christmas* on the late movie. And when I headed upstairs to go to bed, I got this sudden picture in my head of the staircase in that lady's house. The lady we robbed.

The staircase was dark, just like the staircase in her house. I got to thinking about those rubber strips on the edge of the steps and wondered if they bothered her feet if she ever went downstairs barefoot. I wondered if she had been able to get Christmas presents for her granddaughter. I wondered if she had more than one grandkid. I wondered if how happy me and my family were this Christmas was at the expense of her family.

The feeling kept gnawing at me. Guilt, I guess. And instead of feeling better over time, I kept feeling worse and worse. Over the next few weeks, I spent nearly all the rest of the money. It was like, if the money wasn't around, maybe it wouldn't bother me. I enrolled in that computer school and paid my whole tuition up front. Then I paid the whole kit and kaboodle for the hall and the caterer and the wedding invitations. And I paid more money on my mother's mortgage. I just didn't want the money around me anymore. I had one envelope of cash left, hidden in the back of my closet under my old baseball glove and cleats and some other stuff. There was only about one hundred fifty dollars in it. That was all I had left. One envelope. And all the good things I had done with the money didn't change the fact that I had still done this thing, this really bad thing. The money being gone didn't change what I done.

Near the end of January, we got hit with a monster blizzard. This thing was a snowstorm for the ages. From Tuesday night to Friday, nobody went anywhere or did anything. I sat in the house with Cathy while she studied and talked to me. Mom was stuck in the hospital, where she had been working since Tuesday morning. It was a nightmare.

Blizzards challenge me just as much as they challenge you. They make me creak and crack. Do you know how heavy the shovel is when you go out to clear the snow? Imagine that shovel of snow multiplied by 1,000,000,000. Imagine the weight of all that snow on top of you.

On Thursday morning, Cathy and I were sitting around the living room watching TV. She had finally given up studying, because even Youngstown State was closed. It was like the whole world was closed. We were both just hanging around in pajamas and sweat shirts, looking like a couple of scrubs. It kind of felt like we were kids again, sitting around on a Saturday morning in our pajamas watching cartoons. And then, out of nowhere, Cathy turns to me and asks, "Where did you get the money for my tuition?"

For some reason, my heart started pounding faster, but I stayed cool. "I told you, I've been working for a mover."

"They must be paying you really well," Cathy said.

"Well, it's under the table, so I'm taking home more than I would have if I was a regular employee. No taxes. And sometimes people give us tips."

"Those must be some pretty hefty tips."

"Well, people are moving out of Youngstown. They're happy to be leaving," I said and threw a pillow at her. That was enough to start a quick pillow fight. I even let Cathy beat me up a little bit to keep her from asking about the money. But that didn't stop me from thinking about it.

The only way I could think of to get whole thing off my conscience was to go to confession. Even if you don't believe in God or sin or anything like that, I thought maybe telling someone what I had done would make me feel better.

I never thought about the whole meaning of words like "confession" and "absolution" when I was a kid. I mean, you're in second grade when you make your First Confession, and what horrible things can you have done when you're seven? My sins were always something like, "I teased my sister three times and disobeyed my mother twice." At St. Columba, everybody always tried to go to Monsignor Walsh for confession because he always gave the same penance: three "Our Fathers" and three "Hail Marys." No matter what you had did, he gave you the same penance. If I were able to track down old Monsignor Walsh right now and told him I had stolen ten thousand dollars from an old lady, I'll bet he'd still tell me to say three "Our Fathers" and three "Hail Marys."

I couldn't go to confession at St. Columba. Mom and Cathy still went there. I went with them sometimes, when I let my mother convince me to go. I didn't want to talk to anybody I knew or might see again. I know priests aren't supposed to talk about what they hear in confession, but I felt like if any of the priests at St. Columba heard me confess about stealing the money, they'd look at me different for the rest of my life.

Denise and her family go to St. Christine, which is near where they live. That's where we're getting married, so I sure wasn't going there. Then I remembered this article I saw in *The Vindicator* a couple months ago about the pastor at St. Cyril and Methodius who's going to El Salvador as a missionary. I've never been in that church and never met the guy. He seemed like the perfect priest for me because once I confessed to him, he'd be leaving the country. I was pretty sure I would never see him again.

When the weather was good and I could have been doing stuff around the yard or looking for work or something, I stayed in the house for days at a time. But having to stay inside for a few days because of the blizzard made me crazy to get out of the house. By Saturday morning after the blizzard, the streets were plowed enough to get through, so I went. I didn't tell my mother or Cathy where I was going. If I told them I was going to confession, they'd automatically know something was wrong. And it was. My conscience felt all wrong, but they didn't need to know that.

Most churches have confession on Saturday afternoon for maybe an hour or two before the four o'clock mass. I wasn't exactly sure when they had it at St. Cyril, so I got there in the mid-afternoon and just hung around. The only people who go to church on Saturday afternoon are old folks. They'll sit there for hours just saying the Rosary or

These are my favorite kind of people. Not because they're religious, but because they believe in something and don't mind showing it. You have to believe in something. You go crazy if you don't. I've seen it. If you don't want to believe in God, believe in me. Believe in the power of my concrete and steel and brick and glass and earth. Even if you tore down all my buildings, I'd still exist. Here's something you didn't know about me: I've always been here. I existed long before John Young gave me his name. You didn't call me into existence, you just gave me a name that suited you.

whatnot. I guess it gets them out of the house. We'd just had a blizzard that people were saying was the worst in forty years, so you'd think the church would be deserted. The church parking lot hadn't even been plowed yet. I had to park around the corner. But when I walked into the church, there were two old ladies with black boots and huge overcoats and hats and the whole nine yards sitting in the front row. They must have walked through all that snow just to get to church. They were praying up a storm when I got there.

I picked up a church bulletin and saw that confession was from two thirty to three forty-five. I had a little time to kill so I picked a pew somewhere in the middle of the church and took a seat. It was kind of neat to sit and look at the church when it was empty. It was smaller than I thought, but really pretty. I took a little walk around the church, just to check out the paintings and statues and stuff. A tall guy, maybe in his sixties, shuffled into church and almost bumped into me by the baptismal font in the back of the church. I couldn't get over how these old folks would trudge their way through the snow mounds and the wind and the cold just to get to church. I have no idea what any of those nice old ladies would have to confess. Cheating at bingo? Yelling at their cats? They had to be true believers to come out in this weather. Then I realized that I was sitting in that church, too, that I had driven past a couple other churches through all that snow just to get here. Maybe they thought I was as devout as they were. Or maybe they were as messed up as I am.

Right at two thirty, a priest came out from behind the altar and went into the confessional. St. Cyril is small — there's only one confessional. There's a big door in the middle where the priest sits and a door on either side where you go in so you can confess. Confessionals always remind me of those rows of phone booths that you see in old movies, but instead of opening the door, dropping a dime in the phone, and asking the operator to connect you to some number, you open the door, drop to your knees, and ask the priest to connect you to God.

With a church this small, I figured there wasn't more than one or two priests, so odds were that the priest who was going to El Salvador was in there. The tall guy was waiting outside the confessional too. When I sat down at the far end of the pew, the guy nodded to me. I kind of mumbled "Hi," but he looked down like I was disturbing his praying. The two old ladies were on the other side of the church. With all the snow on the ground, I figured nobody else would show up unless they were coming to four o'clock mass.

I looked up at the confessional door. It was carved in this really elaborate pattern, with angels and flowers and stuff. Really pretty. A couple of years ago, most of the churches around here started giving you the option of confessing face to face instead of anonymously. I remember the first time I went to confession back when I was in second grade. You walked into this dark little box and kneeled down by a grill and talked to somebody you couldn't really see. It felt kind of creepy. We weren't allowed to pick for our first confession, so I made mine with Father Corrigan instead of Monsignor Walsh and his "three Our Fathers and three Hail Marys." It felt like Father Corrigan kept me in there for days, talking to me about being truly sorry for my sins and everything, like I was some delinquent. I was seven — I wasn't old enough to do anything bad. I always thought maybe he had me confused with some other kid, because he couldn't see my face. Whether you have a birthmark or a moustache, if you have something on your face, people generally remember it.

The tall guy went into the face-to-face side. He didn't stay in there all that long, and when he came out, he gave me a smug "I've-got-nothing-to-hide" kind of look. Up until then, I was gonna go to the anonymous side. Maybe it's because the priest was leaving Youngstown and I'd never see him again, or maybe it's because I wanted to feel like I was talking to somebody, not just a shadow, but I went into the face-to-face side.

Father Troha was in his forties, with dark, thick hair and a pencil-thin moustache. He looked like Errol Flynn without the slicked-back hair. There had been a picture of him with the article in the paper. When Cathy and my mother saw it, they called him "Father What-A-Waste." I guess he was good looking for a priest.

"Hello, my son," he said when I sat down in the straight-backed chair across from him. The face-to-face confessional still has half a wall — they just took out the grill and turned on a light. It's a tight squeeze; if the little half-wall wasn't there, our knees would've touched.

"Hi," I said. I almost couldn't remember what I was supposed to say. "Um, bless me, Father, for I have sinned. It's been um ... geez, it's been a long time since my last confession. I mean, years since the last time."

"That's okay. Welcome home. My name is Father Troha." He smiled, made the Sign of the Cross, and said a little prayer. That was his part. Then he waited for me to say my part, to tell him my sins. I realized I must look a little weird to him. Who the hell else shows up at confession for the first time in years with a priest they don't know four days after the blizzard of the century unless they've got a doozy of a sin to confess?

For a moment, I kind of wished I had gone to the anonymous side. I looked down at my hands and my knees and the polished wood on top of the half-wall in between me and the priest. I couldn't bring myself to look him in the eye and say what I had done. Father Troha didn't say anything. He just waited for me.

"I'm not a bad guy," I said finally. "But I've done some bad things." My heart was pounding and all my nerves felt shaky. It was like that feeling when you know your dad is about to haul off and smack you on the rear end for something. I took a deep breath and just said it, just got the worst part out first. "I set fire to a house for the insurance money, and I stole money from an old lady who kept winning the lottery." I looked up at Father Troha, but his expression hadn't changed. Priests probably make great card players because they have so much practice perfecting their poker face. "Some guy was going to pay me and my friend to burn down a house that he owned. Nobody was living in it and we didn't hurt nobody," I added. I didn't want Father Troha to think I was a complete jerk or dangerous. "And it turns out we didn't even do the job right, so he didn't get the insurance money and we didn't get paid."

Father Troha nodded. "Is that why you robbed this woman?" he asked softly.

"Yeah. I saw that she was hitting the daily number a lot. I saw her walk out of a store with a wad of cash a couple of times. So, me and my friend figured out a scam to take the money. We figured she had won it, so it was extra to her. It's not like we took her pension check. We didn't want to hurt her. We both lost our jobs in September ... ." Father Troha just nodded when I said that. Around Youngstown, that's all you have to say to let people know you used to work at the Sheet & Tube. "I'm getting married in May, and I have to pay for my wedding and my sister's college tuition and my mother's mortgage and trade school and ... I used the money for good things. I don't drink — I mean, I drink but I'm not a drunk, you know? And I don't smoke weed and I don't cheat on my fiance and I don't do things like this ... I don't. I mean, I *did* set a house on fire and I *did* steal, but those things aren't *me*."

"Our God is a forgiving God," Father Troha said. "And he knows the goodness in your heart."

"I feel really bad about taking the money. I keep thinking maybe that old lady really needed it, like maybe it was the windfall she was looking for, just like it was the windfall I needed."

"Can you return the money?"

It was a simple question, but it made me feel like a crumb to think I had blown through nearly five grand in two months. It didn't matter that I had spent it on trying to help my family. I spent it. I stole it, and I spent it. "No. It's gone. Almost gone. There's about a hundred fifty bucks left."

"How much money did you take?" Father Troha asked.

"It was almost ten thousand bucks. I got half that."

When Father Troha said "Wow," it was the only time he looked like a regular guy and not like a priest.

"Yeah, wow ... ," I said.

Father Troha asked me if the woman had been hurt. I kind of liked that he said it that way and not "Did you hurt the woman?" Like he realized I wasn't deliberately trying to be mean or anything. But I still felt like I had to tell him the truth. "I don't know," I said quietly. "I accidentally bumped into her and she fell down the stairs. I don't know what happened to her." Both of us just sat there for a minute. I kept waiting for him to say something, and I guess he was waiting to make sure I didn't have any other terrible thing to tell him. Finally, I just said, "I guess that's a big bunch of 'Hail Marys' and 'Our Fathers' I'm gonna have to say, huh?'

"My son, I don't want you to think of prayer as a punishment. Prayer should be a joy, a time for you to renew your relationship with God." He leaned forward a little and rested his hands on his knees. "Do you know this woman's family?"

"No. I mean, I know where she lives, but I don't know her name or anything about her except that she has a little granddaughter

When Bobby said "I know where she lives," I'll bet they both thought "602 Audubon." He didn't seem to notice that the good father mentioned Dolores's family but not Dolores.

who hangs around her house a lot."

"You can't return the money you stole, I understand that. And I want you to hold prayer in a sacred space, not as a punishment. For your penance, I want you to find three ways that you can make amends."

This seemed like the dumbest penance anyone had ever gotten. What was I supposed to do, write a note saying 'Hey, sorry I stole all your life savings?' But I just asked, "How am I supposed to do that? Can't I just say the Rosary a bunch of times?"

"If saying the Rosary would make you feel better, do so. I encourage you to pray and renew your relationship with Our Lord. It's very clear that you feel genuine remorse for your actions. Remember that the seal of confession is absolute — I will never repeat what you've said here today. However, I'd like you to consider that the best way to make amends might be to turn yourself into the police."

As soon as he said that, I stood up. There was no way I was gonna let him turn me in. "Forget it."

"I will never repeat what you've said here," he said again. "I admire you for confessing to me today. Whether or not you confess to the police is your choice." The look he gave me was like your favorite teacher and your dad and your dog all rolled into one, like he knew the worst thing I had ever done and still thought I was an okay person. "If you sit down, I can give you absolution."

I sat.

He made the Sign of the Cross and said, "Repent in your words and in your deeds. Your sins are forgiven. I absolve you from all of your sins in the name of the Father, and of the Son, and of the Holy Ghost. Amen."

"Amen," I said.

"You'll find the right path, my son," Father Troha said. He kept calling me "son" like he knew I didn't have a father. "Open your heart to God, and you'll know what to do."

That sounded half Jesus freak and half hopeful to me. I believe in God — I mean, I believe that there's something up there. I'm not sure I buy into the whole idea that God is watching out for us and communicating with us. I don't need a burning bush or nothing, but sometimes, it'd be nice to have a real sign, something to let you know that somebody's listening. I didn't know what else to say, so I just said, "Okay. Thanks."

"Peace be with you," Father Troha said as I stood up.

"You too," I said and left the confessional.

The church was empty when I walked out of the confessional. I don't know what happened to the two old ladies and the tall guy. With Father Troha shut up in the confessional, it felt like I was a million miles away from anybody. I walked halfway across the church and stopped in the center aisle for a minute and looked up at the huge arches over the altar and the paintings and carvings of saints all over the place. The outside of St. Cyril's is just plain red brick — you wouldn't think that the inside is so elaborate. I know God isn't going to come down and zap you with a lightning bolt or something if you don't do your penance, but I didn't want to start a new life with Denise with this hanging over my head. She was the best thing going in my life. If she knew what I had done to pay for the wedding, she wouldn't marry me.

When I walked out the church doors, that wind hit me like a slap across the face, even with my heavy coat and gloves and hat. The snow plows had come through again, so the streets were a little better, and the church parking lot had gotten plowed, but nobody had gotten around to shoveling the sidewalks downtown. There was nobody on the street, so I just walked down the middle of Wood Avenue and around the corner to Rayen where I had parked. The sky was so cloudy and the snow was piled so high you could look down Rayen Avenue and not be sure where the ground ended and the sky began. It all just got mixed into one mess of white and gray.

I thought confession is supposed to make you feel better, but it didn't. So what if some priest said God forgave me? That doesn't change what I did. Who knows what that humped-back old lady was going to use the money for? That much money could have changed her life even more than it changed mine. I kept thinking about that word "amends." If you break something, you need " a mend" — a fix for something that's broken. I definitely broke something, but I didn't have any idea how to fix it.

Youngstown

You want magic. That's why you're still here, isn't it? That's what you've been waiting for. Everybody wants magic. You like magic for the same reasons you believe in God or astrology or fortune cookies: You want something that you can't see and that you can't explain to be real.

Hope
Winter 1977-78

I didn't know I could do magic until I started kindergarten. Before that, sometimes I would tell my mom that I was going to do magic so it would stop raining and we could go to the playground or so we would get all green lights when she was driving. But every time it happened, my mom would always say "Well, isn't that lucky!" Except I knew it wasn't luck, it was me.

Well, I *thought* it was me. I wasn't *sure* it was me until the first week of kindergarten. I was in Miss Beck's room. I liked Miss Beck because she always read us a book at the end of the day. I heard her tell Mrs. Korzunowski, who teaches first grade, that she read to us to help everybody calm down. Books are kind of like magic.

In Miss Beck's room, we had baskets

You people have made some really terrible things, but books are one of your better inventions. I can't say the same for pet rocks, disco, or machine guns.

on the shelf for our folders and lunch boxes and stuff. My basket was on the top shelf because they were in alphabetical order and my last name starts with "B." I couldn't get my basket because it was too high, and I was too short. Every day for the first week of kindergarten, when we were getting ready to leave and everybody else was in a big rush to get their stuff, I had to wait for Miss Beck to help me. I got tired of that pretty quick.

The only way my basket was going to get moved to a lower shelf was if a bunch of kids with last names that start with an "A" joined my class. I needed to get my basket by myself.

When everybody else was lining up to leave, I stood in front of the shelves where the baskets were. I raised my hand up, as far as I could reach. Even on my tippy-toes, I could only touch the end of the shelf but not the basket. Instead of standing there reaching and reaching, I stood straight on my feet and held my hand up to the edge of the shelf and said very quietly, so nobody else could hear, *"Please move closer. Please move closer. Please move closer."*

The next thing I knew, my basket slid to the end of the shelf. It moved closer just like I asked it to. I could reach it, and I didn't even have to stand on my tippy-toes. That was the first time I really did magic. I can make things move without touching them.

You have to concentrate really hard to do magic, so I only do it when I really need it, like moving my basket in kindergarten, or making the ball go a little farther in kickball so I get on base. I've never used magic to make me kick a home run or anything — *that* would be cheating.

At Susie Cafferty's birthday party last summer, she had a big cake from a bakery — the kind with a bunch of frosting flowers. Everybody was supposed to get one flower, but Maureen Mackey whined and got two because she's like that. I didn't do anything. And then Maureen was bossing everybody around when we were playing games, but I still didn't do anything. When we played Pin the Tail on the Donkey, she held her head back so she could peek under the blindfold. She even pretended to scratch her nose and moved the blindfold up so she could see. My tail was the closest, and she pushed it out of the way when she put her tail on so she would win. And even though everybody knew she was cheating, Susie's mom gave her first prize anyway because he's friends with Maureen's mom. Then I did something.

We had an egg and spoon race, where you have to balance an egg on a spoon while you're running. If your egg falls, you're out. I walked as fast as I could without letting my egg fall. I could have used magic to keep my egg from moving, but I didn't want to cheat. We were in Susie's backyard, so the eggs wouldn't make a mess if they fell. A couple girls dropped their eggs and some of the eggs broke on the ground, but everybody just laughed. I was tired of Maureen cheating at all the games, plus she's always mean to me at school. So I didn't cheat, but I got back at her. I made Maureen's egg fall. It flew hard right into her stomach so that it broke and got all over her dress. Then she cried.

All I can say is if you're going to teach people a religion that celebrates retribution, don't be surprised when they go looking for it.

I felt kind of bad after that.

Kind of.

Like I said, it's hard work doing magic.

Susie and Maureen and I all go to St. Christine, which is a Catholic school. Catholic school is different than public school because you have to wear uniforms and the public-school kids can wear anything they want. Plus you have religion class and you have to go to church once a week during school. They don't teach religion in public schools because of the Constitution. I mostly like my school, except that most of the kids on my block go to public school. I still play with them but I don't ride the bus with them and we don't see each other every day like you do in school. And some of the stuff you do in Catholic school you don't do in public school, so we don't always understand each other. Sometimes it makes me feel a little lonely.

I'm in second grade this year, and in second grade, you get two sacraments — the sacrament of Reconciliation, which most people just call Confession because "reconciliation" is a really long word and nobody seems to know what it means — and First Communion.

With First Communion, one, you get a new white dress with a *veil* and new shoes that match. Two, your family has a huge party and everybody gives you money. And three, you don't have to go to school the next day. Sister Ellen Mary at school says it's the most important sacrament you can make, even more important than getting married or dying, because you're receiving the body of Christ. It's a *really* big deal.

I always feel bad for First Confession. With First Confession, you just show up at church and tell the priest all the things you did wrong and nobody throws a party for you and you don't even get a new dress. It's like nobody cares about poor First Confession.

> It is my considered opinion that nobody cares about First Confession because none of you people ever want to admit you did anything wrong.

I care. First Confession is important because it means you're growing up. When you're a little kid and you do something wrong, it isn't a sin because you don't know any better. You're just a stupid little kid. When you get to be my age, you're supposed to know right from wrong. *Now* when I do something wrong, I'm not just making a mistake, I'm committing a *sin*. I like being old enough to know better, except they didn't tell us in school when the time when we're supposed to know better actually started. I'm guessing at the beginning of second grade.

When I went to confession for the first time, I didn't tell the priest anything about doing magic. I just told him the bad stuff I'd done, which wasn't very much. When you're an only child, it's hard to commit any really good sins because there's nobody around to fight with. It's easier to get in trouble with more people around. My friend Elizabeth Calani at school has two older sisters, one older brother, *and* one younger brother. From what I've seen, they spend most of the day arguing and beating each other up. She has all sorts of good things to confess. Most of my sins have to do with me not listening to my parents or disobeying. It's pretty boring.

The only people who know that I can do magic are my cousins Edie, Lou, and Nico. It was kind of an accident that they found out. They're all older and can do everything better than me. Edie can run way faster than I can, and Lou can throw balls way farther, and Nico can climb trees higher. I can't do anything as good as them. We were all out playing in my backyard when we were having a picnic on Labor Day, and I told my cousins that I could make a rock move without touching it. I had never told anyone that I could do magic before, but magic was the only thing I could do that they couldn't.

So I moved a rock without touching it.

Ever since then, they don't treat me like a little kid. They treat me like one of them.

We haven't told anyone else, not even Uncle Joe. And my other cousins from Cleveland aren't even allowed to know because there are too many of them. Somebody would tell. You have to keep this kind of thing a secret because grownups cannot handle magic.

II

Grownups aren't allowed to know about magic because they'd just mess it all up and try to use it for everything. I've been really careful about doing magic, and I still made two huge mistakes. The first is that my grandma got robbed. Two men came to her house and pretended to be from the Water Department and went in the house and took all her money. They lied *and* they stole, which are two big, big sins. And one of them pushed her down the stairs, which has to be some sort of sin. They must have known she won a lot of money in the lottery, but she wouldn't have had all that extra money if I hadn't picked the numbers for her, so it's kind of my fault.

I didn't know this would happen when I started picking lottery numbers. I thought I was doing something good. One day, right before second grade started, I was helping my Uncle Joe fix a car and some numbers popped into my head. There were two twos and a zero. Uncle Joe was teaching me all about how an engine works, but those twos and that zero kept hopping around in my brain like they wanted me to notice them. I told my Uncle Joe that the number two-two-zero was going to come up and that he should play it. He didn't really listen to me, so I told Grandma because sometimes she and my mom would play the lottery just for fun. She and I walked to McGuffey's and she bought four tickets, all with two-two-zero. Once she had spent *two whole dollars* on my numbers, I *had* to make those numbers come up because my grandma is kind of poor, and she doesn't have two dollars just to waste.

When I got home, I told my mom that Grandma bought four lottery tickets with numbers I gave her. She said I could watch them pick the numbers on TV. I didn't even know they did that. We watched it after dinner. There was a man in a tie talking about the lottery. He was standing behind these three big glass bowls with little ping-pong balls with numbers written on them bouncing around inside them. Then he opened a little door at the top of each bowl so one of the ping-pong balls could pop out, and that's how they get the daily number. I stared at the TV and concentrated really hard. When he went to the first bowl, I said, "*Two, Two, Two*" to myself, and a two came up. Then I did the same thing for the second bowl, and then "*Zero, Zero, Zero*" for the third bowl. And that's how I made two-two-zero come up.

Grandma called my mom the next day. She asked me for another number, but I didn't feel like giving her one that day. The next morning, my mom asked me for a number *again*. I told her I'd think about it and asked if I could watch TV while I ate my breakfast. She said, "Sure," so I got to sit in the den and watch Scooby-Doo while I ate my Cream of Wheat. There's a little notepad in the den next to the telephone so if somebody calls and has something important to say, my mom and dad can write it down. While I was eating, I saw some numbers hanging around on top of the TV, and then a seven and two fives lined up. I liked how that looked, so I told them to stay just like that and wrote seven-five-five on the notepad next to the telephone.

I made *that* number come out *that* day, and my mom and my grandma started getting really excited. Every time I saw one of them, they'd ask me for a number. It was kind of annoying. This is why you can't tell grownups about magic. Sometimes I'd give them a number just to make them leave me alone, but I wouldn't make the number come out and my mom and Grandma wouldn't win. I'd only make the daily number come out if it had two of the same digits, like two-two-zero or seven-five-five. Numbers like that are the best, because it's like two parents and one kid, which is how it is in my family. There's me and my mom and my dad. I only ever made numbers like that come out in the lottery.

All during the whole fall, I got to watch TV in the den while I ate breakfast instead of eating in the kitchen. My mom never let me do that before. I know she didn't change her mind about it because I was getting older and learning how not to be messy. She let me do it because she wanted me to keep giving her lottery numbers. I know this because when I stopped giving her lottery numbers, I had to eat breakfast in the kitchen again.

After I wrote down the number, I'd go to school and my mom would call my grandma and tell her the number and they'd both play it. We'd watch them draw the daily number every night. When we went to visit my grandma on Saturdays, I'd walk up to McGuffey's with her so she could cash in her lottery tickets. She won a lot of money. I guess my mom did, too, but she didn't really give any of it to me. I didn't even get a raise in my allowance — it was still only fifty cents a week. I went with my mom to the bank a bunch of times to put money in my savings account, but I think my mom spent some of it on treats for herself, because there were more Rolling Rock bottle caps in the big jar she keeps in the basement.

Ruthie did everything everyone needed from her and never neglected her family, but she took after her father. They both liked the sanctuary found at the bottom of a bottle.

When Grandma got hurt, my Great Uncle Joe called my mom. She didn't even have time to try and find a babysitter — she just grabbed me and her purse and drove to the hospital. I got to see Grandma before they operated on her. I was with Uncle Joe and he said that she broke her hip. I concentrated really hard and tried to move my grandmother's hip back where it should go, but I don't think I did it right. Ever since they operated on her hip, my grandma's been acting weird, like she isn't always sure what's happening. And she keeps getting sicker and sicker. That's the second big mistake I made with my magic.

I've only done magic once since my grandma got hurt. I made one lottery number come out for a waitress at a restaurant that didn't have any customers, and I didn't tell anybody but her. That's all. Doing magic is too dangerous. If my grandma wouldn't have won all that money, then no one would have wanted to rob her. And if I hadn't tried to use magic to fix her hip, maybe she wouldn't be so sick.

My Uncle Joe and I have been trying to find the guys who robbed Grandma. We investigated at McGuffey's, at church, and at a restaurant near where the Sheeting Tube used to be. We even found out the name of one of the guys who maybe did it, but that's all. This is what we know about him: His name might be Bobby, and he has a birthmark on his cheek and he's kind of chubby. I asked Uncle Joe at my birthday when we could go and look for Bobby with the birthmark again, but he just said we ought to wait until after the holidays.

Here are the bad things about having your birthday in December. One, you don't get any presents for a whole year and then you get birthday and Christmas all at the same time. Kids with birthdays in the summer are lucky, because they get presents twice a year. Two, you can never have a party outside because it's too cold. Three, if you get something like a bicycle, you have to wait months before you can use it. For instance, my Aunt Peggy gave me real roller skates for my birthday — the kind that are like shoes, not the kind that slip over your sneakers and tighten with a key. They were exactly what I wanted, but I can't use them yet because there's too much snow.

My grandma usually gives me a card with a five-dollar bill in it for my birthday, but this year she didn't because she's back in the hospital. Everybody tried to pretend like they were happy at my birthday party, but I knew they were all worried about Grandma. It was my first birthday where she wasn't there. It felt empty.

Dr. Distinguished Moustache who said Dolores would be home by Christmas was full of hooey. She wasn't ever coming home again, and everybody knew it.

Christmas is my mom's favorite holiday, and she almost named me Christine, after Christmas, but then I would have been Christine going to St. Christine's and that would have been horrible, so I'm glad they didn't name me that. Then they were maybe going to name me Noelle, because that's French for Christmas, except we aren't French, and even though I was born on December twelfth, that isn't really *Christmas*. My mom and dad tried for years and years to have a baby before they had me. I think my mom was almost forty when I was born, which sounds awfully old to be having babies. My dad suggested they name me Hope, because that's what they had the whole time they were trying to have a baby. And that's how I got my name. My mom always says that hope is a good thing to have, and I know she means me and not just the feeling that things will turn out okay.

I have lots of hope. Mostly I hope that Uncle Joe and I will find the guys who robbed Grandma, except I'm not sure Uncle Joe is feeling hopeful about that anymore. And I'm trying to be hopeful that Grandma will get better, but my dad says she had a little stroke and is in intensive care. Nobody will tell me anything except my cousin Edie says it means she's going to die. She's almost a teenager, so she knows.

Christmas should have been fun because I got to see all of my cousins at the same time, even the ones who live in Cleveland. I got a lot of neat stuff — Legos, Princess Leia and Chewbacca action figures, plus I got Superstar Barbie and the Superstar Barbie Beauty Boutique. All during Christmas, my dad and Uncle Joe kept calling it the "boo-tikki," and thinking they were being funny. They weren't.

We had Christmas at our house. Nobody said it was because it'd be too sad to go to Grandma and Uncle Joe's house but we all knew. My mom and Uncle Joe went to the hospital on Christmas morning. My Aunt Peggy and all those cousins were in town and went to the hospital in the afternoon so there was somebody with Grandma almost all day, even though you can't really talk to her. She's kind of sleeping.

After dinner, all my cousins and everybody were in the dining room and the living room, and Uncle Joe and I went into the kitchen at the same time to steal an extra cookie.

"I won't tell if you won't tell," Uncle Joe said, and picked the cookie tray off the counter and held it down so I could see better. "What kind do you want?"

"Pinwheel," I said. Uncle Joe took a Cherry Twinkle, which is pretty good too because it has a maraschino cherry in the middle of it. With pinwheels, you have to eat around each ring of the cookie — first the chocolate, then the vanilla, and then the chocolate all the way to the middle. It can take a while to do it right, but you get to have your cookie longer.

We stood there and smiled at each other and ate our cookies, because we both knew that my mom would say we had had too many already. For a minute, it made everything feel normal. I took a break from eating the vanilla part of my cookie and said, "Uncle Joe, when are we going to go and look for Bobby with the birthmark again?"

Uncle Joe ate the last bit of his cookie. It looked like he was thinking hard while he chewed, like maybe he was trying to figure out what to say. "I don't know," he said finally. "It doesn't seem to matter much anymore."

"I think it still matters," I said. I took another nibble of my cookie. Right then, my dad came into the kitchen looking for another cookie too. "Don't tell Mom," he said, and we all laughed and it kind of felt like a regular Christmas. But it wasn't a regular Christmas because Grandma wasn't there and I don't want to forget her, so I keep talking about her and trying to find the guys who robbed her. It seems like Uncle Joe and the other grownups don't want to think about it at all.

"Well, it's getting to be time for me to go," Uncle Joe said.

"You know, you could just stay here," my dad said. "The invitation is always open."

"I don't want to be a bother. And I'm going to stop by the hospital again on my way."

"You're not a bother. I like having you here," I said. Uncle Joe looked down at me and smiled.

"We all like having you here. There's no reason for you to stay in that old house all by yourself."

The university had been making offers to people in the Hollow all year, kind of like the slimy guy who puts the make on every woman at a party. The university keeps taking more and more land and getting bigger and bigger. It makes me feel a little like Dr. Frankenstein with a monster that's getting too big for its britches.

"I'm not in the house, I'm in the garage."

Uncle Joe and I laughed, but my dad didn't. "There's a reason we built the in-law suite in the basement," he said. "And nobody is going to make a better offer for the house on Audubon than the one the university made."

"Let's wait and see what happens with Dolores." Then Uncle Joe looked at me asked if I would make a care package of cookies for him to bring home.

"Sure!" I said. Uncle Joe and my dad walked out of the kitchen, and I put some cookies on a paper plate and got a big piece of aluminum foil to cover it. Before I did, I wrote a note on a piece of paper and put it on top of the cookies. It read "We have to look for them!" I figured Uncle Joe would know what I meant. After that, I went into the dining room and started playing Crazy Eights with my cousins because I just learned how to play that game and I'm pretty sure I'm a natural.

III

Uncle Joe wouldn't go investigate with me, and I couldn't go by myself because I'm way too young to drive. So I had to wait. It was a really snowy winter, and even though that meant I could make a lot of snow angels, it also meant that my mom didn't want to drive me anywhere if she didn't have to. She doesn't like driving in the snow, but she knows *how* to drive. My dad says that back when Grandma was growing up, most women didn't know how to drive. They always had their husband do it. He also said that when Grandma was born, women weren't even allowed to vote for president or for anything. I thought it was another one of his jokes until I looked it up in the encyclopedia.

My grandma used to go to confession once a month. Sometimes I would go with her, even though I'd have to sit in the pew outside the confessional and wait for her. I really, really wanted to know what it looked inside the confessional, and Grandma wouldn't tell me. Sometimes I'd ask my mom and she said was just a little room, like a closet. Uncle Joe said inside it was really huge and that every confessional had a skylight, but I knew he had to be joking. And my dad said he didn't know because he's Presbyterian and they don't have anything to confess.

Now that I've made my First Confession, I know that Mom was telling the truth — the confessional really is just a little room like a closet. I always liked going to confession and Saturday mass with Grandma because only old people and grown-ups go then. They aren't noisy like the kids in my class and nobody's fidgeting next to you. It's easier to daydream when it's quiet. Plus, if you go to Saturday mass, it counts for Sunday. When I used to go to Saturday mass with Grandma, Mom would go to church by herself on Sunday morning and Dad would stay home with me and make French toast and let me watch cartoons or play games with me. Saturday mass is A-okay with me.

Grandma used to say it's good to start off the new year with a clean slate. I know what a slate is because they use them on *Little House on the Prairie*. The Saturday after New Year's, I asked my mom if we could go to confession and Saturday mass so I could sleep in on Sunday, but she said "No" because she didn't want to drive anywhere. Then I asked could we go because the church bulletin said that Father Troha was hearing confessions and I wanted to go to him, and she still said "No." Then I asked could we go because it reminded me of Grandma and she said "Okay" and that we could stop by and see Uncle Joe afterwards.

St. Cyril is in an old neighborhood right near downtown where all the houses are close together. The neighborhood is called Smoky Hollow. My mom said it's called that because it's so close to the steel mills. I think that's why everything in Smoky Hollow looks gray and dirty. I understand the smoky part, but I don't get the hollow part. It isn't hollow. It has a whole bunch stuff in it, like people and houses and buildings.

Uncle Joe and Grandma's house is five blocks away from St. Cyril. It's a gray house with a big porch that goes almost all the way around. The house is on a corner, so the yard is really little, but there's a vacant lot next door where I would sometimes play with my cousins. When they lived with Grandma, they walked to school at St. Cyril and roamed all over the place like a pack of wild dogs. Youngstown State University is practically across the street, and my oldest cousin said she and her friends used to go run around in one of the parking garages there and scream so they could hear the echo. My mom grew up right in that same house, but she says the neighborhood has changed and never lets me go anywhere unless I'm with my cousins or an adult.

One of the things I like about St. Cyril is the outside. It's made of red brick and the church is right up against the sidewalk, so you can walk right in. It's older and prettier than St. Christine. There are statues *every*where and lots of wood carvings that are all shiny and beautiful. My dad says it's too ornate for his tastes. My mom says he only thinks that because Presbyterians have boring churches. I think ornate churches are the best. You get dressed up to go to church, so when the church is ornate, that means it's dressed up for you too. The fancier the church is, the better behaved you are. That's why I'm always good when I go to St. Cyril.

There was a bunch of old ladies and some old men going to confession when we got there. I counted two people besides my mom who weren't really old. I was the only kid there. I don't know why old people are always going to confession. If you're old and you can't move that fast or do that much, how much trouble can you get into?

Father Troha really was doing confession that day. The line was kind of long because he's going to leave Youngstown to go be a missionary in El Salvador. Here is what I know about El Salvador: One, it's in South America, so everybody speaks Spanish. Two, whenever we get little cardboard boxes at school to collect money for the poor, one side of the box always has a picture of kids in El Salvador. Three, the kids in El Salvador have beautiful brown skin like my friend Natalie from school. Father Troha is going to help all the poor people down there, although I'm not sure how he's going to do that. *Every*body wants to go to confession with him and talk to him as much as they can before he leaves. I don't know if Father Antioch feels left out or not. He's the other priest at St. Cyril. Father Antioch went to school with my Uncle Lou, who lives in New Jersey now.

Father Antioch had many long dark nights of the soul, wondering if he should volunteer for the El Salvador mission too. I would hear him praying, talking to himself, asking God if he was a coward for not going. He never got an answer that I heard.

My whole family knows Father Antioch. It's always handy to know a priest because you never know when you'll need a direct line to God, but you absolutely don't want to go to confession to somebody who knows your family. If they know too much about you, they'll give you a tougher penance.

My mom went to confession first. "No monkeying around and stay where you can see me," she said before she went in.

"How can I see you when you're in there?" I whispered. "You have to close the door." Mom gave me a look, so I just said, "Yes, Mommy." I sat up nice and tall in the pew while I waited, which is the way Sister Aloysius tells us we have to sit at our First Communion mass. There are two nuns who teach second grade at St. Christine. Sister Ellen Mary has bright blue eyes and a little bit of blond hair sticking out of the front of her habit. Sister Aloysius will hit you with a yardstick if you talk during First Communion practice. I have Sister Aloysius.

There were three people in line behind me to go to confession with Father Troha. The old lady closest to me smiled at me when she sat down next to me. Old people always act like kids are pets or something. I smiled back and then looked down at my hands like I was praying so she wouldn't try to ask me how old I was and if I liked school and all those other questions grownups always ask. I glanced over at the confessional door once or twice to see if my mom was done, and I thought about whether I ought to tell Father Troha everything or just mostly everything.

When my mom came out of the confessional, it was my turn. I got up and smiled at her as I got out of the pew. She kind of smiled back but she didn't really look happy. Maybe she got a really bad penance.

I decided to go to confession face-to-face. A couple of kids in my class have gone to the anonymous side, and they said it was really dark and kind of creepy, like a haunted house. I like the word "anonymous" because one, it sounds like poetry, two, it lets "y" be a vowel, and three, it has more syllables than you think it should. But I get kind of scared if I can't see someone's face. That's why I don't like costumes with masks or talking on the telephone. Also, if you go to the anonymous side, you have to kneel down, and I have a scab on my knee and it hurts to kneel.

When I went in and sat down, Father Troha smiled and said hello to me. Father Troha is very handsome, and when he smiles, he looks like a Spanish movie star, even though I'm pretty sure he's Slovak or Polish or something like me. I sat down and said, "Bless me, Father, for I have sinned. It has been four weeks since my last confession," like you're supposed to say.

Father Troha said, "It's good to see you, Hope. I'm very sorry to hear that your grandmother is still in the hospital. She was a very big part of this parish." He made the Sign of the Cross and said, "The Lord be in your heart and upon your lips that you may truly and humbly confess your sins. In the Name of the Father, and of the Son, and of the Holy Spirit. Amen," like he's supposed to say.

For a second, I was kind of worried that he remembered my name and knew that my grandma was sick, because I don't know Father Troha nearly as well as I know Father

Antioch. But I guess it's kind of a priest's job to know everybody's name and what goes on. Plus, he'll be leaving soon, so he wouldn't be able to spill the beans about anything I did. I started with the easy stuff. "I talked back to my mother three times, lied to my teacher twice that I wasn't talking in the bathroom when I really was, and lied to my mom and dad about going Christmas shopping with my Uncle Joe when we were really out looking for the guys who robbed Grandma. Oh, and even though I told my mom that I wasn't giving lottery numbers anymore, I gave a number to a waitress who didn't have any customers, so I guess that's another lie. I think there's stuff I'm forgetting, so maybe ... ten lies altogether?"

Father Troha is one of those grown-ups who you can't tell if they think what you just said is funny or if they're taking you seriously. I hate that. "Well," he said. "Ten lies in four weeks isn't too bad, but it's not too good either. When we lie to others, we're also lying to ourselves. Sometimes we lie because we don't want to get in trouble, like lying to a teacher about disobeying a rule."

"Sister Aloysius says we aren't supposed to talk in the bathroom because the noise carries down the hall and disturbs the other classes. If you talk, you have to stay inside during recess."

"It sounds like a reasonable rule. And I know you'll try to do better from now on, but I'm curious about the other sins you confessed — lying to your mother and father?"

"Like I said, Uncle Joe and I are trying to figure out who robbed my grandma. But if I told my mom that we were going out to look for the guys who did it, she'd have a conniption fit. I just told her that Uncle Joe and I were going to see Santa Claus and to do some Christmas shopping. And we did do that, we just also worked on our investigation."

"You've had quite a month, haven't you?"

"Yeah, it's been kind of busy."

"And do you feel remorse for your sins?" he asked. "Are you sorry for what you've done?"

"I know what remorse means," I said. "It means that you feel bad about what you did and will try not to do it again. They taught us all about that." I tried not to sound too mean when I said this, but you can't make your First Confession and not learn what "remorse" means. Our teachers talked about it *all* the time.

"And?"

"I feel bad that I lied a lot, but I don't feel bad about why I lied. Well, I feel bad about lying about talking in the bathroom, but not about trying to find the guys who robbed Grandma."

Father Troha nodded. "Don't you think finding the thieves is a job for the police?"

"Uncle Joe said they have bigger fish to fry, so we're doing it. Except now he doesn't want to."

Father Troha kind of leaned back in his seat and looked at me for a second. I could tell he was thinking up a really hard penance. I had a feeling I was going to be praying for days. "For your penance, Hope, I want you to pray the Rosary. And while you do, I want you think about forgiveness, even for those who have harmed your family."

"Like the guys who robbed Grandma?"

Father Troha nodded. "Yes. What they did was wrong, but you mustn't hold anger in your heart. You must forgive."

"I have to pray a whole Rosary while I think about forgiving those guys?" Doing a whole entire Rosary takes for*ever*.

"Yes."

Wondering the same thing over here. Not that I have anything to confess.

"How come penance is always praying? All the nuns and teachers at school say that you should pray every day and that praying is like talking to God. If praying is a *good* thing that we're supposed to do every day, why do you give it as a *punishment*? I don't get it."

Father Troha looked at me for a long time. At first, I thought maybe what I said made him mad, but then he smiled a little, like he thought it was a good idea. "That's an excellent question. Let me ask you. What do *you* think your penance should be?"

I could tell this was a trick question. Well ... ," I said, "maybe trying not to lie anymore? But your forgiveness thing is a good idea too."

"Thank you."

"You're welcome."

"I'm going to keep your idea in mind," Father Troha said. "I still want you to pray the Rosary while you think about forgiveness. But I also want you to think about telling the truth. Every time you're tempted to tell a lie, take a second to think about how you'd feel if the person you're talking to lied to you. Can you do that?"

"Yeah, I think I can."

"Is there anything else you wish to confess?"

He said it like he knew the real reason I wanted to go to confession that day. I didn't want to say anything but I knew I had to, because this was the biggest thing. "You're not allowed to tell anybody what I say in here, right?"

"Correct."

"Never ever?"

"Correct. Never ever."

My dad always says to just peel the Band-Aid off really fast. This seemed like kind of the same thing, so I took a deep breath and said, "I did magic to try and heal my grandma's hip, but I think I made it worse and that's why she's so sick."

Father Troha looked kind of confused. "Hope, your grandmother's robbery and fall was a terrible tragedy, but none of this your fault. You had nothing to do with it."

"Yes, I did. I tried to move her hip back together because it was broken but I think I must have messed up."

"I don't understand."

"I went to the hospital with my mom because it was an emergency. And when she and Uncle Ed were talking to the doctor, me and Uncle Joe went to see Grandma and that's when I did it."

"Your Uncle let you try to push your grandmother's hip back together?"

"No. I said I did *magic* to try and fix her hip."

"When you say magic, what do you mean?"

I had never told a grownup what I was about to tell Father Troha. I didn't want to tell him, but I didn't want to feel bad about what I did to Grandma anymore either. "I can make things move without touching them," I said.

"Hope, I know you're a very smart and talented little girl, but we are earthly human beings. We can't perform miracles."

"I didn't say miracle, I said magic."

Father Troha kind of thought for a second and then he said, "Can you show me what you mean?"

The confessional is really small, like a phone booth. There isn't much in it, but there was a crucifix on the wall. I looked at it and whispered "*Go to Father Troha*" three times and the crucifix came off the wall and floated down into Father Troha's hands. "I tried to move my grandma's hip back into the right place, but I messed up and that's why she's so sick," I said again.

Father Troha was looking at the crucifix in his hands like he had no idea how it got there. "How did you ... ?"

"I can make things move without touching them." I wondered how many times I was going to have to say that before he believed me.

Father Troha did the last prayer really, really fast, like he wanted to finish or had to go to the bathroom or something. The whole time, he didn't look at me — he just stared at the crucifix in his hand. "You didn't do anything to hurt your grandmother, just stop lying so much. Repent in your thoughts and in your deeds. Your sins are forgiven." Then he made the Sign of the Cross and said "I absolve you from all of your sins in the name of the Father, and of the Son, and of the Holy Ghost. Amen."

I always figured priests daydreamed about finding some little kid who could do miracles. It's an automatic book deal plus a first-class ticket to the Vatican. When Dolores and Ruthie told him that Hope claimed she saw the Virgin Mary in her bedroom, Father Troha listened politely and said to tell him if it happened again. When one of the guys from the Brier Hill Works swore he saw clouds that looked like Jesus Christ coming out of the smoke stacks, Father Troha drove by the mill just in case. But when Hope confronted him with bona fide inexplicable magic in confession, he knew he could never tell a soul. Never ever.

"Amen," I said. "See you."

Finally, Father Troha looked up at me. "I'm not sure what I just saw but use ... please use this power wisely."

"I'm trying," I replied.

IV

Here are the things I've seen die: One, an African violet that a friend of my mom's gave me because she thought I'd like a little plant. I did like it and tried to take good care of it and rubbed water on its leaves because you're supposed to do that for plants but not for African Violets, which I didn't know until the leaves turned yellow and it died. Two, a bird that flew into the picture window in our living room last year. I was in the living room with my dad on a Sunday morning in the summer. He was reading the paper and I was looking at the funnies and all of a sudden we heard this little *thump* at the window. My friend Michael next door and I had a funeral for the bird in my backyard. Three, the people across the street's cat who got run over by a car. His name was Zippy and he always let me pet him.

Those three things don't equal one grandmother.

She died on January 6, 1978. I remember the day because I started going to Michael's after school so my mom could be at the hospital with my grandma. My Aunt Peggy from Cleveland was staying with us, and usually they'd both be home by dinnertime, just like my dad. That day they called Michael's mom and asked if I could stay there for dinner because all three of them were still at the hospital, and that's how I knew that Grandma died.

The funeral was at St. Cyril. All my cousins and aunts and uncles were there and lots of people I don't know. A ton of people came up to talk to me. I didn't know most of them, but they all knew my grandma somehow. Some of them said they were her neighbors or her friends and a couple of old ladies said they went to school with her years and years ago. That was weird. It was the first time I ever thought that my grandma had ever gone to school or was ever a kid like me.

Funerals are weird. One, everybody wears

I remember when Dolores was a little girl. She believed in being fair, in making as many snow angels as possible, and in looking up words in the dictionary when something confused her. But when an eight-year-old Dolores accidentally made a twenty-pound sack of potatoes move without touching it, her Slovak immigrant mother screamed in horror and insisted the devil had gotten into her daughter. Dolores had indeed been a kid like Hope; the only difference between them was fear.

black. Two, everybody whispers. Three, everybody wants to cry but nobody really does. I kept remembering this one time last spring when I got really mad at my mom and dad because they said I couldn't play on my Slip and Slide because it was too cold out. I screamed and cried until my dad said to cut the tantrum or I'd lose TV for two days. I remember him saying, "If you're going to get so worked up over a little thing like this, I hate to see how you'd react if something really bad happened." I don't know why I cried and yelled so much because of that. There was still snow outside, so I guess it really was too cold for the Slip and Slide. I just didn't like that they were right. You'd think that at a funeral people would scream and cry because they have a really good reason to be sad, but they don't. I didn't either. I wanted to. Part of me wanted to cry and scream and kick things and have a huge tantrum. But it wasn't that kind of sad. It was the kind of sad that makes you feel like a robot who can't breathe.

I was allowed to stay home from school for the whole week if I wanted. It was fun and sad at the same time. Every time I felt happy about being home with my mom, I'd remember why I was home and it made me want to cry. Then I missed almost a whole other week of school because there was a huge blizzard at the end of January. Everybody said it was one of the worst snowstorms ever *ever*. It started snowing on a Tuesday morning. I got up and made my dad turn on the news to see the school closings. They play a whole list of them, and St. Christine was on it. Even though the schools were closed, my dad had to go into work because he said the newspaper still needed to go out.

Instead of watching TV, my mom and I sat in the living room and watched the snow. It was kind of scary to look outside and have everything be white. It was snowing so hard you couldn't see the difference between the street or the devil's strip or the sidewalk or anything. And it just kept snowing and snowing and snowing. "Hope, I think we're snowbound," Mom said.

> The blizzard of '78 really did a number on my asphalt. You put on fancy face creams to keep you from wrinkling, but you pour salt on me and wonder why I crack. The only good thing about the snow was the silence. You all stayed in your houses and talked quietly to each other and stopped running your cars and trains and I finally got some blessed peace and quiet. You ought to try that more often.

"I think you're the best person in the whole world to be snowbound with," I said. My dad called later and said he was going to be stuck at work because it was too dangerous to drive. He ended up staying at work for two whole days. We called Uncle Joe and we called my cousins and everybody was stuck inside because of the snow, even my cousins in Cleveland. My mom and I played games and stuff. We had fun being snowbound for the first day and a half, then my mom said I was bouncing off the walls and that I was going to send her to Woodside. That's the hospital where all the crazy people go. I knew she was just joking because I think you'd have to have a whole bunch of kids before you went really nutso. She sent me outside to play in the snow with Michael. He's my best friend even though he's a boy. We aren't boyfriend and girlfriend friends. We just like to play together and that's all.

Our backyards kind of connect, and there isn't a fence or anything, just a row of three big bushes that somebody planted years and years ago. My dad always says that's the divider between our yard and their yard and he always mows the grass right up to the bushes. There was a big snow drift in between two of the bushes, so Michael and I took shovels and piled up more snow until it was taller than we were. It took us two days. Then we dug a hole in the side that was big enough for both of us to crawl into. It was really neat. We decided we lived in an igloo in Alaska and pretended to catch fish and chase bears, and then we went to sleep in our igloo. It was kind of cozy in there, and I liked it because we were hidden. I knew it had to be getting close to dinner because it was starting to get dark and everything outside looked purplish gray. It was really pretty. Then Michael's mom came out and called us but we stayed in our snow fort and she couldn't see us. Unless you went behind the bushes to the entrance, it just looked like a big snow mound. We tried not to laugh so she wouldn't know we were there.

"It's like we're underground!" Michael whispered.

"Yeah," I whispered back. And then I started thinking about being underground and how my grandma was in her coffin underground and I worried if she was cold. I knew she was dead and you don't know it's cold if you're dead, but it still made me really, really sad and I started to cry.

"What's wrong?"

"We're underground!" I said.

"But it's fun underground."

"No, it's not. It's like we're dead!"

Michael stopped smiling. "Like Zippy?" Michael still has two grandmas, but he really liked Zippy the cat.

"Yeah. When you die, they put you in the ground, and it's cold and dark and you're all alone." I don't know why I said that because it made me cry harder and it made Michael start crying too. Then we heard both of our moms walking around back and forth between our two backyards, calling our names. Michael and I tried to crawl out of the snow fort at the same time and the whole thing fell in on us. Our moms had to dig us out of the snow. All my tears froze to my face and I got snow in my hood and Michael's hat fell off and we weren't allowed to build any more snow forts with rooves after that.

I never heard Hope or Michael tell their mothers why they started crying. No mention of frozen tears or cold, dead bodies alone underground. Kind of makes you wonder what other secrets little kids are hiding.

With no school, I had a lot of time to think about what Father Troha said. He said I should forgive the guys who robbed Grandma, but I really wanted to find those guys and yell at them and make them apologize. Forgiving people is hard. There's a boy at school named Robby Galvin who has red hair and all sorts of huge freckles on his face. He's like a big talking Dalmatian. It would be easy to make fun of all those freckles or his hair or his name, and I never have.

The boys at my school call Fridays Friday-Flip-Up Day and they try to flip up the girls' skirts to see their underwear. At the beginning of the year, Robby flipped up my skirt *three times* in one day because I forgot to wear shorts under my uniform.

The third time he did it, I was so mad that I made his pants fall down so that everybody could see *his* underwear. Nobody knew I did it. One second he was running around the playground laughing at me and trying to flip up Susie Cafferty's skirt, and then his pants fell down and everybody could see his blue underwear just like everybody saw my pink and white underwear. Ever since then, I've never seen Robby flip up anybody's skirt, but other boys still do it.

I don't know if I forgive Robby for flipping up my skirt. If you do something bad, you ought to get punished. That's how things are supposed to work. But if he knew I can do magic, he would have to forgive me for making his pants fall down. It seems like you could go around and around forever doing mean things and having to forgive each other for it.

I didn't get to see Uncle Joe at all the whole week of the storm because my mom said it was too dangerous to drive in the snow. I think she was just scared to drive because she sent my dad over to check on him, even though Dad says that Uncle Joe is probably the last person in the world you ever have to worry about because he can fix almost anything and knows a lot about how the world works.

Mom and Dad had been asking Uncle Joe to come and stay with us and he kept saying no, but then he had to because he hurt his back shoveling snow. The same day, some electrical poles got knocked over and his house lost power. There wasn't anything he could do to fix it, plus his back hurt. My mom said he had a slipped disc in his back. She said a disc was a little round thing like a tiny frisbee. The picture of the human skeleton in the encyclopedia had a bunch of little bones sticking out of your back, but I didn't see anything that looked like a frisbee. After what happened with Grandma, I was too afraid to try and fix Uncle Joe's back. Except for the one time in confession, I wasn't doing any magic. I didn't want anybody else to get hurt.

After Uncle Joe had been at our house for a week, my dad came home from work with a big pile of mail. "I stopped by the house on Audubon for you," he said, and put the mail next to the crossword puzzle Uncle Joe was doing. Then he kissed my mom, who was making dinner, and hugged me, who was tap dancing, and then he went to change his clothes because he'll be damned if he wears a tie at home.

> There are thousands of men like Phil Bowers in my streets, men who wake up every day and go to work and quietly do what needs to be done. Some of them are required to tie a noose around their neck before they go out in the morning.

Uncle Joe and I have watched some old movies on TV. I've seen Gene Kelly and Fred Astaire and Ginger Rogers tap dance, so I kind of know how it's done. I know you have to use your heel and your toe. Joey Pavlovich at school said that if you pin metal buttons or thumbtacks to the toe and heel of your shoe, it sounds like you're tap dancing. A whole bunch of us did that once and started tap dancing in the playground, but Sister Aloysius made us take them off our shoes when we went inside. She isn't a very fun teacher.

I found some old buttons with smiley faces and one that said "McGovern in '72" but my mom said I couldn't pin them to the bottoms of my shoes because it would ruin the soles. She didn't know that I had already done it at school and my shoes weren't ruined.

Uncle Joe started whistling a song while he looked through the big pile of mail, and Mom actually sang along with him. She almost never sings except when we're in church. The song was called "Tea for Two," and Uncle Joe said it's a famous tap-dancing song.

"If it's so famous, how come I've never heard of it?" I asked.

"Because you're seven."

"Eight!" Mom and I both said at the same time.

"Jinx!" I said to Mom. "I've been eight for two months," I said to Uncle Joe. "You were even at my birthday party."

"My apologies. I forgot."

"Hey, did you know that Wednesday was Groundhog Day?"

"Yes, I did. And I know that we're going to have six more weeks of winter. As if we hadn't had enough already." Uncle Joe started looking through the big pile of mail again. "Neither snow nor rain nor heat nor gloom of night stays these couriers from the swift completion of their appointed rounds." Uncle Joe kind of mumbled but I heard him because I have ears like a dog.

"What does that mean?" I asked.

"It means the Post Office delivers the mail no matter what the weather," Uncle Joe said.

"Oh. Hey Mom? Do you know what you should do if you find the groundhog sleeping in your bed?"

"No."

"Find someplace else to sleep! Mom, do you know where sick groundhogs go?"

"No, I don't," she said.

"The hog-pital!" Making my mom laugh is one of my favorite things to do.

Most of the mail looked like bills. I know this because all the bills that come to our house have a little window cut out in the front with something that looks like tissue paper where your name and address shows through. I could tell they were mostly bills because of the way Uncle Joe tossed the envelopes into a little pile, saying things like "Ugh" and "Yuck." There was a little envelope that had Grandma's address written on it and two postage stamps and nothing else. It looked kind of thick. "This looks interesting," he said, but he didn't open it.

"Who's it from?" my mom asked.

"It doesn't say. Youngstown postmark."

This was driving me nuts. I kind of crawled onto the table to get a look. "Can I see it?"

"I suppose you can ... ."

"I suppose yo Uncle Joe said.

"Hope, get off the table."

"*May* I see it?"

"Sure."

I hate it when grown-ups do that, but at least I got to look at the envelope. It was one of those short envelopes, but it felt like something thick was inside it. I read the address out loud. "It says it's for 'The Lady of the House, 602 Audubon.' Does that mean Grandma?"

"Yes. Probably just an advertisement," Mom said with a little sigh. She always gets sad when somebody mentions Grandma. She stirred the pot of soup on the stove and put a bunch of rolls in the oven to get hot. It was gonna be a good dinner.

"I don't think so," Uncle Joe said. "The envelope is hand-written."

"Let's see."

I stood and held the envelope up to her so she could see it without having to touch it. My mom is really picky about germs and dirt and won't touch anything when she's cooking until she's all done. She looked at the writing on the envelope and made a little face.

"Can I ... may I open it? Please?"

Ruthie inherited her germ phobia from her mother. Dolores Nagy did not have the means to keep a wealthy house, but she made sure all her children knew that you're never too poor to keep a clean house. 602 Audubon may have been dingy, but it was spotless. After she fell, when she was lying in a heap with a broken hip at the foot of the basement stairs, I heard Dolores mumble "At least the floor is clean."

"Go ahead," Uncle Joe said. He didn't even look up from the rest of his mail.

"Yay! Thank you." I was so excited I could barely open the envelope, but I was really careful to not rip it. When I opened it, there was a whole bunch of money wrapped inside a piece of notebook paper. "Wow!" I said.

"What is it?" Uncle Joe asked.

I pulled the money out of the envelope. "Somebody sent Grandma a bunch of money."

The next thing I knew, Uncle Joe took the money out of my hands. And the *next* next thing I knew, Mom forgot all about germs when she was cooking and took the money out of Uncle Joe's hands. "Holy Jupiter ... ," she said, and she sounded a little like Grandma.

"Why would you send money to someone whose name you don't even know?" I asked.

"Why would you send money to someone other than the bill collector?" said Uncle Joe. My mom gave him the money back and we watched him count it. "One hundred forty-two dollars," he announced.

"How come somebody sent you one hundred and forty-two dollars?"

Uncle Joe looked at the money for a second. "They didn't send it to me. They sent it to Dolores." He looked up at my mom. I could tell neither of them knew why somebody sent money to Grandma, but I did. Before I went to bed that night, I asked Uncle Joe if he'd tuck me in. I needed to talk to him in private.

"Okay, kiddo, let's get you to sleep," he said as he walked in the room and turned out the light. He came over to my bed and gave me a kiss on the forehead. "Goodnight, Hope."

"Uncle Joe? What if that money is from one of the guys who robbed Grandma?"

Uncle Joe gave me a funny look, like he wasn't sure if I was joking or if he thought that was a dumb idea. He sat down on the edge of my bed and said, "Well Hope, let's think about this logically. If you stole money from somebody, why would you bother sending some of it back?"

"Because I felt bad about stealing it?"

"That's a nice thought, but you have to figure that if they're low-down enough to steal it, they aren't going to be giving it back. I'd say it's more likely that someone thinks they're paying back an old debt to your grandmother."

"Do you think the guys who stole the money know that Grandma died?"

"I have no idea." Then he told me I had to go to bed because it was getting late and didn't I want to be all fresh and awake in the morning because tomorrow was Wednesday, and don't you have First Communion practice on Wednesdays? He could try and change the subject and make me go to sleep, but I knew the money was a sign. And that was just the first sign.

The second sign happened at the beginning of March. I was in the living room doing my spelling homework and practicing writing in cursive because cursive is pretty. My dad and Uncle Joe were watching the news. Uncle Joe was also looking through another pile of mail from the house on Audubon. There were a couple of bills and a letter from an old friend, and an envelope addressed to the Lady of the House at 602 Audubon from the Society of the Little Flower in Darien, Illinois, with a Special Living Mass card in the mail. I know that's what it said because Uncle Joe let me open it. At first, I thought it was something important, but it was really kind of boring. "What does this mean?" I asked, as I handed it back to Uncle Joe.

"It means some nuns way off in Illinois are saying mass for your grandmother," he replied.

"That sounds nice. How come they're saying mass for her?"

"Well, people can send money for the mass — it's kind of like sponsoring someone."

"Wait, does that mean the nuns get *paid* to go to mass? Why can't I get paid to go to mass?"

My dad had been listening to our conversation and he kind of sighed because we were talking while he was trying to watch TV. "Hope, sweetie, they're nuns. Their job is to pray and go to mass, just like your job is to go to school and learn and grow. If you want a job praying, you can be a nun when you grow up." He turned up the TV a little bit after that but I heard him mumble, "God forbid."

I didn't bother telling Dad that he didn't need to worry about me becoming a nun because I already knew I was going to be an astronaut. Last year, there was a spaceship called Voyager, and it sent back pictures from Mars. We saw the pictures in school, and my dad and I looked at them in the newspaper and in *Time* magazine. That's when I decided I wanted to go up into space too. Michael next door says I can't be an astronaut because there aren't any girl astronauts, but I think he's wrong. I think there are some somewhere. I didn't mention any of this to my mom because she gets worried if I go around the block by myself, so I bet she'd get really worried if I went up in space.

So the one hundred and forty-two dollars was the first sign. The mass card from the Society of the Little Flower in Darien, Illinois, with a Special Living Mass card was the second sign. The third thing was that somebody left a box of groceries at the house on Audubon on Easter Sunday.

V

We hadn't gone to church at St. Cyril since Grandma's funeral. My mom or Uncle Joe would say "Oh, let's just go to St. Christine's. It's closer," and we'd go to mass there. They didn't say it, but I could tell they were avoiding the house on Audubon. And even though Uncle Joe kept saying he was only staying with us until his back got better, I kind of knew he was going to stay for good because he never seemed to want to go back to the house. That's why my dad always went there to get the mail. It was like they were avoiding it because it made them sad.

When I first woke up on Easter, I got my Easter basket and went around the house looking for eggs. We don't hide real eggs, just the little plastic ones with jelly beans or chocolate inside. My mom made breakfast and Uncle Joe and my dad sat in the living room drinking coffee and saying things like "Oh, you're getting warmer, Hope," whenever I got near a place where an egg was hidden. It would have been easier to do magic to make all the eggs come to me, but doing magic was too dangerous and my parents would have a *lot* of questions. Besides, hunting for Easter eggs is more fun without magic. Once I found all the eggs, I asked Uncle Joe to hide them and I found them all again, and then I hid all the eggs and the grown-ups had to find them. Finding all those eggs took a while and we missed mass at St. Christine, so Mom said, "What if we went to St. Cyril?" like going there was some big new thing. My mom looked at Uncle Joe and Uncle Joe looked at my mom, and my dad said, "If we're going to church anywhere today, we have to leave now," so we did.

It was cold and slushy out. My mom said I could wear my new Easter dress but not the shoes because they're sandals and my feet would get cold and wet. She made me wear my boots. I was mad, but on the way to St. Cyril, Dad went down Midlothian Boulevard so we could drive by the Schwebel's Bread billboard. It has a big picture of a bag of bread, but it looks like there are slices of bread falling out of it. Uncle Joe explained it to me once. He said it's just like a big pinwheel spinning around and around to make it look like the bread is coming out of the bag. I don't care how it works, I just like it.

Father Troha said the mass. I hadn't seen him since I made the crucifix fly off the wall during confession. At the end of mass, Uncle Joe went off to talk to one of his old man friends, but me and my mom and dad got in line to say hi to Father Troha. He was smiling at everybody and shaking hands. When he saw me, he kind of stopped smiling, just for a second, like he was maybe worried I was going to make things fly off the wall again. "Hello, Hope," he said.

I kind of waved at him and leaned against my mom. Sometimes it's hard Ruth Nagy Bower's confessions weren't any racier or heart-rending than anyone else's. Neither are yours. to talk to other people, especially grownups. He smiled at me and then asked my mom how she was feeling. "Better, thank you, Father," she said. She had the same pretend smile she gave me when she came out of confession. It made me wonder what she and Father Troha talked about. My dad put his arm around her and gave her a little hug, like he knew what they were talking about too. Nobody told me anything.

We didn't have time to hang around and talk because so many other people wanted to talk to Father Troha. After mass, we drove by the house on Audubon because Uncle Joe wanted to get some more clothes, even though he always just wears green or white T-shirts and baggy pants and a flannel shirt if it's cold. I guess he wanted more T-shirts or something.

We pulled into the driveway, and I got out first. I could hear Uncle Joe and my dad say something like, "I don't know why you're running, you don't have the key," but they didn't see what I saw. There was a plastic milk crate on the porch, right by the back door. It had never been there before. My mom and dad got to the porch at the same time and then Uncle Joe.

"What have you got there, Hope?" my dad asked.

"I don't know. Somebody left this on the porch." There was a plastic bag inside the crate with the top tied in a knot. I was trying to untie it to see what was inside, but my dad just said, "Hmm" and picked up the crate while Uncle Joe unlocked the door.

"Hey, I was looking at that!" I said and followed him inside.

"It's not yours. It belongs to Uncle Joe."

"That's not mine." Uncle Joe took off his shoes and left them by the wall next to the door. He always does that at our house too. Grandma didn't like dirty shoes in the house. "I won't be a minute," he said as he headed for the stairs.

"Then who does it belong to? Don't you want to see what's inside?"

My mom was looking through the crate. I couldn't believe my dad would let her look through it and not me. She untied the plastic bag and started taking things out. There was a bag of rice and a box of spaghetti, two cans of green beans and two cans of Hormel chili, another plastic bag with a bunch of apples, and a package of Oreos and a little bag of Fritos.

"Oreos!" I screamed. Grandma never let me get Oreos because she always said she made better cookies than Nabisco. She did, but I still like Oreos. I couldn't believe my eyes. "This is another miracle."

"*Another* miracle? Did we already have a miracle that I missed?" Mom asked.

"We had two. The mass card and the hundred and forty-two dollars. Miracles are religious, and the mass card was definitely religious. And miracles are unexplainable, and you can't explain how you got this or the money or the mass card, so they're all miracles."

"Hope, it's not a miracle. Someone just left a crate of groceries for your Uncle Joe. It looks like it's been there a few days."

"Why would somebody leave groceries for Uncle Joe? He doesn't even live here."

"Maybe they don't know that."

"Why would you leave food for somebody if you don't know if they live there?"

My dad talked really gently to me, like he was trying not to get me or my mom riled up. "Now that your grandmother is gone, one of the neighbors probably thought it would be kind to leave a little gift for Uncle Joe."

Uncle Joe came down the stairs right then, carrying a little pile of clothes. I looked, and they were all T-shirts, two flannel shirts, and a pair of pants. "Somebody thinks I'm a charity case," he said.

"Of course not," Mom said. "Someone just wanted to do something nice for you." Uncle Joe didn't say anything, he just took the plastic bag of groceries out of the crate and put his clothes in the crate. He handed me the grocery bag.

"Hope, you wanna carry this?"

"Sure!" I couldn't believe my luck. It was kind of heavy, but I carried it all the way back to the car. On the way home, all of the grown-ups talked and I managed to sneak three of the Oreos. Then my mom noticed my teeth were black from the cookies and said I couldn't have any Easter candy until after dinner.

Uncle Joe went downstairs to his room to put his clothes away. My mom and dad call it an "in-law suite," because there's a big bedroom and a whole other bathroom down there and it doesn't look like a basement. It looks just like a regular bedroom, only the windows are kind of up high. I think Uncle Joe likes it. He said it reminds him of living out in the garage, only warmer.

After I changed out of my Easter dress, I went downstairs to talk to him. He didn't know I was there, and I saw him with the Oreos from the crate. He looked up when he heard me say "Aww, how come you get to eat Oreos and I don't?"

Uncle Joe was sitting on his favorite green easy chair with his feet up. The chair and one picture were the only things he wanted to bring from the house on Audubon. "Because they're mine. But I would be happy to share them with you." He held out the package of Oreos to me. "Don't tell your mother."

"Thanks!" I took a cookie and sat down on the edge of his bed. "Can I talk to you?" I asked.

"You already are."

I sighed and tried to ignore his bad joke because we had more important things to think about. "Okay, we need to talk about our investigation." As soon as I said that, Uncle Joe stopped eating cookies and just kind of *stopped* for a second. Then he said "Hope, I hate to say it, but we aren't going to be able to find the guys who robbed your grandma. It kills me that they're out there somewhere, probably spending my sister's money on booze and God knows what. It kills me, and if we had any realistic way of finding them, I would do it in an instant."

"But we know one of them is skinny and one is chubby with a birthmark on his face and he's probably named

Bobby and we know that he worked at the Sheeting Tube. And what about the crate with the groceries in it? And the money and the prayer card? I think the guys who robbed Grandma feel bad about it and are trying to make it up."

Uncle Joe almost never gets mad. Even when he's watching football or something and the Browns fumble and everybody else yells at the television set, Uncle Joe says something that sounds like "Say-la vee," and doesn't care. I've only ever seen him really mad one other time, and that time he threw snowballs at an empty building. This time it just looked like a big dark cloud came out of his head.

"Dolores is dead. They can't make up for that.' He shook his head. "Anyway, it's just a coincidence."

"What if we go back to that restaurant and ask Bernie the waitress if she's seen him?"

"Hope, no. Those guys could be anywhere. We tried, and it didn't work. That's it. We have to let it go."

"I don't want to let it go."

"Neither do I, but we have no earthly way of finding them."

When you get to be eight years old, everybody starts telling you that you're a big girl and big girls don't cry. I think everybody who says that ought to try not being able to find the guys who robbed their grandma and see how they like it. I was so mad I didn't know what to do. Sometimes crying is just easier. Uncle Joe got up from the ugly green chair, sat down next to me, and gave me a hug with one arm. He held out the package of Oreos to me with the other hand but I pushed it away. "Are you mad because I said no or are you mad because we can't find those two crooks?" he asked quietly.

I didn't really want to say anything, so I just muttered "Both." Then I said, "I'm mad that you're giving up."

Uncle Joe sighed and didn't say anything for a while. "I'm not giving up," he said. "I'm just facing the facts. Let's say we know one of those guys is named Bobby. That's a common name. We don't know his last name or how to find him."

"I'll keep looking for him by myself." I kind of shrugged off Uncle Joe's hug because, if you're going to do something on your own, you shouldn't be leaning on anybody else when you say you're going to do it, otherwise people won't believe you.

"How are you going to do that?"

"I have eyes. I'll keep my eyes peeled. I'm not a quitter like you." I shut my mouth real fast after I said that because calling your great-uncle a quitter isn't very nice.

"That's true, you aren't a quitter," Uncle Joe said. "That's one of your finest qualities."

I should have said, "thank you," but I didn't because I wanted him to know how mad I was. I stood up and walked to the door, thinking of all the magic I could do right then. I could turn the water on in Uncle Joe's bathroom right from where I was standing. I could make the picture of two guys fishing fall off the wall. I could open the windows and let the rain in. Uncle Joe didn't know any of the things I could do. Nobody did. When I went upstairs to my room, I slammed the door shut, and every other door in the house slammed shut too. Nobody knew why but me.

VI

I had been looking forward to First Communion all year long because you get a party afterwards and you don't have school the next day. Uncle Ed and those cousins were coming to my party and so was Aunt Peggy and my cousins from Cleveland. But after my grandma died, having a new dress and a big party didn't seem as important as it used to.

My mom and I got my dress ages ago. I hadn't even looked at it since Valentine's Day, when I asked her if I could wear it to school and pretend I was an angel delivering valentines, and she said I could wear it at home and deliver Valentines to her and Daddy and Uncle Joe but that was all, because the dress wasn't for wearing to school. I think it's kind of silly to get a pretty dress if you're only allowed to wear it once. If I ever get married, I'm going to wear my favorite jeans or maybe my spacesuit.

I wanted to sleep in, but my parents made me get up and have breakfast. Then I went and played school in my room in my pajamas. I was teaching a spelling lesson to two of my dolls and three stuffed animals when my mom knocked on my door and said it was nine-thirty and that I should start getting ready. I said, "Okay," but I didn't get dressed right away because it only takes two seconds to put on a dress. I couldn't play in my First Communion dress because it would get dirty or ripped or something. That's another reason I'm not going to wear a wedding dress when I get married. White clothes are too hard to keep clean.

A little while later, my dad knocked on my door and poked his head in my room. I had all my students lined up on the floor against my bed and a stack of old flashcards from first grade with a bunch of easy math problems on the floor in front of them.

"Dad! I'm teaching a class," I said.

"You're getting dressed. Now."

Whenever my dad says, "Now," you have to do what he says and do it right then or he'll take away TV or something. He doesn't mess around. I got dressed really fast, but my mom had to help me brush my hair because it was all tangly. When I was ready, my mom helped me put on the veil and my dad took my picture in the living room. He made me stand by the fireplace with my hands up like I was praying. I let Dad take my picture about a thousand times until my mom said, "We need to leave now."

"Do you want the flashcube?" he asked after he took it off the camera. He kind of jiggled it from hand to hand because the flashcube is always hot after you take a picture.

"No, thank you," I said. I used to like to play with the flashcubes, but now they seem kind of boring. Dad looked surprised, but he just said, "Mom's waiting" and threw the flashcube in the garbage before we went out to the garage.

When we got to St. Christine, I had to go into the parish center and wait with all the other kids making their First Communion. Here's how First Communion works:

One, we line up on the sidewalk outside the church, two by two, like the animals going onto Noah's Ark. There are two sets of front doors at St. Christine. Outside on the sidewalk there's a little brick bell tower, so you always have to choose if you want to walk around the bell tower to the right or to the left. My line goes to the left, but it doesn't really matter because everybody goes down the center aisle once we go in. When everybody else is inside, the organ player starts playing and we walk in the front doors behind the priest and the altar boys. You can't talk or fidget or fool around, or Sister Aloysius will pull you out of line and you won't get to make your First Communion.

Two, the shortest kids walk in front and the tallest walk in the back. The good part is that my friend Natalie and I are the same height, so we get to walk together. The bad part is that Maureen Mackey is in front of me and she's still a big jerk. We're near the front of the line. We walk up to the altar with our partner and we genuflect, then we split up and sit down. I go to the left side and Natalie goes to the right. We're the first ones in the second row, so that means we get to sit right at the end of the pew and we get to see everything.

Maureen Mackey had a nice mother, a nice little sister, and a decent father who didn't drink too much or yell more often than any other dad. There was no reason for her to be anything other than a nice kid, but she was always a little sourpuss. That's just how some of you are.

Three, after communion, we have to kneel in the pew and pray and then sit quietly and sing "One Bread, One Body" while everybody else in the church goes to communion. I asked Sister Aloysius how we could sit quietly and sing at the same time and she told me she doesn't like show-offs. When the mass ends, we walk out the front door, down the sidewalk, and into the parking lot. Then our families meet us outside.

Four, under no circumstances are we to leave the line or wave to our parents or talk to each other.

It was kind of windy when we were standing outside the church waiting to go in. Two girls' veils actually flew off their heads, and they had to run and get them and Sister Ellen Mary and somebody's mom had to pin them back on the girls' heads. Natalie and I were really excited and kept looking at each other and giggling. I thought Sister Aloysius was going to yell at us, because she really likes to yell, but once we heard the music coming from inside the church, everybody got real quiet. Natalie and I stopped giggling and everybody stopped talking and we all walked into the church, not too fast, not too slow.

I sang nice and loud because Sister Ellen Mary always says that we should sing so God can hear us up in heaven. When we walked down the aisle into the church, there were people everywhere, and everybody was looking at us. It was like being a movie star. Even though they sent a letter home to our parents saying nobody could take pictures during the mass, I saw flashbulbs go off, so *somebody's* parents disobeyed the letter, but mine didn't. I saw my mom and dad and Uncle Joe all scrunched together with some other people in a pew on my side. My mom waved at me, but I didn't wave back. I *did* smile, just a little, so she'd know I wasn't ignoring her. Right before we got up to the altar, I glanced over at Natalie and she glanced over at me right at the same time. Then we genuflected, and she went to the right and I went to the left. We had to go all the way around the front of the altar and into the second row of pews.

Usually I can't see much during mass because I'm too short, but being on the end of the pew was great. I'm going to sit on the end for the rest of my life. The pastor at St. Christine is named Father Kenny. He was wearing a purple vest-thingy over a white robe. It looked pretty. We all sang really loud and paid attention and when it came time for communion, nobody fidgeted or giggled or tripped or anything.

When you go up to communion, you have to stick out your tongue just a little bit so the priest can put the wafer on your tongue without having to stick his whole hand in your mouth. I practiced in front of the mirror in the bathroom so I looked like an expert when I got communion from Father Kenny. He smiled at me and held up the host and said, "Body of Christ," and I remembered to say "Amen," and then I walked back to the pew and that was it. I had my First Communion. I didn't feel any different.

Another great thing about sitting on the end of the pew is that you get to see almost all the people in the whole church come by during communion. Most people just walk along with their head down a little bit to make it look like they're praying really hard. Some of them sing. I like watching people. After communion, I sat in the pew and sang. There were a ton of people, so we had to keep singing the same song over and over until everybody had gone up. I was looking around at all the people, and then something made me look up at the guy who was right next to my end of the pew.

You will never believe what I saw.

I saw a birthmark that looked like a little caterpillar on his cheek. Right when I looked at him, he looked at me. At first he was smiling, but as soon as he saw me, he stopped smiling, because it was the same guy I saw in McGuffey's when Grandma was cashing in her lottery tickets. I could tell he recognized me just like I recognized him and suddenly, I knew he was one of the guys who robbed her. I *knew* it.

I stopped singing and did a big gasp. The guy jerked his head and looked straight ahead like he hadn't seen me. There was a pretty girl with blond hair in front of him. He just stared at the back of her head until he got up to Father Kenny, and then he walked around to the side aisle without looking at me again.

I turned around to see if Uncle Joe had seen him. I couldn't see anybody in my family, but I did see Sister Aloysius two rows behind me. She gave me a nasty hawk look, so I turned around to face the front. I didn't want to turn around again because I didn't want to get in trouble. Instead

I tapped my new white shoes back and forth, heel-toe, first one and then the other, while I thought of a plan. Maureen Mackey was sitting next to me. She shushed me and whispered, "You're annoying." We weren't supposed to talk, but she's the only kid Sister Aloysius never gets mad at.

Before mass ended, Father Kenny talked for a while about God and how this was a big day for us and a bunch of other stuff. The whole time he was talking, I was trying to plan how to get Bobby with the birthmark before he got away. I kept moving my feet back and forth because sometimes that's what you have to do when you're thinking. Maureen shushed me again and whispered in a really nasty voice, "You are so immature." That's when I figured if I actually went through with my plan, I'd have plenty to talk about the next time I went to confession, so why not add to the list, and I pinched Maureen right on her chubby white arm.

It was a joke about the second graders not having school the next day and staying home driving their parents crazy. It wasn't funny, but everyone was in a good mood so they all laughed.

Maureen yelped, but it was right when Father Kenny had said something that made all the grownups laugh, so nobody noticed.

"I'm telling." Maureen's voice sounded like a snake hissing.

"I don't care," I whispered back. "I have things to do."

Right before the end of mass, Father Kenny said something nice about all the second graders, and we had to stand up so everybody in the church could clap for us. While we were standing, I turned around to see if I could spot Bobby with the birthmark. My mom must have thought I was looking for her, because she waved. I didn't wave back — I was too busy looking.

Then everybody else in the church stood up because the mass was over. That's when I looked down and saw a white feather sitting on the pew. I swear it hadn't been there before. It was just sitting all perfect and kind of half-curled up, like it just dropped off an angel. I picked it up. I was pretty sure it was another sign.

"That feather is dirty," Maureen whispered.

"It's from my grandma," I whispered.

"No, it isn't. It's from a dirty bird."

"You're a dirty bird."

The organ started playing and Father Kenny was walking down the aisle and we all had to follow him. The middle aisle at St. Christine seemed awfully long, and it felt like *every*body was walking super super slow. I just wanted to get out of the church with my grandma angel feather and find Bobby with the birthmark before he got away.

Going out of the church, the line was the opposite of how we walked in, so Maureen Mackey was behind me and a boy with dark brown hair that was always in his eyes whose name I can never remember was in front of me. Maureen was still mad at me for pinching her, because when we started walking down the aisle, she stepped on the back of my heel, right on my beautiful new white shoe. I didn't even look behind me. I just did a little hop and kicked my leg back at her. I definitely hit something — I think it was her shin. She yelped again.

We were right in front of Sister Aloysius. She gave me a dirty look and pointed at me, which means you are in big, big trouble. I thought she was going to grab me and pull me out of line, so I kept moving. I looked around at the side of the aisle, way near the back, and I saw *Him*. I saw the guy from McGuffey's, who Uncle Joe and I think is named Bobby, and his fuzzy birthmark. He turned his head and said something to the girl with him, and they started heading for the door at the back of the church. Everybody else was standing and singing and watching all of us kids who had just made our First Communion walk out of the church. And that's when I realized I could do my plan.

Sister Aloysius couldn't say that I wouldn't get to make my First Communion if I disobeyed. It was all done. It's not like I could give the communion wafer back. I already ate it. It tasted like cardboard. She might get mad at me and my parents might punish me and I might have to go to confession and be grounded and have no TV and stay after school for the rest of the year, but nothing *really* bad was going to happen to me if I disobeyed the big rule of First Communion.

I got out of line.

We were supposed to stay in line all the way down the aisle, through the part of the church that my mom always calls the *foyer*, but I call the lobby, and out the front door. Then we were supposed to walk down the sidewalk and into the parking lot next to the church. We weren't supposed to get out of line until we met our families in the parking lot.

I didn't do that. I pushed the boy with dark brown hair in his eyes whose name I can never remember and ran down the aisle, past the priest and the altar boys and the other kids from my class and a bunch of other people standing at the back of the church, through the foyer, and out the front door.

I hadn't done magic in a long time, not on purpose anyway. When I slammed all the doors shut at home, it was an accident because I was so mad. My mom and dad and Uncle Joe all thought it was the wind, but it was magic and it was me and nobody got hurt.

I didn't want anyone to follow me, and closing door magic seemed safe. There are two sets of front doors at St. Christine. I made both of them slam shut and lock. I liked the sound it made — like a big "*Whomp!*" I didn't hear anybody yell "Ow" so I guess closing the church doors didn't hurt anybody. That made me feel better, like maybe doing magic didn't have to be dangerous. It made me want to do more magic.

Bobby with the birthmark and the girl he was with were already walking over to the little parking lot across the street. He was walking really fast, and it looked like she was trying to keep up, like he wanted to get out of there faster than she did. I heard her say something about waiting for her aunt and uncle and little cousin. He said something like "We'll see them at the party."

I tried to keep one part of my brain on the church doors to keep them shut. With the other part of my brain I yelled, "Hey!" and ran into the street. Then I yelled louder and kind of mean, like my dad does if kids are trying to set a leaf fire on our devil's strip. "Hey! Bobby!"

I wanted to help Hope keep the church doors closed, but that isn't something I can do. Try wiggling two hairs on your left big toe. See what I mean? You can't do it. Too small.

They both stopped, right on the sidewalk across the street from the church. The girl looked at Bobby and he kind of shrugged, pretending he didn't know me. I ran up to them, and the girl with blond hair said, "Can I help you, sweetie?"

I looked at her and then took a good look at him. It was definitely the same guy from McGuffey's, and Grandma had said one of the guys was chubby with a big birthmark like a caterpillar. It was him. "I need to talk to him," I said. Even though I only ran across the street, it felt hard to breathe. And it was hard to talk and use my magic to keep the doors closed and be brave enough to finally talk to one of the guys who robbed my grandma all at the same time.

"You need to talk to my fiancée?" the girl asked. I

I'm no fortune teller, but I knew this wasn't going to end well for Denise.

heard that word before. It means somebody you're going to get married to. She kind of laughed and said "Honey, do you have a girlfriend on the side you didn't tell me about?"

"I need to talk to him," I said again. I looked Bobby straight in the eye. He looked scared. I was *really* scared, but I didn't want him to know. I just said, "I know what you did."

"Bobby, what is she talking about?" the girl said. His name really was Bobby.

"I don't know. Some crazy kid stuff." He took her hand and pulled her a couple steps down the sidewalk and into the little parking lot.

"Stop!" I yelled as loud as I could. And they did. "He robbed my grandma." When I said this, I walked closer to them and pointed right at Bobby with the birthmark. He kind of opened his mouth like he was going to say something and then closed it like maybe he really didn't know what to say.

The girl kind of laughed. "I think you have the wrong guy, sweetie."

"No, I don't. Do you know the lady who used to live at 602 Audubon?" I asked.

He didn't say anything for a second. He just looked at me and looked at his girlfriend and then looked back at me again. In my head, I pretended he was like the lottery numbers, like I could make him do what I wanted. I kept thinking to myself, *"Say 'Yes,' Say 'Yes,' Say 'Yes.'"* His girlfriend said something else about how I was wrong and I should go back inside the church because everyone would be looking for me. She was talking so much she didn't even hear her boyfriend say, "Yeah, I know who she is."

The whole time Uncle Joe and I were looking for the guys who robbed Grandma, I never thought about what I would say if we actually found them, so I said the biggest, most important thing I could think of: "She was my grandma and she *died.*"

"Oh my God ... ." he kind of whispered. "I'm ... I didn't mean to... ."

His voice got quieter and quieter and his girlfriend's eyes got bigger and bigger. I thought she would yell, but she asked really slowly and quietly, "Bobby, what's going on? You didn't mean to *what*?"

Some of my old babushkas used to read their grandkids this story called The Tinderbox. It talks about a dog with eyes the size of teacups and one with eyes the size of dinner plates and one with eyes the size of windmills. Looking at Denise as she realized where Bobby got the money for their wedding and everything else, her eyes were somewhere in dinner-plate territory.

I've never seen a grownup look as sad as Bobby with the birthmark looked right then. He looked like he never wanted to say another word for a hundred years. All he said was, "Denise, she fell," so I guess that was his girlfriend's name.

Denise looked really mad and confused. "What happened? What did you do?" Bobby with the birthmark just stared at her. "What happened?" she asked again.

"I was trying to get money for our wedding and for Cathy's tuition ... ." He stopped talking for a second and it looked like he was trying not to cry. Then he said really quietly, "I didn't hurt anyone. She fell."

The two of them stared at each other and didn't say anything. I kept talking because he had to know what he did. "She fell and broke her hip. And they operated on her. And then she died," I said and they both looked back at me. "And she fell when *you* robbed her."

Denise took a couple steps away and looked at Bobby like he was a big, slimy slug she found under a rock. "Denise ... " he said, and reached out his hand to her.

She backed away from him and said, "Get away from me," and started walking down the street without him.

"Denise!" Bobby took a couple steps toward her, like he wanted to chase after her.

"Hey!" I said. "Where do you think you're going?"

He turned around and looked at me. For the first time, I realized that he was a lot bigger than me.

"Little girl ... " he started to say.

"My name is Hope."

"Fine, Hope. Do you know what you just did? You just ruined the one good thing in my life. That woman," and he pointed at Denise. She wasn't that far away yet, and he was talking pretty loud, so I bet she heard him. "That woman, Denise Skernicki, is the best thing that ever happened to me, and you just screwed it up."

I tried really hard not to cry, because crooks don't care if you cry, but I was crying anyway. "I didn't do anything. You're the one who robbed my grandma. You're a big lying, stealing poopy-head." I yelled "big lying, stealing poopy-head," so I bet Denise heard that too.

"You know, I tried to make amends," he said. He was talking a lot more softly now. "I sent yunz the money I had left over."

"The hundred and forty-two dollars?"

"Yeah. And the mass card and the box of groceries. I didn't know she died. I'm sorry."

There was a sound from across the street. The doors. I had stopped thinking about them to keep them locked. Somebody must have found the keys. I concentrated on all the doors to the church, even the ones on the side, and made them close and lock again. Even so, a couple of people made it out of the church, including Sister Aloysius and some grownups I didn't know.

I turned back to Bobby with the birthmark, and he was running down the street after Denise. That's when I got really mad. He was being a chicken and running away. I yelled "Stop!" and ran after him.

I've only ever made things move without touching them. I never moved a person before, but I needed Bobby to stop running away. *Lift him up, lift him up, lift him up,* I thought, and suddenly, Bobby with the birthmark was running in midair. It was kind of funny to see his legs going like he thought he was still on the ground, then he stopped and looked back at me, like somehow he knew I was the one keeping him floating above the sidewalk.

The whole time when I stopped doing magic, it was because I didn't want to hurt anyone. I didn't want to hurt Bobby with the birthmark. Not really. He said he was sorry, but sorry isn't enough, not for what he did. I wanted him to know how it felt to fall like my grandma fell. I let him hang in the air a few feet above the ground until I got closer. Then I dropped him. He wasn't that high up, but he still fell on the sidewalk kind of hard. I knew it was a mean thing to do, but I didn't care. I didn't care that I was doing magic in front of a grownup or doing magic to a grownup or hurting someone. It was like being a whole different person.

Bobby with the birthmark went "Oooff!" when he landed on the ground. He was kind of lying half on the sidewalk and half on the devil's strip and rubbing his leg like it hurt. When I made the egg splat all over Maureen Mackey's dress and she cried, I felt bad. This was different. I didn't feel bad at all. I didn't know what to say, so I just stared at him. He looked really scared. I never had a grownup be scared of me before. I didn't think he was going to try and run away again, but I couldn't be sure. I could lift him up again, but I didn't know where to put him. I had to make a place where he couldn't get out.

We were far enough down the street that we were across from the school instead of the church. There were some potholes in the street outside St. Christine. My school bus hits this big pothole every morning that makes everybody bounce in the seats. It kind of feels like you're in the bumper cars at Idora Park. Uncle Joe says potholes happen when water gets under the ground. In winter, it freezes and expands. When everything warms up, sometimes things collapse and you get a hole.

I knew what Hope was trying to do, and I didn't like it. Do you think it tickles to have your earth and concrete crack open, to have your inner core exposed for all the world to see? No, it doesn't. It hurts like hell. At first I fought her, like you'd fight back if someone was trying to cut you open. But I like Hope, and I like a good dose of comeuppance. I stopped fighting her, opened myself, and helped put Bobby Wayland in a hole in the ground.

I looked at the spot on the ground where Bobby with the birthmark was sitting. He was kind of scooting backwards on his butt like he was trying to get away from me. *Break open, break open, break open*, I thought, and the ground and the sidewalk started to crack in a big circle around him. It was really hard to make the sidewalk and the ground move, but I kept concentrating and thinking *break open, break open, break open* and it got a little easier to move everything. The sidewalk kept cracking and the ground started to open up and the big slabs of stone that make the sidewalk broke in half and turned on their sides. I kept concentrating and concentrating and made the little circle of dirt and broken sidewalk where Bobby with the birthmark was sitting sink down into the ground, like a giant elevator pothole so deep that he couldn't climb out. Now he couldn't run away.

I was really happy because I finally got Bobby with the birthmark. I still had the little white feather in my hand and I looked down at it and thought about my grandma, and it kind of felt like she was there with me. For the first time since she fell, I didn't feel bad about using magic. Then I heard someone yell, "Hope Bowers!" and I kind of froze. Even before I turned around, I knew Sister Aloysius was coming for me.

You wouldn't think that you can be totally happy one second and totally scared and sad a second later, but I was. Sister Aloysius didn't have her yardstick with her, but she was still scary all by herself. She had to be super mad because I just broke a whole bunch of her rules.

"Hope Bowers!" she said again. Every time Sister Aloysius says your name, it makes you freeze because you never know what she's going to do. She walked up to me and said, "Just what do you think you're doing?" and it was like she didn't even notice the big huge hole in the ground behind me.

I didn't know what to say. Right then I wasn't doing anything. I just standing in front of a big hole in the ground. The whole time I was talking to Bobby with the birthmark and doing magic, I kind of forgot where I was. Now I remembered.

"Where did this hole come from?" Sister Aloysius asked me this like she knew I made it. She looked over the edge and saw Bobby with the birthmark sitting in the bottom of the hole. He looked too scared to say anything. "Who is that? What have you done?"

"I got out of line." I thought maybe saying the one thing she already knew I did would make things better, but it didn't.

"I told you I don't like show-offs," Sister Aloysius said. There were a bunch of grownups out on the sidewalk in front of the church and walking into the parking lot and into the street. All the other kids in my class were outside too. I totally forgot about keeping the church doors locked. I knew I was in big trouble, but there wasn't any way to get out of it. For a second I wondered if I could lift myself up the way I had lifted Bobby with the birthmark. Then I could just fly away like Jesus ascending into heaven or Dumbo when he held the feather in his trunk. I held onto my grandma angel feather a little tighter. Except if I did that, then *everybody* would know I could do magic. They'd know that I put Bobby with the birthmark into the big hole. I didn't even have time to think of a new plan because Sister Aloysius said, "We're going to find your parents," and she grabbed my ear and started pulling me down the sidewalk to the church.

"Ow!" I yelled, because it really hurt. Right when I yelled "Ow!" there was a rumbling sound, like a whole bunch of trucks except the sound was coming from under the ground, not the street. The rumbling got louder and the ground started to shake a little. Sister Aloysius stopped pulling me and even let go of my ear. Everybody outside the church just stopped what they were doing and listened. Then the sidewalk right in front of where Sister Aloysius and I were standing started to crack and a hole bigger than a pothole but smaller than the one Bobby with the birthmark was sitting in opened up right in front of us. I leaned over to try and watch it open, but Sister Aloysius grabbed my arm and pulled me back. I guess she thought I was going to fall in or something.

This was my sacrifice to save Hope—more holes. One sinkhole with a two-bit crook in it is suspicious. A whole bunch of sinkholes and the sewer department comes out. Call it a painful *polis ex machina*, just don't call me sentimental.

You could still hear the rumbling sound, and then a big pothole opened up farther down in the middle of the street. St. Christine is on a corner, and I saw a bunch of people who were down near the intersection jump back, like a hole opened up near them. There were holes opening up all over the neighborhood. Some kids in my class who live near school walked around and counted them the next day and said there were seventeen sinkholes. Nobody knew that I made the first hole. I don't know where the other sinkholes came from, but I was glad about them. Instead of everybody looking at me and the big sinkhole and Bobby with the birthmark and thinking I did it, all the grownups thought that there was something wrong with the sewers or the ground or something. I was still in trouble, just maybe a little less trouble.

The only nice thing Sister Aloysius did was keep me from falling in the sinkhole. After that, she found my parents and told them I was going to miss recess for the rest of the year, and they told her that was fine with them.

I guess after I ran out of line, some other kids thought that getting out of line was a good idea and did the same thing. Pretty soon, there were kids running all over the church. Parents started taking pictures and other people went around the church trying to find the keys and everybody thought they could open the doors but they couldn't. Here are the words people used to describe what happened after I got out of line: One, Sister Aloysius said it was *bedlam*. Natalie told me that, and I trust her. Of course, she wasn't able to tell me that for a while, because I was grounded with no TV and no dessert and couldn't go to any of my friends' houses for two whole weeks. Two, my mom said she was *furious*. Even my dad was mad, and he's not into the whole First Communion thing. Three, Uncle Joe said he was *disappointed* in me.

On the drive home from church, my mom and dad gave me a long talk about responsibility and respect. I tried to be quiet and listen, but when my dad said, "I don't want to see those kind of shenanigans ever again," I started laughing. I didn't mean to.

"Young lady, there is nothing funny about what you just did," my mom said.

Uncle Joe was sitting next to me in the back seat because my mom said she was too furious to sit next to me. "What in God's name are you laughing about?" Uncle Joe asked.

I caught my breath and managed to stop laughing just long enough say "shenanigans!" before I started laughing again. It's a funny word.

"Your shenanigans were not funny," Dad said.

"But the word is funny!" I said. "It just *sounds* like people doing bad things." I lowered my voice and said half to myself, "That or a restaurant."

Normally playing the grandma card would throw the whole game Mom's way, but Hope had that trump white feather clutched in her hand.

My mom said, "Do you think your Grandma would have been proud of what you did?"

"She wanted me to get out of line so I could find one of the guys who robbed her," I replied.

"What?" My parents said this at the exact same time.

"Mom, you know how you always say that when you find a white feather, it's from an angel?"

"Yes ... ."

"I found this feather in my pew." I held it up so she could see it. "It wasn't there when I sat down and when we stood up at the end of mass, it was right there where I was sitting. It's from Grandma. And I saw one of the guys who robbed her and that's why I got out of line. I had to find him." I shut up then because I realized if I kept talking, sooner or later I'd have to talk about putting Bobby with the birthmark in the bottom of a sinkhole. It didn't even matter that I stopped talking because all three of them started saying things like, "Hope, sweetie, the men who robbed Grandma were not at your First Communion mass." It wasn't even worth talking about. They didn't believe me. We pulled into our driveway right then. My dad said, "We don't even know who robbed her," and my mom said, "Go inside and change your dress."

I went into my room and closed the door. I sat down on my bed with the white feather and looked at it. After a while, Nico and one of my cousins from Cleveland poked their heads into my room and asked when I was going to come out and play. "I just have to change out of my dress," I said.

I don't know what I expected her to do with the feather. Throw it away? Cry over it? Put it under her pillow? She didn't do any of those things, just sat there, quiet as a mouse, and gazed at the feather like it was her grandmother's face.

I put the feather on my dresser, under the jewelry box my mom gave me two birthdays ago. Then I whipped off the First Communion dress, threw on a different dress, and ran outside to my party.

We still had my First Communion party, but Mom and Dad told everybody what I did so practically every grownup decided to "have a talk" with me. About the only good thing my mom and dad could say about me was that I hadn't gotten my white dress dirty.

All my big cousins thought it was kind of cool that I got in trouble. But I didn't get out of line and ruin First Communion because I wanted to be cool. I wanted to find the guy who robbed Grandma, but every time I tried to say that, everybody said it was impossible.

At the party, we had lots of food and a big cassata cake, which I love because strawberries are my favorite fruit. And we had cold cuts and cheese for sandwiches and macaroni salad and fruit salad. I even got to have orange pop. We almost never have pop in the house because my mom calls it sugar water. For a minute, it looked like Mom wasn't going to let me have any pop as part of my punishment, but my dad said my being grounded and not having any treats could start tomorrow.

I ended up spilling about half of my pop on myself and had to go change again. The second time I didn't even bother with a dress. I just put on jeans and a T-shirt, and then I got to be the only one in jeans and everybody else was still all dressed up. Michael from next door got jealous and went home to change into play clothes too.

By the time we got done changing our clothes all those times, a lot of people were gone. Aunt Peggy and my big cousins left because they had to drive all the way back to Cleveland. Michael's mom and dad said they had to leave because it had been enough excitement for one day, but I think they were worried Michael would get bad ideas from me. And Uncle Ed and those cousins had to leave because my cousin Nico had a report due at school the next day that she hadn't done and Uncle Ed said he was going to give them all a long talk on procrastination on the way home. Procrastination is when you keep saying you'll do something and you don't do it. Kind of the way Uncle Joe kept procrastinating about going to find Bobby with the birthmark.

I said that to Uncle Joe way late in the afternoon. By then, everybody else had left. My mom was inside cleaning up from the party and my dad was in the living room reading the Sunday paper and doing what he called "recovering." All my cousins and I had been out in the backyard playing tag and messing around with hula hoops and some play balls and stuff. I was hula-hooping all by myself when Uncle Joe came out and sat down on the lawn chair near where I was.

"That's some pretty fancy hula-hooping there, Sport," he said.

"Thanks," I said, but I didn't stop. I was on a roll.

Uncle Joe was quiet for a second and then shook his head. "That was quite a scene you caused at the church."

"Uncle Joe, Bobby with the birthmark was there at the mass. I saw him. I *talked* to him."

Uncle Joe looked like he didn't believe me. "Are you sure it was him?"

"Yes. He looked just like Grandma described him *and* it was the same guy I saw in McGuffey's *and* his fiancée called him 'Bobby' *and* he even said he did it. And I decided to do something about it. I didn't *procrastinate*."

"What happened to him?"

"He was the guy sitting in the big sinkhole. I don't know what happened to him because Mom and Dad wouldn't listen when I tried to tell them."

"I think they called the fire department to get him out," Uncle Joe said. "I wonder what caused all of those sinkholes. It was lucky only one person fell in." I didn't say anything. "I heard they're going to close the school for a few days so the city can do some testing to make sure the area is safe."

I could have told him that there weren't going to be any more sinkholes. They hurt too much, but nobody listens to me, either.

"You mean *everybody* gets the day off tomorrow? Not just the second graders? That's not fair. We should get an extra day."

"Sometimes life isn't fair."

I could tell Uncle Joe still didn't believe me. "I'm not lying," I said. "Bobby with the birthmark was there at the mass."

Uncle Joe leaned back in the lawn chair and stretched out his legs. He's kind of tall and has long, skinny legs like a stork. "I never said you were lying, Hope, but I think you're mistaken. The probability of you seeing one of those guys at your First Communion mass is very, very low."

I stopped hula-hooping and looked right at him. "I don't know what probability is, so I don't care. It happened." I picked up my hula hoop and one of the play balls. I figured I had done enough bad things that day so I ought to at least clean up my stuff.

"Probability means the likelihood of something happening. You know how you used to pick the daily number for your mom and grandma? When they pull the daily number, they have three bins, and each of the bins has ten ping-pong balls in, numbered from zero to nine. You've seen it on TV, right?"

"I know that." I didn't tell him that I made the balls pick the number I wanted every time I watched it.

"The *probability* of any number coming up straight is one in a thousand. Whether the number is one-two-three or zero-zero-zero, the number of possibilities and outcomes is the same. There are thousands of people in Youngstown and two guys who robbed your grandmother. That means thousands of possibilities and only two possible outcomes. So, yes, I'd say the probability of one of the men who robbed your grandmother being at church today is very low. I'm sorry."

I had to think for a minute about everything he said. "What did you mean that zero-zero-zero could come up the same as any other number?"

"Just that — the probability of any three-digit number coming up in the daily drawing is one in a thousand. It doesn't matter what the number is. But what does that have to do with the guys who robbed Grandma?"

"Nothing." I walked across the yard to pick up a frisbee that one of my big cousins had thrown. It gave me a minute to think. I handed the frisbee to Uncle Joe and said, "I wrote down o-o-o on the notepad one morning and gave it to my mom, and she laughed at me and said it would never come out. She and Grandma didn't buy tickets and I didn't ... I didn't make it come out."

"Is that why you stopped picking the number?" Joe said.

I said "No" without thinking but then said, "Yeah, that's why," because I couldn't tell him I stopped picking the daily number because doing magic was too dangerous. There was a play ball and a wiffle ball and bat on the ground right by us. I walked over and picked them up and headed for the garage. My mom and dad keep a big plastic bin in there for all my outdoor toys. I heard a ball bounce and saw Uncle Joe walking behind me with the frisbee and another ball. "Thank you for helping me," I said.

Uncle Joe and I put all my toys away and then he said, "Hope, I've been thinking about all that I know about you. You're an honest kid. If you say you ran out of line during First Communion because you saw one of the guys who robbed Dolores, then I believe you."

I was so happy that Uncle Joe believed me I got all teary like I was about to cry. Grownups almost never believe kids, and they should. "Thank you. It's true."

"I'm sorry we didn't listen to you. He ought to be in jail."

I thought for a second about the things Bobby with the birthmark had done and some of the things I've done and about how just because you *do* something bad doesn't mean you *are* bad. One good thing he had done was apologize. It didn't seem like enough at the time, but he did say he was sorry *before* I put him in the sinkhole.

"It's okay, Uncle Joe. I took care of it." I walked back out to the backyard to see if there was anything else that needed to get cleaned up. I felt kind of bad that my mom had to do all the work to make a nice party for me. It seemed like cleaning up the backyard would be a good way to help her. Uncle Joe helped me pick up a few cups and some paper plates and stuff that people had left lying around. While we were picking things up, Uncle Joe asked how I had taken care of Bobby with the birthmark.

"Did you kick him in the shin like you did the little girl in line behind you?" he said, and it almost sounded like he was going to laugh.

I didn't realize my family saw me kick Maureen Mackey. That was one more thing for my parents to be mad about. "No. But he ended up in the bottom of a hole," I said.

"It's not what I would have chosen, but it's not bad."

233

VII

My mom was supposed to take me shopping the next day because I wanted to spend some of my First Communion money on a Paddington Bear stuffed animal that I saw at Strouss', but she said she was still too mad at me and that she wasn't taking me shopping while I was on punishment. Instead she made me go over to the house on Audubon with Uncle Joe and help move stuff because he finally decided to sell the house.

I hadn't been over there since Easter, but I guess Uncle Joe and my mom had been packing up things when I was at school. It was weird when we walked in because the dining room table and chairs were gone. So was the sofa in the living room. There are pretty built-in cabinets in the dining room where my grandma used to keep all her good dishes that she only used on special occasions. They had little green leaves in a pattern going all the way around and a little line of gold on the edge. I remember Mom and Uncle Joe bringing home some heavy boxes and saying they were giving the good china to one of Aunt Peggy's daughters, but I didn't *see* the dishes. I didn't really think that the plates we used every Thanksgiving and Christmas were all packed up and gone until I was standing in the dining room and everything was empty.

"It's all gone." Even though I said this kind of quiet, my voice echoed. "Echo," I said louder so I could hear it again.

"Well, your mom and Eddie and I have been cleaning it out. Come on. We have some tools to drag out of the basement."

"Why do we have to go to the basement?" I never liked Grandma's basement. It was always kind of dark and creepy down there. I didn't say that to Uncle Joe because I didn't want him to think I was scared.

"We have to go to the basement because that's where I have some tools I want to bring back to the house. Let's go."

I followed Uncle Joe to the basement. When I got to the bottom step, I stopped for a second because I knew that's where Grandma fell. Uncle Joe thought I stopped because it was dark because he said, "Hold on, let me get the lights."

"There are lights down here?"

Uncle Joe looked at me funny. "Of course there are."

"How come Grandma never turned them on?"

"She wanted to save money."

"Oh."

It turned out there weren't that many tools Uncle Joe wanted to keep. The rest he put on the curb because he said they might come in handy for somebody else. I only carried the light things. Then we went out to the garage and loaded some boxes with car parts into the trunk of Uncle Joe's car because he said we were going to bring them to Mr. Javorsik's garage. When that was done, we were tired and I was getting hungry, so Uncle Joe said we could walk over to McGuffey's to get a snack.

I hadn't walked to McGuffey's for a long time, but I still knew the way. Grandma's neighborhood used to seem really big and mysterious, but it didn't look as big anymore. It kind of looked empty too. There was a big empty lot in between two houses, and for a minute I couldn't remember if there was supposed to be a house there or not.

"Who's buying your house?" I asked. "I hope it's somebody with kids. Maybe I could come and play with them."

Uncle Joe stopped for a second to look around before we crossed the street and put one hand on my shoulder like he thought I was one of those little kids who run into the street and get run over. There weren't any cars around anyway. "The university bought it," he replied, and we started to walk again.

"Why did the university buy it? Who's going to live in it?"

I don't blame Joe Steiner for selling the old house. I can't control what you do or what you make of me, but I don't have to like it. I don't have to like the university getting bigger and bigger. I'm not big, but I'm no shrinking village. I'm no university town. The university is part of me, not the other way around.

"Nobody. They're going to tear it down to build a dormitory or a parking lot or something." Uncle Joe didn't look at me while he said this, but I looked at him. His eyes were looking straight ahead, like he didn't want to see anything except what was right in front of him, not even me. "They bought all the houses on our block."

"Are they going to tear all the houses down?"

"All the ones they bought."

I didn't know what to say so I didn't say anything. I never heard of somebody buying up a whole block full of houses just so they could tear them down. That seemed mean.

Uncle Joe kind of sighed and said, "Nothing we can do about it now." Then he stood up a little straighter, the way he sometimes tells me to buck up when I think something isn't fair. "Come on. It's warm enough that I'll bet McGuffey has stocked up the ice cream cooler."

I didn't remind Uncle Joe that my mom and dad said I wasn't allowed to have any treats or dessert for two weeks. When we went in the store, Mr. McGuffey was putting milk in one of the coolers along the back wall. I said, "Hello" and

Mr. McGuffey said, "Good afternoon," but Uncle Joe just kind of grunted. We walked past the register, and I stopped for a second to look at the little chalkboard that has all the winning lottery numbers on it. Uncle Joe stopped too and looked at me. He raised one eyebrow, which always makes him look like he's asking a question without saying anything. I didn't say anything either. I had more important things on my mind, like whether to get a strawberry crunch bar or a drumstick. When I opened the ice cream cooler, the cold air felt really good. I held it open until Mr. McGuffey said, "Hey, that isn't the air conditioning."

"Sorry, Mr. McGuffey," I said. I grabbed a strawberry crunch and closed the lid of the cooler. I heard Uncle Joe say, "Don't yell at my niece." He doesn't really like Mr. McGuffey.

The bell at the front of the store rang, and I saw Mr. Krasniak and his daughter walk in. I met her at church once. She's a lot younger than me.

"Hey there, Joe!" Mr. Krasniak said. "Fancy meeting you here."

"Hi, Ralph. How're things?"

"Same old, same old. Still looking."

Uncle Joe nodded and said, "You'll find something."

"Oh, sure. It'll all turn out okay. In the meantime, I get to spend more time with this little bugger." Mr. Krasniak patted Sally on the head. "Sally, do you remember Mr. Steiner and his niece, Hope?"

Sally leaned onto her dad and kind of waved. I waved back and said, "Hi." Like I said, she's kind of little. Uncle Joe and Mr. Krasniak started talking about cars and jobs and ignoring us. I was still holding the strawberry crunch bar, and Sally was looking at it like she was hoping I'd unwrap it and give her a bite.

"How come you don't have school?" I asked.

"I don't go to school yet," Sally said.

"Ohhh, you start kindergarten in the fall, huh?"

"Yeah."

"I didn't have school today because I made my First Communion yesterday," I said. Sally looked impressed. She looked down at my ice cream bar again. "Are you getting ice cream too?" I asked.

"No," Sally said real quiet and looked down at the floor. "We're just getting bread and milk."

"Oh."

Sally's hair was in pigtails, but her T-shirt was too big and had a picture of a motorcycle on it that was all faded. I wondered if it used to belong to one of her big brothers. It made me feel bad for her. I heard Uncle Joe say something about the house on Audubon, and Mr. Krasniak said, "I wish the university'd make an offer on mine. Just my luck, we're on the wrong block." It seemed weird that Mr. Krasniak would want to sell his house just so it could get torn down.

"We might move," Sally said real quietly.

"Where?" I asked.

"I can't remember the name of the place, but my aunt lives there and she said my dad can maybe work where she works."

Mr. Krasniak must have heard us talking because he said it wasn't anything definite yet. Then Uncle Joe said, "What are the job prospects like over in Jersey?"

"Better than here. I just need to get a little something together to finance the move."

Uncle Joe and Mr. Krasniak started talking about money and jobs and stuff. Sally looked bored. I was too. I walked over to the front counter and looked at the board where Mr. McGuffey wrote down the daily number every day. "Have you ever played the lottery?" I asked Sally.

"No. I'm not allowed."

"My grandma used to play the daily number. I used to buy the tickets with her all the time." I always worried about grownups knowing about my magic, but even if I told Sally and she told her parents, they wouldn't believe her. Nobody ever believes what kids say, even when we're telling the truth. "I can do magic," I whispered.

"Really? What kind?"

"You'll see later. It'll help you." Even though my mom told me I couldn't go to Strouss' and buy the Paddington Bear, I still brought some of my First Communion money with me. I took a dollar out of my jeans pocket and said very loud in my most grownup voice, "Mr. McGuffey. I'd like to buy two tickets for the daily number, please."

It seems like I should be leading you to something, building up to something, but I don't build up to — I'm buildings. You build me. There I am. Real life doesn't build up to some satisfying resolution. Life just keeps going and going until you're dead. After you're gone, someone else will live in my houses and drive on my streets and work in my buildings. You go, I stay.

But I don't want you to feel cheated. What do you want to hear? Do you want to hear that Bobby Wayland turned himself in to the police? Do you want to hear that Hope picked a dozen lottery numbers so the Krasniaks could afford to move? Do you want to hear that all the mills reopened and sent everyone back to work? Do you want to hear that Hope magicked all the dirt off my streets and the soot out of my air? Would that make you feel better?

Pretend that whatever you want to have happen happened. Pretend that's how things end, and I'll pretend you can hear me. I can hear you, you know.

Acknowledgements

Many thanks to everyone who read and commented on early drafts of this book, including Christopher Johnston, Becky Kyle, Judith Mansour, Nancy Marcus, and Bob Price. Extra thanks to Monica Plunkett for convincing me that Grandma had to go down. Thanks to Father John Hissrich for insight into the confessional and to Rick Rowlands of the Youngstown Steel Heritage Foundation for lending a stranger U.S. Steel's steel-making guide. I owe an infinite debt of gratitude to my extended family, especially Edward and Ann Adams, Noelle Powell, and Nora Adams Corbett, for sharing their memories and experiences. This book would not have come together without your help. My undying gratitude to Lou Aronica and the Story Plant for the patience and guidance. As always, much love and appreciation to M. and E. for the time, space, and understanding.